Catherine Cookson

The Unbaited Trap

CORGI BOOKS
A DIVISION OF TRANSWORLD PUBLISHERS LTD

THE UNBAITED TRAP

A CORGI BOOK 0 552 08561 8

Originally published in Great Britain
by Macdonald & Co (Publishers) Ltd.

PRINTING HISTORY
Macdonald edition published 1966
Corgi edition published 1970
Corgi edition reprinted 1972
Corgi edition reprinted 1973 (twice)
Corgi edition reprinted 1974 (twice)
Corgi edition reprinted 1975
Corgi edition reprinted 1976
Corgi edition reprinted 1977
Corgi edition reprinted 1978

This book is set in Intertype Plantin

Corgi Books are published by
Transworld Publishers Ltd,
Century House, 61–63 Uxbridge Road,
Ealing, London W5 5SA
Made and printed in Great Britain by
Cox & Wyman Ltd., London, Reading and Fakenham

THE UNBAITED TRAP

Ann Emmerson had devoted her life to her son, and between the two of them was a bond that nothing could break and no one sever, not even John Emmerson – Ann's husband, Laurie's father . . .

When Laurie became engaged, Ann found the situation difficult to accept. After a lifetime of being the only woman in his life, she was going to lose him. And, without realizing it, her son was not the only man she was going to lose. For after years of loneliness and isolation, John Emmerson had discovered a woman of warmth and affection, a woman who could help him to forget the past . . .

Also by Catherine Cookson

KATIE MULHOLLAND
KATE HANNIGAN
THE ROUND TOWER
FENWICK HOUSES
THE FIFTEEN STREETS
MAGGIE ROWAN
THE LONG CORRIDOR
COLOUR BLIND
THE MENAGERIE
THE BLIND MILLER
FANNY MCBRIDE
THE GLASS VIRGIN
ROONEY
THE NICE BLOKE
THE INVITATION
THE DWELLING PLACE
FEATHERS IN THE FIRE
OUR KATE
PURE AS THE LILY
THE INVISIBLE CORD
THE SLOW AWAKENING
THE TIDE OF LIFE

The 'Mary Ann' series

A GRAND MAN
THE LORD AND MARY ANN
THE DEVIL AND MARY ANN
LIFE AND MARY ANN
LOVE AND MARY ANN
MARRIAGE AND MARY ANN
MARY ANN'S ANGELS
MARY ANN AND BILL

The 'Mallen' Series

THE MALLEN STREAK
THE MALLEN GIRL
THE MALLEN LITTER

By Catherine Cookson as Catherine Marchant

HOUSE OF MEN
THE FEN TIGER
HERITAGE OF FOLLY
MISS MARTHA MARY CRAWFORD

and published by Corgi Books

Contents

Part 1

Dinner at Eight

CHAPTER ONE

THE ROOF

JOHN EMMERSON brought his speed down to twenty as he neared the bottom of the Avenue. Although it was only six o'clock on the November evening, there was already a tendency to frost, and he knew from experience the road would be wet near Handley's Place. There was a spring somewhere up on one of his fields and nothing could be done about it. Twice last year he had skidded on the same spot, and around this time of the year, and he didn't want this to happen tonight, not with his new acquisition only a week old. He'd had a Rover car for years, changing it every so often, but this last change had brought with it a thrill, and he had long since felt that thrills were things that happened to other men, and youths. Yes, thrills were the prerogative of youth. But the Rover 2000 had stirred something in him. It was a small stir, but, nevertheless, because such emotional happenings were rare, it loomed as something large. The effect of the car on him was, he imagined, like that caused by a few pep pills.

As he turned into Lime Avenue his headlights picked up the line of trees. Stiff and stark, they marched into the distance, their blackness shades darker than the night sky.

A short way up the road a headlight crossed his own and he swerved to the right, and as he did so he tooted his horn twice, and received the same reply from the other car. Later tonight the driver of that car would be coming to dinner, and this time next year his only daughter would be his own daughter-in-law.

His house was on the opposite side of the road, number 74, 'The Gables', and was quite a way from number 7, 'Syracuse', since each house stood in about quarter of an acre of land.

He had lived in Lime Avenue ten years, moving here when he became senior partner of the firm. It was in a way the insignia of his success; and no little success, he having bought out Ratcliff, Arnold & Baker. Now to all intents and purposes he was Ratcliff, Arnold & Baker, the leading solicitors of the town. And that state would continue, he supposed, until Arnold Ransome bought him out. The junior partner, Boyd, did not come into it at this stage – junior partners had long, long roads to travel.

He turned into his drive, made the S-bend, and came to his front door. Ann had forgotten to put the light on. She was careful about lights, economical about silly little things, and wildly extravagant about things that cost a great deal of money. But in just under two hours' time she would have the house ablaze to greet the Family Wilcox. Her dear friend, May, her future daughter-in-law Valerie, and the scion of the local Bench, James; dinner-at-eight, the same old routine, the same old crowd.

He went under the glass-covered porch and inserted his latch-key in the heavy oak front door, and before he turned to close it he switched on the lobby lights, when he passed into the hall he again switched on the lights. The burnt orange shades of the wall lights warmed the white walls. He could stand the white walls at night, but in the daytime their starkness chilled him. About two years ago Ann had taken this craze for the stripped look; the lounge had become white, the dining-room a pale French grey; the staircase and landing white; her bedroom pale lilac and white. He had checked the attack on his own room, but he had done it gently, as he did everything when dealing with Ann, or anyone else for that matter, but particularly when dealing with his wife. And so his room was left to its overall greenness, and it was the only place in his home that didn't cause his eyes to blink and water.

He went into the cloakroom and hung up his coat and hat, and having washed his hands he bent his tall, heavy body towards the mirror, and, moistening a finger, rubbed it over the hair at each side of his ears. Then he stared at himself, as was his habit. The blue eyes that looked back at him looked slightly washed out and weary. He now drew his finger and thumb down his long nose, then nipped its point before dropping his index finger to the bristle on his upper lip, which he daily prevented from becoming a moustache. But the movement of his finger was like that of a man stroking his moustache. These were private actions, almost unconscious, indulged in daily over the years until now he neither saw nor felt himself doing them any more. The only way he would have become aware of this habit would have been if he had found himself being observed. It was as if some compassionate part of him looked kindly at the whole, like a mother giving praise to the runt of her litter. Last of all, he stroked his hair back. It was very thick and grizzled and was the only strong-looking thing about him.

He now tugged at his waistcoat and went into the hall again, and he was making for the stairs when he heard his wife's voice coming from the kitchen. After a moment's hesitation he went towards the door and pushed it gently open.

His wife was standing at the table. Her hair was done up in a pale blue chiffon scarf, and she was enveloped in a long overall. On his entry she looked up and gave him a thin smile as she said, 'Hello, dear. You're early.'

'Yes, yes. The case was finished much sooner than we expected. I came straight on from Newcastle. My, my! aren't we busy.' He joined his hands together in front of his chest as if he were greeting himself, and smiled his tight smile as he turned towards the woman standing at the stove 'Well, Mrs. Stringer, something smells good. What are you hashing up for us tonight, eh?'

He was always hearty when in the kitchen and speaking to Mrs. Stringer. He felt it was expected of him, a form of appreciation for services rendered; and it pleased Ann, for she was always saying she didn't know what she would do without Mrs. Stringer. Yet he always felt something of a fool whilst adopting this pose.

Mrs. Stringer's conversation always took a staccato form. 'Oh, sir, going to town tonight,' he said 'Aw, yes. But it's not me. I haven't concocted nothing; all praise to the mistress here. Dead beat she'll be afore eight o'clock. What she should do is have a bath and lie down. . . . Yes an' I told her.'

'There now. Sensible advice. What about it?' He looked towards his wife, and when she made no rejoinder he stood awkwardly staring at her. She could do this, could Ann, refuse to make comment. She could carry on with what she was doing in a silence that screamed, and it didn't seem to affect her. That was wrong; it affected her all right. He could almost hear her nerves jangling in her body. As he continued to stare at her, he thought she was still good looking; in spite of everything she had kept her looks . . . and poise. The latter perhaps owed a lot to her tall thinness, that thinness that had always been able to carry clothes like a fashion plate. And her face, too, had hardly altered since he first met her, except for her mouth, which drooped noticeably at the corners now. But her complexion was still as clear as a young girl's, and she forty-five this year. Poor Ann. He jerked his head on this last thought and the compassion that the words released in him.

As he turned away, being unable to find any more small talk with which to fill the void, she said suddenly in her crisp way, 'Just a minute; I'm coming.' As she pulled off her overall Mrs. Stringer took it from her hand, saying comfortingly, 'That's it, Ma'am. That's it.'

He stood aside and held the door open for her, then followed her across the hall into the lounge.

A log fire was burning on the new hearth that stood two feet from the ground, its funnel-like chimney protruding into the room like some accoutrement in a farmyard – a corn shute he always likened it to. He supposed this was one of the smartest lounges in the town. It should be, too, for the alterations and furnishings had cost him a staggering sum. The new teak floor glowed reddishly along all its thirty-five feet, which took in the dining-room as well. The dividing doors were open and the long dining-table was gleaming with glass and silver. Beyond the table, dull gold velvet curtains shrouded one wall completely, and in the lounge itself the curtains broke the white expanse of wall in three places. If there was an emotion in him strong enough to be called hatred, then he could say he hated this room.

He looked towards her as he said now, 'Would you like a drink?' His voice, no longer hearty, had a tentative sound to it.

'No. No thanks.' Her body made a nervous movement. Then sitting down abruptly on a mushroom-coloured couch, she leant her head back and after a moment said, 'Yes, I think I will, after all. Just a small one.'

He went into the dining-room and beyond the table, and to what looked like a corner cupboard with a carved counter roughly hewn out of a length of oak standing in front of it. When he opened the door of the cupboard, there was displayed a sparkling array of glasses and bottles. The bottles started from floorwards, and the glasses from above his head, all graded sizes and all standing on their particular shelves. He took down two and placed them on the counter; then lifting up a bottle of sherry, he filled the glasses and carried them down the room to the couch. After handing her a glass, he stood with his back to the fire and again the silence descended on them. With the second sip from his glass, he asked quietly, 'What are we having tonight?' It didn't really matter to him what they had, he wasn't very interested in food – he'd had to learn to eat less and less to keep his bulk down – but she spent a lot of time thinking up menus for her dinners, and again he felt it was expected of him to be interested.

'Oh, nothing elaborate.' She shook her head. 'Sole with wine sauce, and pineapple ham and apple rabbit, with the usual accessories; then French pears.'

Nothing elaborate, she had said. There'd be about six vegetables, and a sauce with everything, and wines in their right places, and a platter with eight different cheeses. Nothing elaborate! And all for the Wilcoxes, whom she saw at least every other day.

The Wilcoxes had been her friends for years, long before he knew her. She and May Wilcox had gone to school together and had remained inseparable since, but a battle for social supremacy had grown up between them, and the giving of little dinners such as was to take place tonight was part of that battle. Nothing elaborate! If May's dinners started with shrimp cocktails or hors d'oeuvres you could be sure that in his house those items would not be allowed on his table for many months.

In this covert and genteel battle his wife, John knew, had always been on the winning side, whether it was planning a meal, or being re-elected chairman of a committee, or organizing the coffee mornings. That was, until James Wilcox promoted himself from the position of assistant accountant in the firm of Baxter and Morton, to starting a business on his own. This was achieved by the sudden death of his father-in-law, a widower who had dabbled more than a little in property. Following this unexpected rise in their fortunes it became obvious that May Wilcox could no longer be tactfully patronized, so the battle between the two friends had become more balanced.

But the battle, John had thought of late, had reached a point where a definite cease-fire must be called, for the implements of it had moved from dinners to interior decorating, and he had the strong feeling that the next choice of weapons was going to be headed mink. Yet he was aware, from experience, it was one thing to decide the line he must take, and quite another to carry it out, for he knew, and she knew, oh yes she knew, that he owed her this one outlet.

As he emptied his glass there came the sound of a deep laugh, a guttural, jolly laugh, from the direction of the hall. John did not look towards the door but kept his eyes on his wife's face. At one time her face had brightened when she heard that laugh. It was as if a light were shining under her skin and illuminating her eyes, yet since the wedding date had been fixed between their only son and the daughter of her dearest friend the light in her face had dimmed. She could have been overjoyed that her son and her closest friend's daughter were going to cement their parents' friendship, but she wasn't. She had never said one word to him that would betray her feelings for her future daughter-in-law, but he knew that she didn't like the girl. But there, would she like any girl who would take from her the one thing that had made life bearable?

When Laurance Emmerson came into the room he was still laughing. 'Hello there,' he said. He included his father in the greeting, but only just. Then without pausing he went on, 'Stringy's priceless. Talk about the honour of the house. "No one can do pineapple ham like the missus." ' He was mimicking now. ' "Are you suggesting that my future mother-in-law is not a good cook?" said me. "Ain't suggestin' anything, merely telling you." '

His laughter rose as he flopped on to the couch beside his

mother. Then gradually it faded away. But his face still showed his merriment as he bent towards her and kissed her cheek, saying, 'How are you?'

'Oh, all right.' She kept her eyes on him.

'Tired?'

'Just a little; nothing that a bath won't cure.'

He turned his head and looked towards the dining-room. 'Looks wonderful.' He was gazing at her again, his eyes tender and full of concern. 'You are tired,' he said. 'Go on up now and have a rest. You've got a good hour-and-a-half; go on with you.'

As he pushed her gently his father went out of the room, and he turned and looked towards the door, after which he sighed and lay back, his head leaning towards his mother's.

He always felt better, more relaxed, when his father wasn't about, although nowadays his presence didn't affect him as it used to, for he had come to the conclusion that there was nothing in his father to be affected by. He was too colourless, too inane – too gutless. Yes, that was the word that summed up his father. It was hard to believe that a man so big could make so small an imprint on others. Yet they said he was good in court, that he talked well. It was a pity he didn't make use of his legal versatility at home; it would make things a little more lively for his mother. He wondered how she had stood it all these years. The big bulky quietness of him, his soft voice, and that soundless laugh. Why didn't he laugh, really laugh? It was odd, but he had never heard his father laugh outright in his life.

He now put out his hand and picked hers up from where it was lying by her side as if waiting. Without moving she said, 'What kind of a day have you had?' She was sitting with her eyes closed.

'Oh, the usual. . . . You know, between you and me old Wilcox is a pompous beast; he makes me sick at times.'

'Ssh! Ssh!'

'Well, no one can hear us.'

'It doesn't matter. If you think it, don't say it.' She moved restlessly. 'It's a pity you ever went into his office. But then, you didn't know he was to become your father-in-law, did you? Perhaps you should have gone in for law after all.'

'No. No.' His cultured, pleasing voice was gruff now. 'Not law for me.'

She remained quiet for a moment. It was as if he had said, 'What! Be like my father.'

She moved restlessly again. 'Once you're married he may offer you a partnership.'

'I'm not banking on it; if that was in his mind he would have broached it before now. He loves to be top-dog and have a lot of little puppies running round his heels.'

'Ssh! Ssh!'

'Don't keep saying Ssh! Ssh!' He wagged her hand, and they laughed softly together.

'Does Valerie know how you feel about him?'

'I think she guesses.'

'He's very fond of her. When once you're married she'll likely persuade him to . . .'

'Oh, no, she won't.' He sat up and turned to face her. 'Look.' He wagged his finger like a pendulum before her face. 'I don't want any favours through my wife. Don't forget that where Papa Wilcox is today is solely because of Mama Wilcox's favours, and she's never let him forget it.'

'Oh, Laurie, don't be silly. And don't call May Mama Wilcox; you might come out with it sometime without thinking.'

'Oh, that would be too bad. But I'm not being silly, and you know it. He's the big boss in the office, but out of it. . . . Oh, boy! Who wears the trousers in the house, and who keeps the finger on the purse strings? I know what I know, dear Mamma.' He nodded at her, smiling broadly now. 'Anyway' – he pulled himself up from the couch – 'there are other jobs. If he doesn't make himself plain about my prospects at the end of another year, well I can always move.'

'You wouldn't leave . . . leave the town?'

He turned to her where she was sitting on the edge of the couch staring up at him, and he put his hand out and gently touched her cheek. 'No. Don't worry, I won't go far away. There are at least four other accountants' offices in the town. . . . Anyway, I may set up on my own. All I need to do is pinch a few clients and rent an office.'

She lowered her eyes and dropped her head as if in shame.

'Come on.' His voice was cheerful, bracing. 'Upstairs you go, and get ready for the fray.'

He still had her by the hand as they entered the hall, and there saw his father crossing it with a brief case in his hand.

'I'm . . . I'm going back to the office for a little while.' John looked at Ann and she looked up to the half-landing at a clock encased in a gold-starred frame, like the home of the eucharist in a Catholic church. 'It's twenty-to-seven,' she said.

'I won't be more than half-an-hour. I want to collect some papers. The case was finished today; I told you. And I . . . I want to tidy up.'

'They'll be here about quarter to.'

'Oh, I'll be back before then.'

'You're not changed.' She looked him up and down.

'It won't take me long. I'll give myself half-an-hour. I'll be back on time.'

As he went out of the door into the lobby, he knew that they were both watching him. He got into the car and drove out of the drive on to the road, not taking so much care of the frost now, which was much harder.

After turning out of the avenue, he drove down the lane which still clung to the country, then on to the main road, past the park; past Brampton Hill, that mansion-studded hill, a relic of bygone days, a hive now of building speculators, who vied with each other to see how many flats they could get out of a house; past the old town, bordering on Bog's End; past the new town, with its brash shopping centre; over the main bridge that spanned the river; and to Greystone Buildings.

Greystone Buildings consisted of five four-storied houses. They had been built by one Arthur Greystone, in 1874, primarily as dwelling houses for better-class citizens, men say, who worked in Newcastle and could afford to drive there by coach and pair. The only remaining evidence of this particular splendour was the coach houses at the back now making admirable garages. Four of the houses in Greystone Buildings were taken over as offices; only number ten still carried out its primary use, and this had been turned into four flats.

John's office was in number eight, and somewhere within

him, unacknowledged but nevertheless known to be there, was the fact that this house spelt home to him more than did 'The Gables', 74 Lime Avenue.

His fingers trembled as he inserted the key in the Yale lock. The hall into which he stepped was the usual office hall, bare but for a list of slotted names in an oak board attached to the wall, and it had that dreary air that seems to permeate most solicitors' offices, at least the entrance to them. He went up the brass bound stairs, past the door marked Enquiries, up another flight, past a number of doors here, one with a nameplate on which said 'J. A. Ransome', and another 'M. O. Boyd'. Then up a third flight of stairs to the top floor.

There were three doors on the top floor. One bore his own name, a second led to a storeroom, and the third to an antiquated lavatory with an equally antiquated wash-basin.

As a young man he had been put on this top floor, and together with two other clerks he had shared the one large, chilly room. When, in the course of years, he received promotion and the staff was moved round, he asked to stay on the third floor. There had been nothing unusual in that request, for he was still not very important, but now, as head of the firm he should have been occupying a room on the floor below, the one his junior had, but he had stated a preference to remain on the third floor. This had been considered odd, and, what was more, not good for business. Influential clients were used to lifts; there were no lifts in Greystone Buildings and never likely to be.

Yet people climbed the stairs to the top floor and business grew so much that at times he passed work on to his less fortunate colleagues in the town.

The room he entered was warm from the central heating. It looked what it was, an office, but a comfortable one. It had a good carpet on the floor, four large leather chairs, and a great mahogany desk. One of the walls was covered by a high glass-fronted bookcase, and round the remaining walls were a collection of prints, some sporting, some so faded that their pictures were hardly discernible.

He switched on the metal-angle-poised desk light, then returned to the door and switched off the main light.

After this, he lowered himself slowly into one of the chairs;

then, with his hands covering his face, he sat perfectly still. He shouldn't have done it, come back here. And so little time. But he felt he would have gone mad had he stayed in the house. After he had changed he couldn't have stayed upstairs until the others actually came, and if he had gone downstairs, there they would have been, the two of them, holding hands, or laughing with each other, or talking over his head. He couldn't stand it much longer, he would go mad. Would it be better when he was married and out of the house? No, it would be worse, because then she would be entirely lost and he'd feel her agony and not be able to lift a hand to ease it.

But he shouldn't have come out tonight. He knew what stock she laid on these dinner do's. That's all she asked of him: to be there at the head of the table when she gave her dinners. He knew, too, that in her own way she was grateful to him if he smiled and talked and generally made himself agreeable. And he always tried, knowing that the one fear of her life was that the state that existed between them should ever become public knowledge.

He was sure that even May Wilcox knew nothing whatever about the pattern of their real life. The Wilcoxes just considered him a quiet, withdrawn sort of fellow. . . . Did Laurie talk to Valerie about the situation in the house, a situation that had not altered from when he was a small child? No; somehow he didn't think that Laurie would discuss his mother with anyone, not even his future wife. At least he would say nothing that might cause her to probe his mother's façade, that well-bred, cultured, ready-for-any-situation façade that effectually hid an intolerable situation. Instinctively he knew that his son was as protective of his mother's image as was she herself.

But he must get home. Why the devil had he to come out tonight of all nights? He'd take the papers and do some work later after they had all gone.

His hand dropped from his face to the arm of the chair, and he went to rise; then stopped, one leg stretched out, one shoulder forward. Slowly now he brought his hand towards his ribs and held it there, and after a moment, during which he remained still, he asked himself how long it was since he'd had a turn. About two months. But this could be indigestion; that lunch had been too heavy.... He'd get into the air; he always felt better if he could get into the air. But he couldn't drive the car like this. Get up, get up, he said to himself. Take it slowly. But he remained stationary, and it was some time later when he moved.

He hadn't taken his overcoat off, just his hat, but he did not pick it up, nor yet put the desk light off when he got to his feet.

On the landing he slowly turned the key in the lock, put the key case in his pocket, and went towards the stairs. There was a good light over the stairs, it picked out every step down to the next landing, but as he stood with his hands on the top of the balustrade he knew he couldn't go down them. He closed his eyes and went back to his door and stood leaning against it for a moment, his breathing short and sharp now. He would have to get air, he wanted air. The roof. Why hadn't he thought of it before? Of course the roof. He went slowly past the store-room door, past the lavatory door and towards eight steps wedged in the corner of the passage, which mounted up to a fanlight. He had only to stand on the bottom step to release the bolt that secured the glass frame. When he stood on the second step his hand pushed the frame upwards, and from the third step his head came into the open, and the frame dropped back on to the roof none too gently. He leaned his arms on the flat roof now and bowed his head as he gulped at the air, and after a while he slowly drew himself up on to the roof proper. That was better; that was better.

He knew the roof as well as he knew the room down below; it had been a sort of bolt-hole to him for years. In the summer he kept a deck chair up here. Sitting with his back to the chimney, he could look over the town to the river, and beyond to the fells, to that part which hadn't as yet been encroached on by housing estates. He considered the view from the roof one of the pleasantest in Fellburn.

But there was no chair up on the roof tonight, so he stood leaning with his back to the chimney breast for a moment before making his way to the low stone parapet that was the only barrier between the houses. Then sitting on it, he bent over and rested his elbow on the top and cupped his head in his hand.

There was a wind blowing, a gusty, rough, iced wind, but it didn't affect him, for he was sweating. He could feel the moisture running down under his shirt.

He became aware that there was a noise coming from somewhere, a strange noise for up here, like people laughing, and singing. It could be coming from the street; yet it wasn't, it was too muffled. It was likely coming from the flats. Yes, from the flats. All the years he had used the roof he could count on his two hands the times he had seen anyone else up here. That was, except for the warm summer a few years ago when his clerks and typists discovered the building had a roof; as did those in the offices of Wallace & Pringle, and the wholesale firm in No. 1.

He wanted to lie down; he would have to get back. It had been mad to come up here, but he'd wanted air. If he lay down he could be here all night. Well, would it matter? No. No, not one jot. Best way in fact. Yes, the best thing that could happen. And when they found him, they couldn't say he had tried anything, could they? Not like before. He was tired, oh, so tired of it all.

He heard the music again and the laughter. It was still distant, still muffled. Then as if someone had turned the volume of a wireless to its full pitch a voice screamed over his head, 'LOVE ME, LOVE ME OR I DIE.'

He slid down on to the flat of the roof with his head leaning against a low parapet, and as he did so he thought he heard a child's voice shouting, 'Mam! Mam!'

There was a blank space in his thinking, as if his heart had stopped and he had died, and then he felt someone lifting his head up and a frightened voice from a long distance, saying, 'Is he dead?'

Now there were different voices all floating around him, and some part of his mind was trying to put faces to the voices. He was very sensitive to voices; when he met clients for the first time and they opened their mouths, he came to decisions about them, and he was very seldom wrong.

'Is he dead?'

'No, no. And get out of the way.'

'I saw his hand, Mam, in the light from the stairs, hanging over the wall. Eeh! I got agliff.'

'Be quiet, Pat, and get downstairs. Can you get him on his feet, Ted?'

'He's a big fellow, I'll try. . . . No, it's no good; I could never get him over the parapet on me own. What about old Locket? Give him a shout.'

'No, no, he'd have a heart attack. He couldn't get up here anyway. Look, we'll manage him together.'

'Wait a minute, he's coming round.'

'How are you feeling?' It was a soft, warm voice. He opened his eyes and whispered to the dark figure, 'Better, thanks.'

'Do you think you can get to your feet? We'll help you.'

'Thanks.'

They sat him on the wall, and it was the woman who lifted his legs, one after the other, over the low parapet. The man started backwards down the steps, similar to those up which John had come from his own landing and the woman held the shoulders of his coat tightly in her fists to steady him from above.

He was swaying and blinking as they brought him across the landing and into a room, which was crowded with people, at least so it seemed to his fuddled mind.

Now he was laying down and the woman was loosening his collar and tie. It was years since anyone had touched his neck. He felt shy and wanted to protest. The voices started up again, muted and soft now, but each different, forming mental pictures in his mind.

'Aw, he looks bad.' This was an old voice, a thick North-country voice, a workman's voice. 'Reckon he could peg out any minute.'

'Don't talk daft, Bill. Trust you to say something sensible. What if he hears you?' Another thick voice, a woman's, but kindly. He put a fat figure to this voice.

'Do you think we could give him a drop of brandy, Ted?'

This was the voice he had first heard. He wanted to open his eyes and look at the source of this voice.

'Don't see that it could do much harm. Of course, it all depends what's wrong with him. I think we should get a doctor.' A clipped, precise voice this. North-country too, yet different from the other man's. This was a voice that was used to talking.

'Why, I know him.' The high exclamation caused him to flicker his eyelids. 'He's Mr. Emmerson, the solicitor from next door. You know, I've told you, my people's daughter, Miss Valerie, is going to marry his son. You mind, Cissy, me tellin' you about their engagement?'

This voice was thin and fussy, and brought him to himself. He opened his eyes and looked at the faces around him. They were all slightly blurred, but the nearest one he knew belonged to the woman with the nice voice. Yet she wasn't quite a woman, and yet she wasn't a girl either. And beside her stood a thin, dapper man. He was the one who had helped him down the ladder; he had the voice that was used to talking. At the foot of the couch stood an old couple. They were likely the owners of the North-country voices. And to the side of them stood another two women. The thin, small one was smiling at him. She, he felt, was the one who knew him. Her companion was equally small, but fat with it. And then standing to the side of this fat woman was a boy. He was slight and thin and very fair and looked about nine years old.

'Do you feel better?'

'Yes. Yes, thank you.' He looked up into a pair of warm dark brown eyes in an oval face, the cheeks flanked by two long strands of fair hair.

'Would you like a drop of brandy?'

'Thank you . . . please.'

No one spoke until the brandy was brought to him, and as he tried to sip it, it spilled down his chin and on to the front of his shirt.

'Drink it all up, it'll do you good.' She held her hand round his to steady the glass.

In a moment or so he felt better, stronger. His heart wasn't beating so fast, although it was still thumping hard.

'Look, I'll put a cushion behind your head.'

She put a cushion behind his head, then said, 'Will I phone for your doctor?'

'No, no thanks. I'll . . . I'll soon be all right. I'm so sorry. . . .'

'Oh, don't be. . . .' He felt she was going to add, 'silly', but she smiled and changed it to bothered, and repeated, 'Don't be bothered about anything . . . Look.' She sat down on the edge of the couch near his legs, and, bending forward, asked softly, 'Will I phone your house?'

This question was like an injection, giving him life. He pulled himself a little way up on the couch and said quickly, 'No, no, please. I'll be all right. If I . . . if I could just stay a moment longer.'

'Oh!' He watched her throw her head upwards, an action suggesting that her whole body was relaxed, loose. 'You're welcome to stay as long as you like.'

'Thank you.' He looked from one to the other of the company now, and it came to him that they were a mixed group . . . this wasn't a family. And his voice was troubled as he said, 'I've interrupted something?'

'You haven't. You haven't.' Again she tossed her head, smiling widely now. 'They were all about to go, weren't you?' She looked round the company, and one after the other they nodded and said in their own particular ways, 'Yes, yes, we were just going.'

Then the old woman spoke to him. 'It was Cissie's party,' she said; 'we just came up for a cup of tea, but as always happens when we get in here we forget to go. We need a reminder.' She nodded at him.

'Oh, Mrs. Locket!' The young woman looked at the old woman, and again she said, 'Oh, Mrs. Locket!'

'It's true, Cissie; we always stay too long.' Mrs. Locket now took her husband by the arm, and she nodded towards John before making her way to the door, almost on tiptoe, as if afraid to disturb him further.

Now the little fat woman and the little thin one made to depart, and the little thin one looked at him and wagged her head as she whispered down to him, 'I hope you'll soon be better, Mr. Emmerson.'

The man, called Ted, followed them. Then came the sound of a door closing, and the man came back. 'How are you really feeling?' he asked gently, bringing his face close to John's.

'Much better. Much better. Thank you.'

He did feel better, but so tired. He wanted to sleep, and he felt he could sleep, he was so comfortable and so relaxed. He had put these people out, broken up their party and yet he didn't feel disturbed by the fact, which was strange. His eyes were now drawn to the boy who was standing staring at him. He could see he had a nice face; it was like the young woman's. He connected them as mother and son. They had the same colouring, the same shaped face, the same brown eyes. In fact, they were replicas of each other.

The young woman was saying, 'Do you think you could manage a cup of coffee?'

'That's kind of you. Yes, I think I would like a cup of coffee.'

'I'll make it, you stay where you are.' The man put out his flat hand towards her, then disappeared round the head of the couch.

John blinked rapidly, then tried to focus his tired gaze on the young woman again. She was sitting down, but even so she looked tall. He said to her, 'Your husband's very kind.'

The laughter of the boy brought his head slowly round and he looked from one to the other. They were exchanging broad smiles. He watched her put out her hand and push at the air between them, as if to stop the boy's laughter, the action also indicated that they were sharing a joke. She said soberly now, 'He's not my husband; that's Mr. Glazier from the ground floor flat.'

'Oh, I'm sorry.'

'Oh, you weren't to know. He's a traveller. He's very rarely here, but he always comes up and sees us when he comes home.'

He inclined his head towards her but made no further comment.

She now bent slightly towards him and began to identify the late company to him as if it were important he should know them. 'The old man and woman,' she said, 'are a Mr. and Mrs. Locket. They live on the second floor, No. 3 Flat. They're old-age pensioners, and they get lonely at times. I often ask them up for a cup of tea.' Her head moved as she spoke. 'Then the other two, the one who knows you, she's Mrs. Orchard. She works as a daily for Mrs. Wilcox, and she lives with Miss O'Neill, that's the fat one. Miss O'Neill's a cook in the school canteen. They live on the first floor.' She pointed her finger downwards. She paused here, then looked towards her son and smiled again as she said, 'And up here among the gods, there's Pat and me.'

Pat and me, she had said; no mention of a husband. She could be a widow, or perhaps not married and the child illegitimate. Yes, very likely, for she had the kind of personality that attracted people seemingly; old and young, cooks and commercial travellers.

'I'm tiring you. You don't want to hear about all us here, but I thought I would explain. Look, wouldn't you like me to ring your home?'

'No, no thank you very much.' He moved restlessly now, and as if coming out of a drugged sleep he stretched his eyes wide and asked, 'What is the time, please?' As he did so he fumbled for his watch, and she turned her head and looked at a grandfather clock in the far corner and said, 'Twenty minutes to nine.'

'Twenty minutes to . . .!' With a jerk he was sitting upright. 'It . . . it can't be.' He looked at her as if he were begging her to tell him she was wrong. 'I came to the office just before seven and . . . and I was out again within ten minutes . . . at least I . . .'

'You must have lain on the roof for some time?'

'No, no.' He shook his head. He had lost an hour, and he had lost it in the office, not on the roof. It wasn't the first time he had lost an hour when this had happened to him. He'd have to see about it. But now he must get home, and at once. What would she say? He felt very tired again as he thought she would say the same if he went home now or in another hour's time, or tomorrow morning, because he hadn't been home at eight o'clock. He'd have to tell her about these turns he was having, then perhaps she would understand. . . . But no she wouldn't; she would never forgive him for this. He couldn't do even this one thing for her, she would say. And she would say it quietly, and the echo of that quietness would seep deeper into them for months ahead; the fact that he had conformed to her pattern of social etiquette for years would bear no weight. He had missed conforming this once, and it was always the once that mattered.

'There.' The man came to the couch with a tray in his hand. 'I've made it strong. Do you like plenty of sugar?'

'One spoonful, please.' As he took the cup from the man's

hand he said, 'I must get home. I wonder if you'd be kind enough to phone for a taxi as I don't think I'll be fit enough to drive my car?'

'You've got a car downstairs?'

'Yes.' He nodded at the man.

'Well then, I tell you what I'll do. I'll drive you home and Cissie here can come on behind in my car and bring me back. How's that?' He looked at Cissie now and she said quickly, 'Yes, that's the idea.'

'Can I come with you, Mam?'

'Yes, yes, of course.' She smiled at her son.

'I'm putting you to too much trouble.' John made to move his legs off the couch, and when she bent down to assist him he became hot with embarrassment. He wanted to say, 'No. No, don't do that, please,' but that would have made things awkward, so he let her bring his feet to the carpet.

'By the way, what is the make of your car?' asked the man.

'A Rover 2000.'

'Really? Oh, boy! I'm going to enjoy this. I used to have a Rover; but a Rover 2000! I hear they're spanking. You don't mind me driving her, do you? I'm a good driver, that's part of my living.'

'I'm sure you are, and you're very welcome to drive it ... particularly tonight.' He smiled weakly.

They had the room to themselves now, as the young woman and the boy had disappeared, getting dressed he surmised, and the man took this opportunity to praise his hostess. Bending down to John, he said in a confidential whisper, 'She's a good sport, is Cissie, none better. They don't come like her the day. A good sport.' He jerked his head and winked his eye.

The nod, wink, and information could have suggested many things, but he was in no frame of mind at the moment to analyse them.

He stood up now and steadied himself on his feet. He still felt a bit rocky. He was aware of his overcoat being creased, and he smoothed it slowly downwards with his hands, then buttoned it up to the neck.

The boy and his brother now returned to the room, and the boy, coming up to him, said, 'Wasn't it lucky I went up for the ice-cream?'

He looked down on the fair head and smiling face and repeated, 'Ice-cream?' He was unable to follow the child.

'We had two blocks of ice-cream. I keep things up there in the winter, I haven't a fridge.' She was pulling a hat carelessly on to her head as she spoke, tucking the strands of hair behind her ears. She looked like an overgrown schoolgirl, not the mother of the boy. So it was lucky we went up, wasn't it? How are you feeling now?'

'Oh, much better.' He did not comment on her reference to luck. But for two blocks of ice-cream he would have lain up there all night, and that would have been the finish. He had wanted it that way, but two blocks of ice-cream had baulked his intention. It was odd how things, little things, could interfere with one's life, or the desire to be rid of it.

'Careful how you go.' Ted had him by the arm now, steadying him firmly, as if he were an old man, down one step after another until they reached the street. There John handed him his car keys and he felt the man's excitement when he took the wheel of the car. He tried to explain the mechanism to him. 'It's a bit different,' he said. 'Quick off the start compared to . . .'

'Oh, I'll get it, never you fear. There's never been a car yet I couldn't drive. There, that's it.' He pressed the starter, then turned his face to John, saying, 'You can hardly hear her, she's a beauty. I've read a bit about her. I bet you what you like I'll not rest until I have one. There'll be some second-hands coming along shortly. . . . Now, where to?'

'Do you know Lime Avenue?'

'Oh yes. Yes, I know Lime Avenue. Nice houses there. What number?'

'Seventy-four.'

He looked through his mirror and said, 'I'll just wait a tick until Cissie comes round the corner. . . . Aw, there she is. Now off we go.'

John thought the man handled the car as if he had driven it for years. He was a natural driver, and he didn't talk while he was driving. As the journey neared its end he wondered about asking them in. It might ease things, help to explain without words. They were in the drive now, going round the bend and into the blaze of light from the windows. And there was Wilcox's car right opposite the door. They always came by car; the comparatively short distance down the road was not to be walked when going out to dinner. He said to the man, 'This is very kind of you.'

'No, no, not at all. Sad world if we can't help one another. Anyway, it's put me in your debt, and what's more it'll likely put me in real debt afore I'm finished.' He laughed. 'For as I said I'll not rest until I have one of these.' He patted the wheel.

'Would you care to come in?'

The man hesitated, then said slowly, almost shyly, 'Well, not tonight, if you don't mind. I'm off early in the morning. I leave around six and I've got things to see to.'

John was out of the car now and he looked towards the gate, from where he could see the reflection of the headlights of the other car. She hadn't got out and he didn't feel able to go to her and thank her. He said, 'I would like to thank Mrs. . . . what is her name?'

'Mrs. Thorpe.'

'Will you tell her . . .?' His voice trailed away on a feeling of weakness.

'Don't you trouble about her; she doesn't need any thanks. Get yourself inside. Good night now.' He pushed him gently towards the porch. 'Sure you'll be all right?'

'Yes, thanks. I'm all right, and I'm very very grateful.'

'Go on, go on.' The man spoke as if he were addressing an old pal; then added, 'I won't be back for another few weeks or so. Going down south this time, but I'll be interested to know how you get on.'

John nodded, there was nothing more to say.

He fumbled in his pockets and found his key, and as he opened the door he heard the man's steps crunching away down the gravel drive.

He drew in two deep breaths, then opened the lobby door into the hall and there, confronting him, were the guests of the evening, together with his wife and son and partner. They all stood as if transfixed, staring at him, all silent. And he stared back. At least he stared at his wife. Her face looked like a piece of alabaster and as stiff, and expressionless, all except her eyes.

The first glimpse they'd had of him had swept the fear from them, and now deep in them he saw a white anger, that quiet anger that he knew so well. Quiet people were always more forceful, more dangerous than noisy ones.

James Wilcox was a noisy man, a fussy little man. He showed it now by crying, 'Well, well! This is a nice kettle of fish. What happened to you?' He did not add, John, which would have tempered his demand for an explanation. 'Come on. Come on, man; don't stand there. What's all this about? Everyone of us distracted here. Poor Ann nearly out of her wits.' He flapped his hand upwards over his shoulder to indicate Ann.

'I . . . I went to the office and I didn't feel very well.' Even to his own ears the truth sounded inane. Silence, full of disbelief, met his statement. And then May Wilcox spoke.

May had a pseudo-refined twang. She was a petite-looking woman with greying hair, tightly dressed over her small scalp. Everything about May was tight and small. John had always thought that she and James were well matched. Couples nearly always paired off together, he had found that. It was an oddity of human nature that you should choose for your mate someone who reflected yourself, as you saw yourself, or your mother, or your father. Yes, it was odd. He brought his eyes fully to bear on May as she said, 'Arnold—' she inclined her head with a genteel movement towards his partner— 'Arnold went to the office. Ann phoned him; she was very worried. There was no one there, not at the office . . . was there, Arnold?'

Arnold Ransome swallowed hard and pushed his hand over his well-oiled hair, then he moved towards John as he said, 'Perhaps you had gone by the time I got there. It was about half-an-hour ago.' He was looking him straight in the face, and his eyes were saying, I'm trying to work in with you; whatever this is about I'm trying to work in with you. And he nodded as John said, 'I had left before that.'

He turned from them now and unbuttoned his coat and dropped it over a chair, and when he turned towards them once more they were all eyes again, all staring at his neck. With the realization that his tie was hanging slack and his collar was open, he felt the colour rushing to his face like a wave of guilt. As his hand went to his neck he looked again towards Ann, but he was more aware of his son then he was of her at the moment. Laurie was standing by her side, his face looking grim and pugnacious, as if he wanted to hit out at him. He'd felt that often about Laurie lately, that he wanted to hit out at him. He turned from them all and made his way towards the stairs, his gait slightly unsteady, and as he did so he saw his wife go into the lounge and his son follow her. When he passed James Wilcox he heard him sniff audibly a number of times, like a dog which had caught a scent, and he was half-way across the top landing when there came to him the scarcely muffled whisper: 'Well! What do you think of that? Did you smell him? He's been drinking . . . brandy!'

Down in the hall, Arnold Ransome shook his head and repeated, 'Brandy? He doesn't drink brandy.'

James Wilcox drew in his lips, thrust out his chin, and said in no small voice, 'I know the smell of brandy. He's drunk.'

'But John doesn't drink brandy; it isn't his drink,' Arnold Ransome persisted.

'Well, it mightn't have been before tonight, but it certainly is now. I tell you he's been drinking brandy. What is he up to, does he think?'

Arnold looked back at the little man. He had never liked Wilcox, or his wife, or his daughter, and so he couldn't keep the sharpness out of his tone as he said, 'How should I know? As he said, he felt ill. Likely when he left the office he went for a drink.'

'And loosened his collar and tie? Did you see the condition of his overcoat?' It was May Wilcox speaking now, and with an exaggerated, gracious movement of her hand she indicated the overcoat lying on the chair. Then picking it up, she held it for their inspection. 'It looks as if he had been rolling in the gutter, doesn't it?'

She was right there. Arnold Ransome moved uneasily. There was something behind all this, but he hoped whatever it was it wouldn't afford these two any more satisfaction. Self-righteous prigs, both of them. And him on the Bench. How in the name of God had that come about.

'Well, we'd better go in to Ann and see if we can sort this thing out.' May Wilcox now marched towards the lounge, her husband following her, and reluctantly Arnold Ransome followed them. But before he entered the room he glanced towards the stairs and thought, 'What if he is bad, he's looked off colour for months now? Somebody should go up to him.' But it wasn't his place to say so.

* * *

Laurie walked Valerie round the bottom of Lime Avenue and up the lane that led to Handley's smallholding. The ground was hard and slippery, and as he was holding her arm they slithered together. They walked to the end of the lane, turned the corner, and stopped at the back of Handley's barn.

There had been silence between them since they left the house, but now as she stood within the circle of his arms she gave a small laugh and said, 'Well, what do you think of it all?'

'You mean father?'

'Who else could I mean?'

There were shades in her voice which at times indicated undercurrents he could not fathom, and this had the power to nettle him, as now.

'It could have been as he said. He felt bad, and then went out for a drink.'

'Oh, Laurie, don't be naïve. You don't come in like that, collar and tie awry. . . . And look at his coat. You don't get like that by going for a drink. Imagine loosening your collar and tie in The George, or at the club.'

'He needn't have gone to The George, or the club.'

'But would he have loosened his collar and tie in any bar . . . your father, in his position?'

'Oh God Almighty! He could have loosened it in the car coming back.'

'All right, all right.' Her voice was controlled. 'I thought you might have seen the funny side of it.'

He peered at her through the darkness. He could just see the outline of her face. He knew that there would be laughter lurking at the back of her round dark eyes. He had never been quite able to make Val out; that was part of her attraction for him. She had quite a bit of her mother and father in her make-up, yet she laughed at them, criticized and scoffed at them on the quiet. This did not displease him at all, especially when it was directed at her father. Yet he couldn't bear the thought of her taking the mickey out of his own parents. He might think what he liked about his father, but the situation changed when other people began to express their opinions of him, for any adverse criticism of his father reflected, he thought, on his mother.

'I was sorry for Aunt Ann, as it was her turn to score.'

'Score! What do you mean?'

'Oh, Laurie, for heaven's sake don't pretend you don't know what I mean about this an' all. You play dumb on so many things. What's the matter with you? You know for a fact that mother and Aunt Ann have been scoring off each other over these dinners-at-eight for years.'

'Oh, that! But I don't see it as competitive. They put on good meals, and . . .'

'Oh, be quiet. Kiss me.'

He kissed her, his mouth covering hers, one hand under her arm pit, the other across her buttocks. It was a long kiss, the length extended by her rather than him.

After it was over there was no breathlessness about her, and she said evenly, 'There'll be no dinner-at-eight for us, I'm a stinking cook.'

'I'll have to eat, so you'll have to learn.' He pulled her closer to him.

'Learn to stand two days in the kitchen preparing a meal? Can you see me? No, darling, that's not for me. Except for drinks and perhaps a snack, our guests will be invited out.'

'That'll run into something, won't it? How often do you think we can do that?'

'Oh, we'll be able to manage it . . . between us.'

He stiffened inside. 'Between us.' That was something else that irked him. She was earning more than he was, at least at this stage of their careers. She had been teaching for two years now in the High School, and she intended to go on teaching after they were married. There was to be no family for the first five years; they had talked it all out. He sometimes wondered if he was a little bit square, for this kind of cold-blooded discussion was distasteful to him. He was all for family planning in principle, but these things could be arranged without a lot of discussion, at least without making a debate of it. Her raw outlook on many things surprised him so much at times that he wondered if there wasn't some prudish trait in him, inherited from his father. Not that he could actually pin such a trait on his father; but he wanted to find no facet in himself that touched on sexual weakness; that was inefficacious.

'You shivered; are you cold?'

'No.'

'You are. Let me warm you.'

She jerked him to her, flattening herself against him.

This was another thing. She always took the initiative, she never waited for it to come from him. There were so many things he liked about her, loved about her. She was cute, smart, and clever, but he wished her cuteness stopped short at this particular line. This was his line. This was the line where he should take the lead, be the master.

'What's the matter with you tonight?' Her voice held a sharp note now.

'Nothing. What could be the matter?'

'What happens to them doesn't touch us. They're living their own lives, we've got ours to live. Let's get on with it.'

There was a space while she held him tightly. Then releasing her hold, she said bluntly, 'Don't you want me?'

He paused before answering, 'What do you think?' Then he pressed his body against hers as if aiming to push it through the barn wall. But quite suddenly the pressure eased and he asked, 'Did you and young Clark have this?'

Her two hands on his chest, she pushed him slowly away from her and he knew that her face was screwed up as she asked, 'Why do you want to know?'

'I just wondered.'

'You've never wondered before. At least, you've never asked.'

'Well, I just wanted to know now.'

'Why? Why now?'

'I just wanted to know if I am the first . . . or not.'

'God!' He heard her laughing in her throat. 'You're funny. What difference does it make? I love you, I want you.'

'You loved Tony Clark.'

'Tony's gone, married, dead to me. That was two years ago. I could ask you if you've been with Susan Lumley. You knocked about with her for years.'

'Not years, and just on and off.'

'You went with her for about four years. When I came back from college on vac I remember seeing you both together several times. So I'm asking you now, did you have her?'

'No, I didn't. And now you answer my question.'

'It's the same as yours. No, I didn't.'

They both knew they were lying.

'Do you want me or don't you? I'm getting cold.'

Oh, God. It was like a groan within him. Slowly he fell against her, and let his hands move over her. But as the minutes passed there rose in him a feeling bordering on panic when he realized that the whole process was tasteless.

CHAPTER TWO

THE FAMILY

ANN got out of bed, put on her dressing-gown, then drew the curtains. As she finished, the clock on the stairs struck eight. She walked towards the dressing-table and sat down, and the reflection she saw in the mirror annoyed her. She put her fingers over her cheekbones, then stretched the muscles of her face, trying to get rid of its stiffness. Except for fitful dozes she hadn't slept. The anger was still boiling in her. He had to fail her in the one thing left she asked of him. She would never forget last night as long as she lived, nor would she forgive him.

There came a tap on the door and Mrs. Stringer entered, bringing in her early morning cup of tea.

'Good morning, Ma'am.'

'Good morning, Mrs. Stringer.'

Mrs. Stringer did not, as was usual on these occasions, begin, 'Well, what did they say, Ma'am? Did they say they enjoyed it? Hard to please if they didn't.' She was silent this morning. As was usual on dinner nights such as last night, Mrs. Stringer had stayed and served the meal, and washed up before going home, so she knew all that had transpired, and all she said this morning was, 'Drink that up while it's hot, Ma'am.'

Ann nodded, and Mrs. Stringer left the room.

As she sipped her tea she listened for movements from across the landing, but she heard nothing. He was sleeping it off. She took a quick mouthful of the tea and it scalded her throat, and she had a hand to her neck when the telephone bell rang.

She sat on the end of the bed and lifted the receiver from the table.

'Ann? . . . That you, Ann?'

'Yes, yes, it's me, May.'

'Well, I thought I'd better phone you straight away. Mrs. Orchard's just come in, and you know what she's just told me?' There was a pause, and Ann waited. Then May's voice went on, 'He was ill last night. John was ill. He went up on the roof and collapsed. The people in the flats took him in. I thought I'd tell you; fair's fair after all. . . . Are you there?'

'Yes.'

'Well, that's what she said. She lives there, down below, and the young boy went on to the roof for something and saw him lying there. They were all up in the top flat, there was a birthday party or something going on, and they carried him down. One of the men drove him back.'

'Oh, May. . . .' Ann was still holding her neck. 'But . . . but James, he said he could smell brandy on him.'

'Well, yes.' May's voice was crisp now. 'He did smell of brandy; they likely gave him brandy. And you must admit he looked a sight. What was anyone to think? It was natural. Anyway, that's what Mrs. Orchard says happened and she was there.'

'Thanks, May. . . . Thanks for telling me.'

'I'll come along presently, dear, as soon as we have breakfast over.'

'Yes, do. Thanks, May.'

She put down the receiver and sat gripping it. He was ill and nobody had been near him; he could be dead. She hurried across the room, out on to the landing and to the far door. Discarding her usual procedure, she entered her husband's room without knocking; then she stood with the door in her hand and looked towards the bed. He was awake and he didn't move as she went towards him. When she came to the foot of the bed she stopped and her mouth opened. She was about to say, 'Why didn't you tell me you were ill?' But he had told her. She said instead, 'How are you feeling?'

He blinked. Then his eyes widened slightly as if he hadn't heard what she said. She knew he had; it was her concern that had surprised him.

She said now, 'I'll get the doctor.'

'No, no.' His voice was low, weary. 'I'm all right now; just a bit tired. I think I'll have the day off. Would you phone Arnold for me, please?'

'Nevertheless, I'll get the doctor.'

'No, Ann.' He pulled himself up on to his elbows and leant towards her, saying, 'Please don't bother; I'm all right.'

She put her hand up to her lips and patted them a number of times and her eyes dropped before she spoke again. 'I'm sorry I . . . I didn't really understand that you had been ill.'

He looked puzzled, and she raised her eyes to his and explained. 'May's just phoned. She told me about you being found on the office roof. Mrs. Orchard apparently was one of the people in the flats.'

'Oh!' He lay back and he could not prevent the slow smile spreading over the lower part of his face, even though it was a facial expression of his which he knew annoyed her. She'd have to have outside proof that he was ill. He hadn't presided at her table, so the evidence before her eyes had been ignored.

She said now in her usual clipped tone, 'You can't blame me for last night. You didn't explain anything, and coming in like that. You could have got the people to let me know.'

He closed his eyes; then said softly, 'It's all right, Ann. It's all right.'

'It isn't all right. You're putting me in the wrong and it isn't fair.'

He opened his eyes and after a moment during which he didn't look at her, he asked, 'Do you think I might have a cup of tea?'

'Yes . . . yes, of course.' Her voice was polite now, as if talking to a guest. 'I'll bring you some breakfast up.'

'No. No, thanks. I just want a cup of tea.'

She remained staring at him. Then with an impatient movement she went out, but she closed the door quietly after her.

Laurie was crossing the landing towards the bathroom and she beckoned him silently into her room.

'What is it?' he asked under his breath.

'Close the door,' she said. She turned and faced him now, her hands fastening and unfastening the bow of her dressing-gown. 'He was ill . . . he is ill.'

'What?'

'May's just phoned. Apparently he was on the roof and collapsed, and the people from the flats found him.' She jerked her head, and her voice rose slightly as she said, 'But he should have explained, he should have told me. He's put me in the wrong.'

When he made no comment she turned and said, 'Shouldn't he?'

His face was straight, his heavy brows drawn together, and he ran his hand through his hair before he replied, halting, 'Well ... when you come to think of it, he didn't get much chance, did he? We all stood gaping at him as if we'd never seen anyone drunk before.'

'Well, you'd never seen him drunk.'

'No, that's right.'

'You're blaming me for ... for what happened?'

'No, no I'm not.' He went swiftly to her and put his arm around her shoulder. 'Don't be silly, dear. Of course I'm not. I felt I could have slain him myself when he didn't come back to dinner after all the work that you'd put in.'

'It was James, James that said he was drunk. The whole situation put him in his element, it gave him a handle.'

'A handle?' He seemed to be picking up the conversation from last night when Val had said, 'Poor Aunt Ann. It was her turn to score.'

'Well, anyway,' she stretched her thin neck and tilted her chin upwards, 'he's found his mistake out this morning. I hope he feels silly.'

Laurie patted her shoulder and turned away, saying, 'I suppose I'd better go in and see him.'

'Yes. Yes, do.'

Out on the landing he paused. It was true what she had said: old Wilcox had acted as if he'd got a handle over them when he thought his father was drunk and had been in a scuffle. He'd likely seen it as the beginning of the steep road down. He could almost hear him in the club, commenting on it. 'Pity. Pity. But I've expected it for a long time. He's always been an odd bloke, has Emmerson. Deep, I could almost say furtive. And he's had cause to be for he's been on the secret drinking line for years. But now it's out.... The one I'm sorry for is Ann. Fine woman, fine woman. She was one of the Coopers, you know, Bailey & Cooper. Yes, yes, the shipbuilders. Of course the Coopers have gone down over the years, dropped out of the firm some time ago, but still they were people of note in the county at one time.

And what did she do? Marry Emmerson, a farmer's son. Oh yes, quite a decent farm, but after all they were only tenants of her father. It never pays. It never pays. I've seen it again and again.'

Laurie rubbed his hand tightly over the side of his head, shutting out Wilcox's voice, then pressed his fingers on his eyeballs for a moment. He was all at sixes and sevens this morning; he hadn't slept well last night, in fact he hadn't got to sleep until two o'clock, for he had been troubled about another member of the Wilcox ménage. He had been thinking about Valerie and himself, funny thoughts, odd, disturbing thoughts. He drew in a long breath, then walked slowly towards his father's door, knocked gently, and went in.

He felt awkward, as awkward as he used to be when, as a boy, he tried to talk to this man. It was a strange facet in their relationship that when he was away from him he could think and speak of him as his father without feeling unduly disturbed, but when he was physically close to him, as now, he was filled with feelings of resentment, and dislike, above all with the knowledge that he despised him as a man.

'How are you feeling?'

'Oh.' John smiled at his son, the same smile that he had given to his mother, the smile that rarely spread his mouth beyond the edge of his teeth. 'I'm all right. There's nothing wrong.'

'You want a holiday.'

'It's only two months since I had one.' The smile remained stationary.

'What I mean is, a long one, six months.' He heard himself speaking in an abrupt manner. It was always like this.

'Yes, yes.' John nodded. 'I'll take a year off some time.' It was meant to be funny, and with anyone else Laurie would have picked it up and said, 'Well now, that's what you want to do, take a year off. And you can you know. The business won't drop to bits because you're not there.' Instead, he said, and politely, 'Can I get you anything?'

'No. No, thanks.'

'I'd stay in bed today.'

'Yes, I'm going to.'

'I'll look in and see you later.'

'Thanks.'

On the landing, Laurie pulled at the collar of his dressing-gown as if it was tight, then went on into the bathroom. He wanted to be sorry for him but he couldn't. Did that mean there was something lacking in himself? Because this man could stir no good emotion in him, no feeling that should be between a father and son – a good father, because by all the rules of the book he was a good father – did it point to the fault being in himself?

He slipped off his dressing-gown and stood looking at his naked body in the long mirror, and not for the first time he was thankful that he did not see before him a replica of the man across the landing. He was two inches shorter than his father, being five foot eleven. His body had no bulk about it or superfluous flesh as was on his father's. He was cut to a symmetrical pattern; his shoulder were broad, his hips were narrow, his whole body looked hard and compact. There was hair between his breasts, and a little on his legs. The hair on his body had remained fair, while that on his head had turned from blond as a boy, to light brown as a youth, and was now shades darker. He opened his mouth and drew his fingers down one cheek, then the other, feeling the heavy stubble on each. He could never understand why, with a mother as beautiful as his, he hadn't inherited one feature of her face, but he hadn't. His face was the same shape as his father's, and his features almost identical, yet, on his father's face they resulted in a soft, insipid look, while, on his, the combination looked pugnacious. He'd always been thankful that was so.

The tinkle of the breakfast bell came to him, and brought a picture of Stringy standing at the bottom of the stairs, the bell in her hand. He was still staring at himself in the mirror when he said aloud, 'Once I'm married I won't hear that.' He could see them scrambling their breakfast at a service counter in the kitchen; then Valerie would dash into her Mini and away to school, and he'd take a bus down to the office, for they wouldn't be able to afford two cars; and he'd as likely as not have to clear up before leaving. He didn't like the picture at all. His life up to now, under his mother's management, had been ordered and gracious. They lived as few people lived today, and, once he left this house, the pattern of his life would alter drastically. Valerie could scoff at 'Dinner-at-Eight', but, for himself, he

CHAPTER THREE

MOTHER AND SON

'MAM, I heard a funny one yesterday.'

Cissie Thorpe, standing at the sink, with her hands in the soapy water, stopped rubbing at the hardened yolk of egg on a plate, and, letting her head fall back on her shoulders, opened her mouth wide before she called into the next room, 'Tell it me. Come on, tell it me.'

There was a scrambling sound, and the boy came into the kitchen in a hunched position, attempting to tie his shoe lace as he walked. Just within the kitchen door he dropped on to the floor and hastily knotted the lace, then getting to his feet, he came to her side and looked up into her face and laughed. 'Well, it was like this,' he said. 'There was a Catholic priest fell off a six-storied building, a big high one.' He demonstrated with his hands. 'An' he prayed all the way down past five of the stories that he'd be saved, but as he passed the last one he made the sign of the Cross – you know, Mam, like Catholics do' – he demonstrated again – 'and he said, "Oh, my God! Now for the blooming bump!" '

'Ooh! Pat.' She had her arms about him and he had his arms about her, tight round her waist, his head down and pressed into her stomach, and they rocked together. Then leaning against the sink and pushing him from her, she said, 'Tell it again, I must remember this one for Ted. You know I forget half of them you tell me. Who told you that one?'

'Barry Rice. An' he's a Catholic an' all, Mam. . . . Well, like I said, there was this Catholic priest . . .'

She was still laughing loudly when she turned to the sink and started to rub at the plate again, and she said now, 'But you shouldn't say my God! It's like swearing.'

'Well, I don't say it, Mam, just when I'm tellin' the joke.'

She raised her eyebrows and smiled to herself as she looked out between the frilled curtains of the window to where she could see a silver streak beyond the roofs and chimney tops, the river with the sun shining on it. It was a grand morning, crisp, frosty, bright. She tossed her head back to get her hair from the front of her shoulders, and asked, 'What you going to do this morning?'

'I was going round to Mr. Bolton's to see if he wanted any jobs done.'

She looked at him over her shoulder, her face straight now, saying, 'You'll get wrong, you know. You're not supposed to work yet, so be careful.'

'He always keeps me in the back, weighing up, nobody sees me.'

'Well, that's all right. And Pat,' she turned round as he was making for the room door, 'what you doing this afternoon?'

'I was going to play football on the pitch.'

'Will Tim Brooks be there with the others?'

'I suppose so.'

As she watched his chin move downwards, she hastily dried her hands and went towards him, and, dropping on to her hunkers, she held him by the shoulders, her face level with his as she said, quietly, 'Pat, you're not going round with him again, are you?'

'No, Mam. 'Struth.' His head went lower and his eyes screwed up tightly against her scrutiny, and his voice mumbled as he said, 'He comes up to me and talks, and hangs on. I dodge him. . . . I dodge him all the time.'

'Well, go on dodging him.' For the first time there came a stern note into her voice. 'Now listen to me.' She shook him gently. 'Go on dodging him. Don't be seen talking to him. Just remember what nearly happened. That boy's bad.'

'Ah, Mam, he's—'

'Don't tell me what he is, Pat. He's bad. You just take my word for it, he's bad. . . . Promise me you'll steer clear of him.' There was pleading in her voice now.

'All right, Mam, don't worry.' He smiled, and the smile had an adult quality about it. It could have been a smile of understanding on the face of someone twice his age. 'I'll do what you tell me.'

'Good boy.'

She bent forward and kissed him, and they clung together for a moment before, pushing him on the side of the head, she said, 'Go on now. And mind, don't stuff yourself with bruised fruit. Remember your tummy last Saturday night.'

'Oh, aye. Coo! yes.'

She walked behind him, through the long room and into the hallway, and from a narrow wardrobe she took out his coat and scarf, and as he put them on he grinned up at her and said, 'I'll eat nothing but the best the day, so I won't have the belly ache.'

Again she pushed his head, then opened the door, and he was away.

She listened until the sound of his footsteps faded at the bottom flight of stairs. Then closing the door she sighed and lifted her arms high above her head and stretched. Aw, Saturday morning. She loved Saturday mornings. To lie in, do what she liked. She could lie in on Sunday too, but Sundays were different. The shops weren't open on a Sunday, and there were few people about, whereas Saturday was a live day. She liked live things.

She went into the long room again and looked about her. Everything that met her eyes gave her a feeling of satisfaction, and she sighed. Then stretching her arms above her head again, she planned her day. She would finish the dishes, then tidy up. Not that there was much to do. She had worked at the place until after twelve last night. That was her usual Friday night routine so that she could have Saturday free for herself and Pat. Then she would have a bath and go out and do some shopping. What would she get for dinner? She stood with her back to the fire, legs apart, her hands joined behind her head, and looked up to the ceiling. He liked sausages. But he was getting too many sausages; she'd get something more substantial this week-end. Chops, chump chops, and a bit of kidney, and one of those small chickens for tomorrow, yes. She swung round swirling her dressing-gown into a tent, and as she gathered up school books and magazines from the couch and banged up the cushions she began to sing: 'I love you because you understand me and all the little things I try to do.'

She was singing while she had her bath. She was singing as

she put on her make-up and dressed herself; and when the bell rang she didn't stop singing as she went to the door to answer it, for it would be either old Bill Locket, or Clara, or Miss O'Neill. It wouldn't be Mrs. Orchard, because she always worked up till one on a Saturday, and it wouldn't be Ted because he wasn't expected back yet.

But when she opened the door it was no one of these.

She gazed at the tall, heavy man with the grey hair. Then her mouth falling open, she exclaimed, 'Why! Why, I didn't know you. Come in. Oh come in. Are you better? Well, you look better.'

As she closed the door he said, 'Yes, thank you, I'm quite recovered.'

'Come on in. Come on in.' She was walking sideways away from him now, her arm extended towards the room, and he followed her. But within the room his step was checked with amazement at what he saw. He couldn't remember any part of this room, although he knew he had been here.

'Sit down, sit down.' Again her arm was extended, but towards the couch now. 'I was just going to make a cup of coffee, would you like one?'

'That is very kind of you. Yes, yes, I would.'

She turned away, almost at a run, then turned back again, saying, 'Oh, I am glad to see you looking better. My, you did give us a scare that night, you looked so ill. Have you been in bed since?'

'Yes. Yes, for the last few days; the doctor thought I should have a rest.'

'I'd say you needed it.' She shook her head slowly at him, then said, 'I'll just put the milk on, I won't be a tick.'

She was the same as he remembered her. He hadn't been able to get her face straight in his mind, and yet now he knew her image had been there all the time. But he had remembered her voice clearly, that airy, bright, warm voice. A caressing voice. A deluding voice, because it had that quality about it that made others think they mattered to its owner. During the last few days the memory of her voice had stayed with him, the tone, one of concern for a sick man. Yet he was no longer sick, and the quality he remembered was still there; it hadn't been imagination. And now this room. He hadn't remembered anything about the room, and if he had, and had remembered it as he was seeing it now, he would certainly have put that down to his imagination. He looked at the walls, papered deep blue, a sort of midnight blue he supposed they would call it, and dotted all round the room were pieces of antique furniture. Almost opposite to him at each side of one long window was a pair of Sheraton mahogany card tables with satinwood bands down the legs. He turned his head to where she had disappeared into the kitchen and saw a double-pillared dining-table with a set of Hepplewhite chairs around it. On a small grand piano in another corner stood a pair of inlaid tea caddies he took to be Regency.

It was fantastic, the whole room seemed full of antiques. He knew about these things, he had been brought up among similar things. A number of pieces like these were still in the family. Some in his elder brother's house in Oxford, and others in his sister's in Dorset; but to see stuff like them here, in a top-floor flat and belonging to this girl . . . woman . . . young woman – he hadn't got her right in his mind yet with regards to age – seemed utterly out of place, out of character. Yet why, why should it?

'There, it won't be a minute.' She came hurrying towards him, as if she wanted to hurry towards him. And when he rose to his feet she said, 'Oh, please, sit down.'

She did not sit on the couch but on a pouffe near the fire, and then she said, 'Now tell me all about it.' And as she did so she lifted the tongs and took a large piece of coal from a bright copper coal scuttle. 'There.' She dusted her hands as if they were dirty, and gave him her whole attention. 'What was it? A heart attack?'

He smiled at her. 'Well, a little lead-up I should say. The doctor wasn't quite sure himself, as I was better when he came.'

She shook her head at him. 'I thought about you all night after you'd gone. Just imagine, if I hadn't put the ice-cream up on the roof. You could have been there all night and died, it was bitter.'

'I suppose so.' His head moved slightly.

'You suppose so! I'm sure of it.'

'Well, I've got you to thank for saving my life.'

'Oh, I didn't mean that.'

'I know you didn't. Nevertheless, I'm grateful. That's what I came to say.'

'Oh, but you shouldn't have bothered about that. Oh, not that I'm not pleased to see you, I am, but you know what I mean.'

Again they nodded.

'The coffee will be ready now.'

He turned his head and watched her this time as she went towards the kitchen. She was tall, almost as tall as himself, slightly taller than Ann he thought, and somewhat of her build, even thinner, but so different, oh, so different. She was mobile. Yes, that was the word that described her, mobile, every part of her body, while Ann was all repose, repose without rest. Repose that frightened you and stretched your nerves to screaming point.

'I've done milk 'cos I like it white; perhaps you prefer it black?' She was hurrying towards him again, carrying a tray.

'No, I like half and half.'

When he took the cup from her hand he said, 'You've got a very beautiful home.'

'You like it?' Her wide mouth stretched, showing large white teeth, apparently all her own, for one at the side was overlapping another, and one at the bottom showed a sign of stopping.

'Yes, I . . . I don't think I've seen so many pieces of antique furniture together in one room before, except in a sale room.'

'Perhaps it is a bit overdone.' She looked around the room now, her face unsmiling, and he put in hastily, 'Oh, no. No, I wasn't inferring that; I think the pieces are beautiful and the arrangement equally so. Oh, please believe me.'

'Oh, I do.' The smile was back again. 'But I sometimes wonder myself about there being too much. But I like old stuff, I love it.'

'I can see that.'

She took a sip from her cup then leant towards him, her mouth twisted slightly as she said, 'I bet you're wondering how I came by it all.'

For the first time since entering this room he found himself reverting to his professional training, and the process surprised him because he hadn't realized that he had been acting and talking naturally, spontaneously, talking without first stopping to think. But now he said in his professional manner, 'No. No, I hadn't really thought about it. But if I had, I should have supposed that they were left to you. These things usually are . . . passed down.'

'You're right.' She stretched her eyes wide. 'But not in exactly the way you mean. I didn't inherit them from my father, and he from his, not like that, yet I did get them from my father. You see, he was a second-hand dealer.' She looked away from him towards a small Georgian mahogany sideboard and said slowly, 'Ours was a rubbishy shop, not what you could call an antique shop, all bits of odds and ends. But he came across nice pieces in his travels, which he never put inside the shop, he always fetched them home.' She brought her eyes back to him once more, and laughing gently she said, 'My mother used to play war with him, because, she said, there was the profit all stuck round our walls, but me dad looked upon these pieces as a sort of investment.'

'And he was certainly right; they would bring some money today.'

'Yes, yes, I think they would too. In fact, I'm sure they would. I've had dealers after them more than once. But I'll never sell any of them. When I don't need them any longer they'll go to Pat. I think that's the kind of profit on his investment Dad would have liked best.'

'I hope when your son is an old man you're still surrounded by your beautiful furniture.'

'Oh.' Her head went up and back. 'There's not much chance of that. . . . Will you have another cup of coffee?'

'No. No, thank you, I feel I have intruded on you long enough.'

'Oh, but you're not intruding.' Again her head moved from side to side, and the action seemed to sweep away all opposition. 'I look upon Saturday as my day. I make it a lazy day, I haven't to go to the office, I enjoy Saturdays. . . . Not that I don't enjoy my work. I suppose it's unusual these days for anybody to say they enjoy their job, but I do. I suppose it's because I've got a good boss.' Without pausing, she went on, 'I work for Holloways, the wholesalers. You know, in the market. I've been shorthand-typist there for thirteen years.'

'Yes, yes, I know Holloways.' He inclined his head. 'We handle their business.'

'Well I never! But, of course . . . Ratcliff, Arnold & Baker. I've written to them often. But to a Mr. Ransome.'

'He's my partner.'

'Well I never! It makes us sort of connected.' She leaned towards him, and he was forced to laugh, and was not a little surprised by the noise he made – he couldn't remember when he had last heard it. Then, his eyes crinkling with inquiry, he said, 'You did say you had been working for them for thirteen years?'

'Yes.' She nodded.

'But . . . but you must have started very young?'

'No, I was seventeen when I went there. It was my first job after the secretarial course . . . I'm thirty. I was thirty the night you put in your appearance.' She dropped her head slightly towards her shoulders, but there was nothing coy about the action.

He stared at her. Thirty! He couldn't believe she was thirty. Of course, her boy must be nine or more. He was curious about the boy. If she had worked for Holloways for thirteen years it pointed to her not being married.

The next minute she startled him by saying, 'I was married when I was nineteen, but I kept my job on and went back shortly after Pat was born.' It was as if she had been reading his mind and he felt a warmth on his face which deepened when she added, 'My husband was killed when Pat was three. He was driving a lorry and a bus ran into him on the Low Town bridge and he went through the parapet into the river.' Her voice was now flat, unemotional, her face straight.

Low Town bridge. A lorry plunging into the river. He remembered. Yes, of course. The contractors sued the bus company. The bus had slithered on to the wrong side of the road. The widow of the deceased driver had been awarded quite substantial damages. Yes, he remembered.

There came a little embarrassed silence between them. He supposed she was dwelling on a painful memory. He broke it by saying, 'Have you always lived here?'

'No, no. I've only been up here about six years.'

'It's an unusual flat; this room is so large, larger than any in our office. But then in the old days they built largely, didn't they?'

'I understand this was two rooms at one time. Would you like to see round?' She was on her feet, looking down at him. And he noticed again how all her movements seemed to flow. Although quick, they weren't jerky.

'It's very kind of you but I feel . . .'

'Now I've told you, you're not putting me out. Look, this is the bedroom. I have two.' She preceded him into another large room, and here again there was old furniture on which the patina was soft to the eye. A bow-fronted tallboy stood cornerwise near the window, and what was evidently a Queen Anne cabinet stood in the opposite corner. The only modern article in the room was the bed, but flanking it, looking like bedside cupboards, were two small Georgian Davenports. He recognized these particularly because in his mother's bedroom at home there had been one. It had known some rather rough wear yet his brother had been offered a hundred pounds for it recently.

'I had to have a modern bed. I bet you wouldn't believe it but Dad had a four-poster. Mam kicked up over that. Oh, but there were some laughs over that four-poster. Mam said she was always afraid of dying in it. And she did die in it, and Dad wasn't long following her, and in the same bed. I think that was the reason why I just couldn't sleep in it. And it was a pity for it fitted in with the rest of the stuff, while this. . . .' She waved her hands towards the plastic-headed double divan. 'It sticks out like a sore thumb, don't you think?'

'Oh no. I think it's feminine, nice.' They were smiling at each other, and she turned away and walked into the long room again and across it to another door.

'This is Pat's room.'

'Yes, this is a real boy's room.' He looked about him, and saw that even here there were pieces that would have graced a drawing-room, one being a sofa table, another a four-tiered whatnot which was being used for a display of miniature aeroplanes. The walls he saw were plastered with pictures of aeroplanes in all situations.

'I see your boy is very air-minded.'

'Oh, he's crazy about aeroplanes.'

'Is he heading for the air force?'

'No, not particularly. He wants to be an engineer. He's very good at maths, he's at the top of his form, and his teacher says he should get through to the grammar school next year. He's only ten now.'

'Oh, that's excellent.'

'He's a good boy.' She was looking straight at him, her face unsmiling as she said this, and when she turned from him she again said, 'He's a good boy.'

He felt he detected something in her voice. Was it a trace of anxiety about the boy?

She showed him the bathroom that held a pink bath with matching basin and which was half-tiled in black. It was startlingly modern and in sharp contrast with the rest of the house. The modern pattern was repeated in the kitchen, but here the colours weren't black and pink, nor yet the stark clinical greys and white of his own kitchen. Here various colours met and mingled, blue, lilac, primrose, soft green.

'What a lovely kitchen!' he said.

'I did it myself.'

'You did?'

'Yes. I went mad with eight colours. There's eight colours in here. And look,' she said going to the window, 'you can see the river from here. Just a little bit of it, but I love to see the river gleaming in the sun.'

As he followed her pointing finger he said, 'I often go on the roof to have a look at the river, and the air always seems fresher up here.' He turned to her now. 'That night I took ill, that's why I went up there, I wanted air.'

She looked back into his eyes, her own soft with innate kindness, her voice expressing it too, as she said, 'And you were ill, weren't you. As I said, I couldn't get you out of my mind all night, and I kept wondering about you. I nearly phoned, but I didn't like to. I had a call from Ted last night and he asked after you. He'll be pleased to know you are better.'

'He was such a help I remember. I would like to see him and thank him.'

'Oh, that's all right, Ted doesn't need thanks. He's a good sort, a real good sort, but you've got to get to know him. He might appear a bit brash at first but he's not, he's a good man at rock bottom.'

Ted had extolled her virtues, and now she was extolling his. It was good to hear people speaking well of each other. There was likely something between them. And why not? Again, why not indeed?

'Well, I mustn't keep you any longer. I have really outstayed my welcome.'

'Not a bit of it.' She led the way out of the kitchen. 'You've made a most interesting break in my day, something different, you know what I mean?' She glanced over her shoulder. 'I generally know exactly what I'm going to do on a Saturday. I usually do some shopping and then. . . .' She swung round towards him. 'You wouldn't believe what I do on a Saturday afternoon.'

He smiled, waiting.

She leant towards him. 'I go round the junk shops.'

They were laughing again loudly, and again he was surprised at the sound of his own voice, and as he laughed he gazed at her. He had never met anyone like her, oozing life. That was the only word he could find in his mind for her, life. She personified it. Sometime before the war, right far away back he must have felt life like this, lived it, while being unaware of living it, expressing it in every moment, walking, eating, smiling, sleeping. Yes, sometime in his existence he must have unconsciously expressed life as she was doing now, but in one searing moment it had been burnt out. That moment was with him yet, and would remain with him until he died.

He took his eyes from her as if unable to bear the sight of her. And he felt descending on him the sadness that would portray itself on his face and translate itself to others as inanity. He must get away from her before it showed. He had felt happy here, different.

In his conventional manner he now held out his hand and said, 'Thank you for the coffee, and for being so kind to me. Good-bye.'

'Good-bye.' She seemed a little nonplussed by his change of manner. She handed him his hat from the hallstand and held the door open for him.

When he had passed on to the landing he turned to her, his

eyes not looking into her face now but lowered towards her feet encased in high, spindle-heeled shoes, and again he said, 'Good-bye.'

'Good-bye.'

She watched him until his head disappeared from her view down the stairs; then she went in and closed the door, and after a moment she walked across the little hall and to the sitting-room door, and there she stood looking round the room. He had been impressed by it, very impressed. He knew old furniture. He was a nice man, oh such a nice man. A gentleman. Oh yes, a gentleman. She could tell. But there was something about him she couldn't quite fathom, a sort of sadness or something, as if he was lonely. That was daft . . . him lonely! The leading solicitor of the town, living in the posh end where he did, and bags of friends. . . . Lonely!

She walked towards the fireplace and moving the pouffe with her foot she sat down on it and held her hands out towards the blaze, and her own action seemed to interpret him in some way which she couldn't explain. And again she said, don't be daft. Him a big pot in the town. Fancy thinking he looks lost and lonely. She moved her hands in front of the blaze. It was funny about him calling. She had felt happy and full of life this morning, and even all the time he was here, right up to those last few minutes. And now she felt flat.

Aw well, this wouldn't get the shopping done. She jumped to her feet. It had been a very nice break anyway, and he was a very nice man, and it was good of him to call. Now she would get her things on and go out and everything would go as usual.

But when she was dressed for outdoors she paused before leaving the hall, and there came to her, as she termed it, a funny little thought. The usual Saturdays were finished it said. You're crazy, she said; you get the daftest ideas.

After she had closed the door she started to sing as she went downstairs.

CHAPTER FOUR

A LITTLE PERFUME

JOHN finished his breakfast and went to renew his cup with more coffee when he realized that Ann was sitting at the table. He could never get used to her being down for breakfast. She had done this two or three times of late. Why, he didn't know, except perhaps that with the approach of Christmas she had had so much to do that she'd needed more time, and today being Christmas Eve she had more than the usual preparation to contend with in connection with tomorrow's dinner. Yet she hadn't put in an early appearance other years and the arrangements had been the same.

He handed her his cup, and as she filled it she said, 'I'll have to leave my car in, there's something wrong with the brakes. Could you run me into town this morning?'

'Oh! Well ... Yes.' There was a pause between each word. Then he added rapidly: 'I can drop you on my way to the office, I won't be going for another hour or so.'

He was drinking his coffee when she said, 'Arnold doesn't go in Saturday mornings, is it necessary for you to do so?'

He blinked a number of times before looking at her, then said, 'Arnold doesn't happen to be responsible for my clients.' Without rising he pushed back his chair, and the action made a screeching sound as the legs scraped over the polished boards.

'Excuse me.' He now rose to his feet but did not look at her, yet he was aware that the sound of the scraping chair had brought her face into a grimace. He went past Laurie, who had his head bent over the morning paper, and out of the room, across the hall and up the stairs, and when he reached the upper landing he pursed his lips and whistled the first bar of Mozart's Sonata No. 3.

Back in the morning room, Ann looked towards Laurie, and he was looking upwards. The sound of the whistle had been as startling to them both as if a ship's siren had suddenly let blast in the hall.

* * *

It was close on eleven o'clock when John reached the office. He entered the room in a hurry, threw his case on to a chair, then went to the seat behind his desk and, sitting down, removed his hat, rubbed his two hands over his head, then looked at his watch. He had about five minutes, he never went up before eleven, although she wouldn't have minded what time he went up, he was sure of that. He leant back in his chair unaware that he was smiling, his lips wide, exposing all his teeth. How many times had he been up there since that first time? Five, six, seven? He had lost count. It seemed now that every Saturday morning in his life he had mounted to the roof, gone over the parapet and down her stairs. Yet he would never have gone down those stairs a second time if it hadn't been for the chance meeting in the market square. He had been passing the electric showrooms when he saw her standing gazing in the window. He could have passed on but he hadn't. He had raised his hat, and with what appeared to most people old world courtesy had bowed slightly towards her as he said, 'Good-morning, Mrs. Thorpe.'

She turned a delighted face towards him, and her 'Fancy seeing you!' did not grate on him. 'I'm looking at fridges,' she said; 'I should have got one years ago.' To which he replied, 'Don't you think it's as well you didn't?' And she laughed outright, a high, infectious laugh.

'What do you think about that one?' She pointed to a small refrigerator in the middle of the window. 'I would like one of the bigger ones, but you see it's the room. That's why I haven't had one before. What with my washing machine, and the spin dryer, and then my stove and the sink, that wall is all taken up. You see?'

He saw. And together they admired the small refrigerator, and he commiserated with her when she said, 'The cupboard behind the door will have to go, and where I'm going to put the china I haven't the least idea. And it's good china, Coalport, and I've some pieces of Dresden . . . just a few.'

What about her lovely china cabinet, he had suggested, for her overflow of china?

But that was full. He had seen it was full. But perhaps he hadn't noticed. Why should he? She was silly. Again her high laughter.

They walked a little way round the market square until they came to a café, where she stopped and said, 'I've got to go in here. This is where Pat comes and picks me and the shopping up after he's finished at the greengrocer's.' To this he wanted to say two things: 'Well I could do with a cup of coffee, and what's to stop me running you and your shopping home?' But the training of years checked such indiscreet spontaneity, and again he raised his hat and inclined his head towards her and bade her good-bye, and the morning once again became November, raw, bleak, with no break in the overhead leaden sky.

It was the following Saturday morning that he had gone up on the roof. He knew what had taken him there; and it wasn't to get the air. When she pushed open the fanlight he imagined his thoughts had drawn her from the room below. And from his side of the parapet he watched her hand reach out to the meat safe, then become stationary. He watched her face light up. As he stepped over the dividing wall she exclaimed, 'Well, I never! you're up here again. Aren't you afraid of getting your death?'

He assured her that he wasn't, explaining that he had come up for air and to enjoy the view.

She had pointed to the wire-mesh-fronted box, saying, 'Well, this is the last time I'll be using this, I've got the fridge coming on Monday. And I've got something else, guess what?'

'I haven't an idea.'

'Another china cabinet.'

'No!'

'Yes.' And to this she added, 'Come on down and see how you like it.'

And like a boy climbing into a cave, into an Aladdin's cave, he went down her steps and into the long room again, and, of all things that morning, she had finished up by playing the piano to him.

He had noticed the open piano and the music on the stand and had remarked, 'You play the piano, Mrs. Thorpe?'

'Oh, play it,' she said in her airy way; 'I should be able to, I learned long enough. My mam put me to it when I was five, and I passed all my exams up to the advanced stage of Trinity College, but to tell you the truth I've no touch. Technically I'm all right, but my teacher used to say my fingers were like hammers. She used to say they were all right for Beethoven, but, you know, I don't like Beethoven, I like Mozart or Chopin. You always like the things you're not fitted for, don't you?'

She hadn't to be coaxed to play; she had played for him and given to the music her own interpretation. Perhaps her touch was slightly hard, perhaps an authority on music would have writhed and tried to shut his ears to certain passages, but as he sat on the couch, his head resting in the corner of it, his eyes focused on the mantelpiece where stood, in artistic isolation, the jade figure of a Chinese lady, her playing had soothed him, stimulated him, and excited him. Here was this girl who not only lived with beautiful furtniture, but who knew and appreciated it, who could sit down at the piano without any fuss and play. What else could she do? She appeared to him at that moment like an uncharted island, mysterious, alluring. ... This girl whom Ann, without a moment's hesitation, would have dubbed common.

That particular morning before he had climbed the ladder to take his departure she had looked at him, her expression and whole manner serious, as he was finding it could be at times, and she said to him, 'Don't think this is cheek, or that I'm being forward or anything, Mr. Emmerson, but you're welcome here any time you've got a mind to drop in. I'm always in on a Saturday.'

He had thanked her for her invitation with a gravity similar to that with which she had made it, and although during the following week he had told himself that he must not go into her house again, the next Saturday morning found him, like some furtive lover, kneeling on the roof, tapping at her fanlight.

During his first three or four visits they had been alone together, and he couldn't now recall anything they had talked about. Then one Saturday morning the old man, Mr. Locket, came up, and this had made him ill at ease, but only for a short time, because he realized that Bill Locket had not been at all surprised to find him here. Yet this fact, when he came to think about it later, disturbed him.

Bill had stayed about half an hour, drunk four cups of treaclish tea, given him an insight into the workings of the gas works, by which company he had been employed until his retirement. Together with his version of why the last war had gone on for so long, and lastly a whispered appreciation of their hostess, who left the key for him under the mat, so that when his wife was out he could slip up and make himself a pot of tea.

This generosity on Cissie's part, and the necessity for Mr. Locket to avail himself of it, was explained by Cissie after the visitor departed. Clara, Mrs. Locket, had to make ends meet, but, in her efforts she not only made them meet, but managed to make them overlap. Clara was careful. She bought a certain quantity of tea each week, and that had to last them. The irony of it all, Cissie had explained, was that Clara's saving was to enable her to leave something to her only son, who was in Canada and apparently comfortably off. People were funny, weren't they, she had said to him. And he agreed heartily with her . . . people were funny.

Then last week Mrs. O'Neill had dropped in.

Mrs. O'Neill's presence really had disturbed him; women always put the wrong construction on things. Mrs. O'Neill was jolly and laughed a lot, and on that occasion she had seemed determined to outstay him. And he hadn't imagined it was because she enjoyed his company.

He had come across her again this morning, in Danes' store, at the perfume counter of all places. She had been profuse in her greeting as if they had known each other for years. 'After Christmas boxes?' she had said. Yes, he had replied, that was what he was after. She said she liked lavender water, it was so refreshing; and he agreed with her; and this after receiving very little change out of a ten-pound note for a bottle of perfume.

The thought of the perfume brought his eyes to the chair, and he rose and took the small package out of his case. As he stood looking at it lying in the palm of his hand he hoped she would like it. He didn't know what perfume she used; there was always a fresh smell about her, but he didn't associate it with anything in particular.

He went hurriedly into the wash room now, washed his hands, smoothed down his hair, stroked his nose, moved one finger to each side of his upper lip, and he was ready.

He had to make his way carefully over the roof. Heaps of last week's snow was still lying frozen hard in the corners, and the roof itself was like a sheet of glass.

There had been no arrangement for leaving the fanlight open, no arrangement whether or not he should come down if he heard voices, nothing surreptitious about his visits, but he tapped gently on the fanlight before opening it, and when he stood in the hall he called gently. 'Are you there, Mrs. Thorpe?' She was still Mrs. Thorpe, and he was still Mr. Emmerson.

'Yes. Come on in. I won't be a minute.'

He went into the long room which now held an enchantment for him. There was something about it that cried to him of home as no other room had done since, as a boy, he sat before the fire in the big farm kitchen surrounded by the close unity of his family.

She put her head round the kitchen door and smiled widely at him as she said, 'Sit yourself down. I'm trying to turn a blancmange out without breaking it; I won't be a tick.'

He had taken off his hat, but he never took his coat off until she asked him. He sniffed at the air. There was a Christmas smell pervading the room, and as he sat down he called to her in a soft voice, devoid of the heartiness that he used to Mrs. Stringer, 'Something smells nice. Are you roasting your goose?'

'No, no,' she called back, 'not till tomorrow. And it's a turkey. I've been making brawn this morning.'

'Oh, brawn.' He was looking towards the fireplace, his eyes on the leaping flames. She made brawn. He had never heard of anyone making brawn since his mother had made it; he thought everybody bought that kind of thing now, there were at least three cooked meat shops in the main street.

'There.' She came hurrying towards him. She was wearing a deep mauve coloured woollen dress, and round her waist she had a pink apron. Her fair hair was tied back, young-girl fashion, this morning, with a ribbon; her arms were bare past the elbow. The whole sight of her hurt him.

'Well, it's nearly here. I've done as much preparation as if I'd ten bairns. Anyway, it only comes once a year.'

Because it was she who had said the threadworn phrase there was nothing trite in the remark.

'Why don't you take your coat off? I'm always telling you.' She put her hand out, and he rose from the couch and took off his coat. But as he gave it to her he exclaimed hastily, 'Just a minute; there's something in the pocket.' When he withdrew the small parcel he looked at it for a second before handing it to her and saying, 'I hope it's right. A Merry Christmas.'

'For me? Mr. Emmerson, you shouldn't, now you shouldn't. . . . Oh, but thanks.'

'You haven't looked at it yet, it might be a cracker.' He watched her intently as she undid the brown paper, then the expensive-looking coloured tape with which Danes' always wrapped up their goods, and when she came to the plain oblong box with the simple word 'Chanel' written across it she stared at it for a moment, then looked up, her dark eyes moist, her whole face drooping in soft lines. 'Oh!' she exclaimed under her breath, 'Oh, you shouldn't have done it. Not Chanel, it costs the earth. Oh, Mr. Emmerson.'

He saw her body sway slightly towards him, and for a second he thought she was going to kiss him. It was a terrifying second. The anticipation checked his breathing, and when the movement of her body stopped it was her hand that touched him, and there swept over him a feeling of relief, yet mixed with it a sense of loss and a wide emptiness. But it wouldn't have done. No, it wouldn't have done, the little voice was piping at him. If she had kissed him that would have been the end of their association. He wanted this to go on for ever, the way they were now, but it couldn't have gone on if she had kissed him, because he would. . . . What would he have done? What? . . . Told her? Yes. Yes. Strange, but he could have told her. She was the one person in the world he had met whom he could have told, and in the telling he knew that he wouldn't have been enveloped in shame.

'I've never had Chanel. I've always wanted it, mind you, and I could have bought it for myself many times over, but I wouldn't afford it. It must have cost the earth; look at the size of the box.'

'Nonsense.' His voice was a little hoarse as if it had been affected by the raw fog from outside. 'It's a very small appreciation for all your hospitality and kindness.'

'Oh, that.' She folded her arms around his coat while she held the bottle in her hand, and she gazed into his face as she said, 'Anything I've done for you you've repaid a thousandfold. I'm going to say it now. . . . I've never met anybody like you, not to talk to. What I mean is, outside of business. I meet men like Ted, who prattles, and my husband wasn't much of a talker. No.' She shook her head now and repeated, 'No he wasn't much of a talker.' He felt her words conveyed something other than what they said; her face was in its rare unsmiling state. 'And there's been the music. I've never had anyone to listen to me before. I play for myself sometimes, but it's different when you're playing for somebody else. . . . And then the books. Oh, I've read novels of all kinds but I've never read an autobiography until you mentioned they were your favourite reading.'

'I'm glad,' he said. 'Perhaps I should have got you a book or two?'

'No. No.' She flapped the hand at him that held the scent. 'I can get them from the public library.' Her head went back and she laughed, and clutching the bottle to her again, she cried, 'Oh! my scent. Oh! won't I smell lovely.' Then, 'You're so kind,' she finished. Solemnly she turned from him and went into the hall with his coat, and he watched for a moment before sitting down again. One small present – and compared with what he gave Ann it was small – yet what a difference in the reception and the thanks.

'What are you doing over the holidays?' she asked as she came back into the room.

'Oh, the usual thing. Tonight we go to my son's fiancée's place. That's been the usual procedure for years, even before they got to know each other . . . at least well. Then tomorrow we don't have dinner until the evening, when we have a few personal friends in.' He felt somehow as if he were excluding her by saying that, and he put in quickly, 'I must admit I don't enjoy it very much, I mean dinners and things.'

'Do you go to many cocktail parties?' Her head was on one side.

'For my sins I have to attend a few, but if I can get out of them I do.'

'I suppose you're kept at it every night at this time of the year; I've never known such a town as this for parties. Everybody seems to want to throw parties. I'm going to one on Boxing Night; one of the girls in the office is having a do. I don't care very much for parties. Too many people saying nothing, if you know what I mean.'

'I do. I do. And I go to one on Boxing Night too,' he inclined his head towards her. 'My partner's having a do, so we're both going to suffer, though I must say that Mr. Ransome's do's are more bearable than most.'

She sat down on the pouffe at the side of the couch and said musingly, 'You know, I think Christmas is overdone, it's just become a racket for the shops. Would you believe it?' Her eyes widened. 'I've spent over twenty-five pounds on Pat.'

'Twenty-five pounds!' he repeated. 'That's a lot of money.'

'But, I've bought him things that'll last, like a set of encyclopaedias.'

'Oh, that's sensible.' It came to him at this point that he'd forgotten to buy the child anything, and he said, 'I didn't know what to buy him but I thought a little extra pocket money wouldn't come amiss, not if I know boys.'

'Oh, Mr. Emmerson, you mustn't. No, you mustn't. After buying that scent, no, you mustn't.'

He was about to protest again that it was nothing when there came the sound of a door opening and Pat came in from the hall in a rush.

'Oo! Mam. Coo! it's cold. Hello, Mr. Emmerson. Oh, Mam, I'm freezin'. How long's dinner going to be? I've got to go back to Mr. Bolton's this afternoon, he's up to his eyes in orders. He let me off at eleven 'cos he had to get the place cleared afore I could do any more, and . . .'

'All right, all right.' She hadn't moved from the pouffe, and when he came round to her side she put her arms about him and pressed him to her as she said, 'One thing at a time, and I'll answer one thing at a time.' Again she hugged him to her, and bouncing her head at him and laughing she said, 'Yes, it's cold, and dinner won't be ready for another hour, and I'm glad you're going back to Mr. Bolton's this afternoon. Go on now into the kitchen and have a sausage roll; that will fill up the space until dinner-time. But, mind you' – she pushed him from her – 'no more than two. I said two, mind. I've counted them.'

The boy grinned at John, and John grinned back at him, and as he ran towards the kitchen he cried, 'You said two and two, that's twenty-two, twenty-two sausage rolls.'

She looked at John and shook her head and was about to make some comment when Pat's voice came from the kitchen door, muffled now with food, saying, 'Forgot to tell you, Mam, Ted's back. . . . Saw his car outside the stables.'

'Oh is he? Oh, that's great. He said he'd try to make it. Now he won't be stuck in some hole by himself for Christmas.' She looked at John. 'He gets lonely. Commercial travellers do, you know. People wouldn't believe it, but by what Ted tells me it's one of the loneliest occupations on earth.'

He watched her face intently as she talked. She was pleased that the man was back; what were they to each other? It was not the first time he had asked himself the question, and he gave himself the same answer now as he had before. It was nothing to do with him. She was a young woman, free, and could live her own life. Nevertheless, as before, the answer increased the loneliness within him.

'I'm off to play for a bit, Mam,' called Pat. 'All right?'

'All right,' she said. 'But don't be long.' Then turning back to John, she continued, 'That'll mean we'll have a bit of fun over the holidays, Ted being back. They're all coming up, the others you know, Miss O'Neill, and Mrs. Orchard, and Mr. and Mrs. Locket; but it wouldn't be the same without Ted; he makes things go, he's got that way with him. As I said, he prattles, but he's funny in company.' She leant towards him. 'I . . . I suppose you wouldn't like to come in one evening when . . . ?' She straightened up and ended quickly, 'Of course you wouldn't. You'll have all your spare time planned over the holidays.'

He caught her statement as an excuse and said, 'Yes. Yes, my wife generally works out all my spare time.' He widened his eyes and shook his head as if it was funny, and she smiled understandingly back at him.

Quite candidly he told himself that even given the time he would never accept an invitation to join in one of these gatherings, informal and natural as they were – and there was a craving in him these days for the informal and the natural. The small voice told him he was going beyond the bounds of propriety in visiting her at all. In the beginning he had hoped to keep his visits secret, yet he had acceded to this in one way only, by coming over the roof. Even this, he felt, was proving more clandestine than if he came boldly up the stairs, for his visits were known to the other inhabitants in the flats. And what if they put the wrong construction on things? It wasn't the first time he had put this question to himself, and again he shied from giving himself an answer.

In his work he dealt with all types of cases, among which divorce was frequent, and slander not infrequent. The latter, in nine cases out of ten, was dealt with privately. Slander always started in a whisper. That was no legal phrase, he had first heard his mother use it. He wondered now if there was already a whisper going through the building. He had been vitally aware from the morning Ann had come into his bedroom, after hearing through May that he had really been ill the previous evening, and not drunk, that Mrs. Orchard could quite easily start a whisper about him. Yet he felt certain that if she had said anything to her mistress, May would have passed it on to Ann quicker than a shot from a gun.

For the past few weeks he had been holding his hands out towards a flame; and that was all he told himself he ever meant to do, just hold his hands towards the flame and feel the comfort of it. Yet how many people would believe him? And could he expect anyone to look upon his motives as altruistic? He would find it hard to take this view were he surveying such conduct in someone else. If a client in the same position were to say to him, 'I didn't stop seeing her because my conscience was clear. There was nothing between us but friendship, just friendship,' he would smile at him, his professional smile, and reply quietly, 'The public don't want to hear about clear consciences, they don't want to know about the good people, they're only interested in the bad, and once they get a smell of any kind they follow it, hoping at the end they'll find something rotten. That is human nature.'

'You look miles away.'

'Yes.' He blinked his eyes. 'Yes, I think I was. This ... this couch is very comfortable.' He moved his head against the back of it. 'It induces one to relax. But you were saying?'

'Oh, I forgot what I was saying. I suppose I've been thinking too. Yes, yes I was. I was thinking we're going to have a jolly Christmas. I've got a tree for Pat.' She was whispering now. 'He doesn't know yet. I've got the lights and things, and I've had to keep moving them so he wouldn't find them. I'm going to have it all ready for when he comes in tonight. I don't like trees set up days before Christmas ...'

She was interrupted by a sound from the direction of the outer landing, of someone singing 'Good King Wenceslas', and he watched her spring up from the pouffe, her face alight with laughter, and fling out her hand towards him in her characteristic way, saying, 'That's Ted larking on.'

He watched her as she ran towards the hall, then heard the door open and her crying in mock indignation, 'No carol singers the day, thank you'; then the man's voice, deep and pleasant-sounding, singing now, 'I wish you a merry Christmas, I wish you a merry Christmas, I wish you a merry Christmas and a happy New Year.'

'Get in. Get in. Oh, you are a fool, Ted. Go on with you. Mr. Emmerson's here.... Get in.'

Ted came into the room. He had a wrapped bottle in the crook of one arm and a number of parcels in the other, and he cried to John, who had risen to his feet, 'Well, hello there. I'm glad to see you better.'

'Thanks. It's nice to see you again.' John felt his own greeting sounded too polite and formal. But Ted had turned to Cissie. 'Here,' he said, thrusting the bottle into her hand; 'that's to be kept exclusively for Irish coffee.'

'Oh, thanks, Ted, thanks, Irish coffee! It's a long time since we had Irish coffee.'

'And here; these are for the Christmas tree.' He piled the parcels into her arms. 'Those two are for you, and those three are for his nibs. And mind, nothing to be opened until tomorrow morning. I was going to play Santa and visit all the beds in the house, but then I thought that if I got into Millie's and Maggie's downstairs I would never get out.'

He laughed heartily, and Cissie laughed with him. And John thought, the usual prattle of commercial travellers.

'Oh, it's good of you, Ted, but you shouldn't have bought all these things.'

'Aw, go on with you. I'm looking for a free dinner. Anyway, you don't know what's in them, so don't get all effusive until after you've opened them.' He pushed her, then came towards the couch.

'Well, well, I wouldn't have known you. You feeling all right now, Mr. Emmerson?'

'Yes, thank you. Yes, I'm quite recovered.'

'By, that was a night, wasn't it? How's the car behaving itself?'

'Oh, splendidly.'

'By, I'd give me ears to have one like that.'

'Would you like a coffee now?' Cissie was leaning over the back of the couch between them.

'Would I like one? . . . Two, but Irish.' Ted stretched out his hand and touched her nose. 'Have you any cream in?'

'Yes, I got a pot fresh this morning; I must have known you were coming.'

'That's the ticket. . . . Do you like Irish coffee?' He leant towards John.

'Yes, yes, at times, but I'm afraid I'll have to be going.'

'Oh, nonsense, Cissie won't be a tick brewing it, will you, Cissie?'

'No; and do stay, Mr. Emmerson. Go on.'

Looking up into her face, he inclined his head and said, 'Since you insist, I will.' He couldn't help but be aware that his form of speech always sounded stilted, sort of old-fashioned, as if he was of another generation. Well, he might be compared with her, but not with the man.

'Aw, it's nice to be back.' Ted stretched out his legs and buried the back of his head in a cushion. 'You know, I often think of this room when I'm stuck in some dreary hotel. It's funny but I never visualize my own place downstairs, although it isn't bad, but this room has something special, don't you think?'

'I do indeed. Yes, indeed, it's a beautiful room. I've never seen so many good pieces of furniture in one room before. I've told Mrs. Thorpe so.'

'Yes, yes. But if they were just egg boxes I'm sure Cissie could do something with them, make them home-like. You know what I mean?'

'Yes, yes, I do. Do you travel much in your work?'

'Yes, length and breadth of the country. I didn't used to when I worked for Randalls, but I changed over last year. This is a new paint firm I'm working for and I'm pushing it, it's all very uphill but the prospects are good. They're pleased up top with what I've done this year and they're talking about me training representatives.'

'Oh, that's good; it should make you feel very pleased.'

'Aw, I don't know. Do you smoke?' He pulled out a packet of cigarettes.

'No thanks; I gave it up about a year ago and I'm trying not to start again.'

'I wish I could. But as I was saying, it's funny the things that please you. If this opportunity had come up ten years ago I would have been over the moon, but now . . . well. You've got to have somebody to work for.' He turned his head towards John. 'Don't you agree?'

'Yes, yes, you're right there.'

'I used to work like stink when I was young, but I picked the wrong job.'

'Oh, I wouldn't say that, you seem to have made a go of it.'

'Well, I suppose I have in one way, although I've had to pay for it. It's cost me my family.'

John made no comment on this and Ted went on, 'You, being a solicitor, come across my case every day in the week I suppose: wife left too much on her own, goes after other blokes. But it wasn't quite like that in my case, until me daughter married.'

'You have a married daughter?' There was genuine surprise in John's voice.

'Yes, she'll be twenty-one this month. And I've a son nineteen. After the girl married, Gladys, that's my wife, told me bluntly she'd had enough. Of course, I knew she'd had enough for a long time, and I knew what had been going on, but when you have two kids and want to keep a home together and give them some sort of a chance you close your eyes to lots of things. The boy went into the air force; then, as I said, Claire got married, and what was there left for us? But she said nothing about a divorce until a few months ago, and now that's going through. So there you are.' He spread his hands wide. 'As they say, that's life. But, you know, they can have it for me. I'm forty-six and I've been on the road since I was nineteen . . . life! . . . Still' – he sat up and pulled at his waistcoat – 'here and there you meet one of the rare ones.' He now thumbed over his shoulder towards the kitchen. 'The best there is.' His voice was a whisper. 'They don't come any better. You take my word for it.' He now leant towards John. 'You believe me?'

'Yes, yes, I do.'

'She's rare.'

'Yes, as you say, she's rare.'

It did not appear ludicrous to him that he was discussing the qualities of this young woman with this strange man. For weeks now he'd had a personal view, an unprofessional view, of how the other half lived, and in this moment he felt an active participant in their way of life, and the candour, the honest, unpretentiousness of it, appealed to him.

Cissie now came into the room with the tray, and John got to his feet, and she said to him, 'Sit down, sit down.' But he took the tray from her and put it on a side table.

'I'm going to let you put your own cream and brandy in it.'

'Good idea. Let me get at it,' cried Ted.

When they had each helped themselves to the brandy and the cream, they sipped at the coffee in silence, their eyes moving from one to the other. Then John said, 'Excellent, excellent.'

'Haven't tasted better.' Ted winked at Cissie and jerked his head. Then putting the cup sharply down on a small table she had placed to the side of the couch, he cried, 'Aw, I've got a funny one for you, priceless. It's about two spiritualists . . .'

Perhaps it was something in John's face that checked his flow, for now he turned to him and said, 'Oh, it's all right, it's clean. It's funny, real funny, but clean. I'm not the kind that ladles out muck to women.'

John wanted to say that he was sure he wasn't, but he

remained silent, his face slightly flushed, as Ted, addressing himself solely to Cissie, began:

'Well, it was like this. There were these two spiritualists, and they made up their minds, a sort of pact, that whoever died first would try to get in touch with the other, because they believed that they would change form once they died and they wanted to pass on the gen. Well, Johnnie was the first to go, and Bill set about his stuff. He tried, and he tried, and it was a long time before he made contact with his pal, but one day, after saying, "Are you there, Johnnie? Can you hear me, Johnnie?" he heard Johnnie's voice coming through, saying, "Yes, I can hear you, Bill." "Aw, good," said Bill. "By! I've had a hard time contacting you. Where are you, Johnnie?"

' "Oh, I'm in a wonderful place, Bill," said Johnnie, "wonderful. It's hard to describe to you, but it's simply wonderful."

' "No kiddin'," said Bill

' "No kiddin'," said Johnnie. "The weather's perfect. Sun all the time. You've never seen anything like it. And the food, man ... there's lashings and lashings and lashings of it. ... As for the women. Oh, boy! Dames never ending."

'Bill could hardly believe his ears, and in an awe-filled voice he said to his late pal, "Johnnie, it sounds marvellous. And it's done something to you; you sound changed. What are you really now, Johnnie?"

' "Well ..." said Johnnie. "I'm a bull in the Argentine, Bill. ..." '

John watched Cissie's head go back as she laughed. He himself knew that he was expected to laugh, to roar; he made a good pretence at it, widening his mouth and covering his face with his hand. And as he did so he listened to Ted's rollicking mirth and his voice choking on 'A bull in the Argentine! A bull in the Argentine'.

The inference of the joke, its masculinity and virility, touched him on a spot that was painful. He hadn't ever cared much for jokes; and jokers, the type that spouted the tales that bred the club-room guffaw, had always been distasteful to him. As he looked at Cissie again he felt that she hadn't really enjoyed this joke either, and he was glad. He understood that women, when they got going, could out-do men in their relating

. . . of good ones. He had never been able to imagine women telling each other dirty stories, yet he knew that they did. But, as Ted had said, this wasn't a dirty story, yet he felt it was unsuitable for mixed company.

'Going to have another coffee?' Ted was leaning towards John now, and John knew that the man was aware of his feelings about the joke.

'No thank you. No thank you. It was delightful, and the brandy very good indeed' – he nodded towards him – 'but I must be getting along.'

As he got to his feet Cissie also rose, saying, 'It's a shame you've got to go so soon.' But as she spoke she went towards the hall, adding, 'I'll get your coat.'

After some seconds, when she didn't return to the room, John held out his hand to Ted, saying, 'Well I hope you'll have a good Christmas and enjoy the rest.'

'Thanks, and the same to you; the same to you.'

As John reached the room door. Ted's voice came at him loudly, 'Mind, if ever you want to get rid of that beauty of yours, remember me, won't you?' and John looked over his shoulder, smiled, and said, 'Of course, of course.'

Cissie was standing in the hall near the door, which seemed to indicate that she wanted him to leave by this way, and he felt strangely hurt, she had never done this before. She held his coat ready in her hands, and he made a small movement of protest when she went to help him on with it. Then handing him his hat she said softly, 'Thank you for your present. I still feel you shouldn't have done it, but thanks all the same. And I do hope you have a good Christmas.' Her hand came out to his and he took it. It was the first time they had shaken hands. It was also the first time he had consciously touched her. His eyes were blinking rapidly, and he said under his breath as if he was whispering some endearment, 'And you too.' He relinquished his hold on her hand and she opened the door, and again they looked at each other.

'Good-bye, Mr. Emmerson.'

'Good-bye. Good-bye.'

As he went down the stairs he pulled on his trilby. It was a good job he had been holding it in his hand, for if his two hands had been free he would surely have clasped hers with both of his. Yes, it was just as well he had been holding his hat.

Back in the hallway Cissie stood looking at her hand. For such a soft-spoken, quiet man he had a firm grip. She laid great stock by handshakes. She never trusted the jelly-like handshaker or those who tried to wring your fingers off. The latter were usually big-heads. But his handshake had been firm with a kind of tenderness about it. She liked him. Oh, he was a nice man, such a nice man.

She went into the room to Ted. By, it was going to be a nice Christmas.

CHAPTER FIVE

THE JOKE

THERE were three Christmas cards on the mantelpiece. They had been chosen for their lack of ostentation. The only other indication of Christmas that Ann had allowed play in her lounge were three red candles. These were arranged within a floral display, termed, apparently because of its meagreness, Chinese.

There were no crackers on the long dining-table, such signs of low-class frivolity would have been quite out of place. The table displayed the usual glass and silver, the latter supplemented on this occasion by two candelabra. The candles they held were of a delicate cream colour, their wicks as yet unsinged.

The men stood around, with drinks in their hands, waiting for the ladies to come downstairs. The male company was made up of James Wilcox, Arnold Ransome, and the junior partner, Michael Boyd, together with Laurie, and John himself. On occasions such as this it was very often Laurie who inquired of the guests their different tastes; then passed round the drinks; but tonight his father had forestalled him.

When they all had glasses in their hands, and had told each other how boring they had found Christmas, which attitude seemed to be the right one to take with regard to this festive season, there fell upon the company, as is often the case, a quietness. It was the kind of quietness which tells a man that he must do something. So when young Boyd and Arnold Ransome spoke together it was as if they had combined to create a unique witticism, so loud was the laughter that ensued.

'Go on.' Still laughing, Arnold nodded towards Michael Boyd, and the young man, knowing his position, shook his head, saying, 'No, no, it was nothing. You first.'

'Oh, well, I was just going to say I heard old Rawlins speak the other night at a dinner in Newcastle and wondered if you had heard him, John?'

'Yes.' John nodded. 'A long time ago. But never at a dinner, mostly from the Bench, and I dreaded being on the receiving end of his rapier tongue.'

'I bet, I bet. I've never heard him in court, as he's been in London for years, but I can imagine it. He had the whole place roaring. And can't he imitate dialects. He told the case of an Irishman who had been brought up for fighting on St. Patrick's Day and assaulting a policeman. And he talked as broad as any Irishman I've ever heard. Apparently a priest had come to speak up for the man. . . . Oh, if you had heard him doing the priest. I could never imitate him, but he went something like this: "Yer Honour, Shane O'Grady is a peace-lovin' man; he's at his duties every week, an' he's sober in his habits. But you must remember, yer Honour, that this happened on St. Patrick's Day, and for anyone to question the land of your origin on such a day is an insult."

' "Would you enlighten me?" said old Rawlins.

' "Well, it's like this," the priest said. "When a countryman of his, who had not long since landed, asked him if he was English green or Irish green he saw red. For your information, yer Honour, I'll explain. There are Irish Catholics and English Catholics and as God knows they both adhere to the green, but it's the Irishman that knows that the dye in the green of the English Catholics is not to be compared with the real thing, if you know what I mean. So the doubt put upon his true colour was too much for Shane, and he up with his fists and down went his countryman. But there were no hard feelings, it was just unfortunate that the polis man should come along at that moment, and that he shouldn't happen to be of either dye, an' blood, as you know, is thicker than water, and green, yer Honour, whatever its shade, is thicker than blood." '

They all roared.

Still laughing, Laurie took a sip from his glass. He could tell a story could Arnold. What was that one he had heard the other day about the tax inspector and the brewer. He was searching his mind rapidly for the telling point of the story when he heard his father say, 'I heard a funny one too about an Irish priest the other day.' Only in time did he stop his mouth squaring from his teeth, but his eyes narrowed as he gazed in astonishment at the man standing with his back to the high hearth looking down into his glass as he began to tell the story. His father, to his knowledge, had never told a yarn in his life; he would have said he wasn't capable of telling a story. There were men who could tell stories, and there were men who couldn't, and his father was one of the latter.

Well, there was this Catholic priest who fell off a six-floor building, and as he dropped rapidly past five of the stories he prayed like nobody's business to be saved, but when he came to the sixth he suddenly made the sign of the Cross and shouted, "Oh, my God, now for the bloody bump." '

James Wilcox was laughing. He didn't want to laugh, but he was laughing, while in the back of his mind he was saying to himself, 'Ah, I was right about that night. He may have been ill but he'd had a skinful nevertheless, and he's been at it again today or I'm a Dutchman. . . . Emmerson telling a joke!'

Arnold too was laughing, and he too was saying to himself, Fancy old John telling a joke, and in the back of his mind he thought, he's changed lately; he's more relaxed, easier. And he recalled the two Saturday mornings when he phoned the house to have a word with him, and Ann had said he was in his office, and when he had phoned the office he had received no reply. He had made no comment on this, but the second time he had thought it odd.

Michael Boyd was thinking, That was very funny, the way he told it. Now for the bloody bump! I must remember that one. Fancy the old man telling a yarn. He had always thought him very stiff and strait-laced, sort of old-school. Yet there was nothing in the story; it wasn't one of those, it was the kind that could be adapted to any kind of telling. But fancy the old man telling a story at all. He didn't seem that type.

Laurie had laughed at his father's joke. He had not wanted to laugh, but not to laugh would have seemed odd. His father had stood there in company and told a joke, and yesterday morning he had heard him whistle. There was something different about him lately. Was it a defiance? No, no, he couldn't call it that. Yet he was changed. Nothing that happened would surprise him after this . . . his father telling a joke.

The sound of the men's laughter had penetrated the bedroom upstairs, and on hearing it Valerie, turning to Mrs. Boyd, who was only a year or so older than herself, said, 'I think we are missing something, come on.' And looking over her shoulder she added, 'We're going down, Mother . . . Auntie Ann.'

'All right, dear, we won't be a minute.' May Wilcox turned from the dressing-table seat and beamed on her daughter, but she made no attempt to rise.

After the two young women had left the room, Ann stood looking down on her friend and she asked softly, 'What do you mean, May, I'm not wearing it? You don't expect me to wear a mink stole tonight, do you?'

'Don't be silly, dear.' May slapped her arm. 'I wasn't meaning the stole, I was meaning the perfume . . . the Chanel.'

'Did Laurie tell Val that he was going to buy me Chanel? He bought me these.' She flicked a treble strap of pearls encircling her thin neck.

May screwed up her face in a puzzled way. Then her eyes dropping to her hands, she turned round to the mirror and, patting her hair into place, said quietly, 'It's been some mistake. I'm sorry I spoke.'

Ann looked at May in the mirror, but May would not meet her eyes. 'What's this about Chanel?'

'Now look, I don't want to cause any trouble, Ann.' May looked up now.

'Tell me what this is all about, please.'

'Look, Ann, you've got a dinner facing you. There are people downstairs, not just James, Valerie and Laurie. We'll talk about it after.'

'We'll do no such thing.' With a quick movement Ann placed her hand on May's shoulder, and said below her breath, 'You'll tell me now. What do you mean about this perfume?'

'Oh my God!' May shrugged herself from Ann's hold and, rising to her feet, put her hand to her brow. Then turning on Ann she said, 'Well if you must know, you must. It happened that Millie, Mrs. Orchard you know, rooms with a Miss O'Neill, and this Miss O'Neill happened to be in Danes' yesterday morning when John was there at the perfume counter, and he was buying a bottle of Chanel, a large bottle, nearly ten pounds she said it cost. Well naturally. . . .' She spread her hands wide. 'I thought it was for you. I knew it wasn't for Val, as he had bought her and Laurie the joint present of the chair, and you don't go round buying ten pound bottles of Chanel for . . . Oh what am I saying?' She beat her forehead with the palm of her hand, then ended, 'Aw, don't look like that, Ann. Come on, pull yourself together.'

Ann had her eyes fixed tightly on May's face, and when she tried to speak her voice made a croaking sound. Then she gave a little cough to clear her throat and said, 'May, you're not to mention this to anyone, James, or Val, or anyone. Promise me?'

'All right, all right.'

'Don't just say all right, all right. May, I want your solemn promise you won't mention this to anyone.'

'All right, Ann, I promise you. Now don't get upset.'

'Not to James?'

'I won't mention it to James.'

'Nor to Val?'

'I've told you, I've told you. Now come on, pull yourself together; we'll talk about it after.'

'I'm all right, I'm all right.' Ann turned towards the mirror, but she couldn't see herself, only the fuzzy outline of her face. But May was waiting, and her guests were waiting, so she walked with apparent calm out of the room and down the stairs. And just as she entered the lounge she heard young Boyd's high voice exclaiming, 'A Bull in the Argentine!' Everybody was laughing. Her husband was laughing; for the first time in twenty-six years she heard the sound of his laughter. It stood out against all the other sounds in the room.

CHAPTER SIX

PAT

OH it was hot, more like a summer day than one towards the end of spring. Cissie dropped her shopping bag and handbag on to the landing floor while she took the key from under the mat and opened the door; then picking up her things again, she went inside.

When she reached the room door she went to call Pat's name but checked herself, her mouth half open. He wouldn't be in with the key under the mat. But what had happened to him? He had never failed to turn up at the café before. Perhaps Mr. Bolton had been busy and kept him on; even so he had been busy other Saturday mornings, but things had always slackened off before quarter past one, the time he was supposed to meet her.

She put her shopping away, then went into the bathroom. Standing in front of the mirror, she lifted the hair from her forehead. She was sweating, it had really been hot walking from the market, and it would be this morning that that little monkey hadn't turned up. Wait till he came in. She washed her hands, applied a little fresh make-up, then returned to the kitchen again.

Where could he have got to? Oh, stop worrying, she said to herself, and get on with the dinner. He'd likely come dashing in in a minute and not a thing ready. . . .

An hour later she was standing at the window looking down into the street. From this position she could see Albany Road and Cromwell Street. He would come down one or the other. Five minutes later she saw him, and her hand went to her throat and gripped it, for on one side of him was a policeman, and on the other a man in a fawn mackintosh.

'Oh my God! Not again. No, no, Pat, not again.' She found she was shouting her thoughts aloud.

She was waiting for them when they reached the top landing, and it was she who spoke first. In a gabble she said, 'What's the matter? Where've you been?' She put her hand out making to grab Pat and shake him, but he stood stiffly between the two men as if petrified. It was the man in the mackintosh who said, 'Mrs. Thorpe?'

'Yes, yes, I'm Mrs. Thorpe. You know I'm Mrs. Thorpe.' Her voice was rising.

'Can we come in a minute?'

'Yes, yes, come in.' She stood aside until they were in the hall, then closed the door and said, 'Go into the room.'

In the room she stared at the plain-clothes man and asked, 'What is it? What is it now?'

'Now don't get distressed, we're only making some inquiries.'

'He wouldn't do anything, he wouldn't. He promised. Anyway he didn't do it before. . . . Pat?' She appealed to him, and of a sudden the boy flew to her, and, putting his arms round her waist and looking up into her face and fighting his terror for a moment, he gasped, 'I didn't, Mam, I didn't do anything. I swear, I swear I didn't. I've been at Mr. Bolton's all mornin'. I was just talkin' when they came. I didn't, I didn't.'

She held him tightly to her for a moment before pushing him aside. Looking from the policeman to the other man, she said, 'What is it this time? He's never been near Woolworth's or Smith's, I would swear on it.'

'Sit down, missus.' It was the policeman speaking again.

'It's a little more serious than Smith's or Woolworth's this time I am afraid, Mrs. Thorpe.' The plain-clothes man's voice was flat, and unemotional. 'It's to do with a little girl.'

'A little girl?' Cissie screwed her face up at the man.

'Yes, a little girl was interfered with this morning in a shed round by the old dump, the car dump near the children's playground.'

'My Pat in-ter-fere. . . .' She looked from him down at her son as she said, 'You're mad . . . Pat' – her voice was a whimper – 'you didn't?' She was appealing to him now

'No, Mam, I swear; I swear I didn't. I know nothin' about it.'

'You see, you see. Don't you believe him?' She was confronting the men again.

The plain-clothes man now looked at her coolly, and said, 'We've got another two of the boys. There were four of them in this altogether, and after questioning they admitted that your boy was one of the gang.'

'Who said that— Who said he was? Tim Brooks?'

'Yes. Yes, it was the boy Brooks.'

'I knew it. I knew it. That boy hates Pat, he hates him. He got him into trouble before; he planted those things on him. He knew what he was doing.' She was wringing her hands.

'Listen a moment. Listen a moment. We have more than Tim Brooks's word that your son was involved in this. . . . You see the little girl has made a statement.'

'She said she saw him then?' She turned to Pat. 'She couldn't, oh you didn't. . . .' Her voice cracked, and he whimpered back at her, 'I didn't. I tell you, Mam, I didn't. Honest, honest I didn't.'

'She didn't exactly see the boys' faces, Missus,' said the policeman now. 'They were wearing stockings, gangster-like.' He nodded slowly at her. 'But she recognized Brooks by the clothes he was wearing and his unmistakable hair. She also recognized your son by the tie.'

Before Cissie could repeat 'The tie?' the plain-clothes man put his hand in his pocket and drew out a blue and red striped school tie.

'Is this your son's?' He handed it to her and she held it across her two hands, saying, 'Yes it is. It was. That's the one. . . .'

She again turned her eyes towards Pat and he cried, 'It's the one that was pinched, along with me pullover, a fortnight ago after gym. You remember? You made me go and report it, an' I did. I did. I've never seen it since.'

Cissie was turning up the corner of the tie and she pointed to some loose threads. She tapped at them quickly before she brought out, 'Look. Look, his name's been taken off. I put a name on everything because of the pinching. His name's been taken off.'

'Yes, the tag's been taken off, but there's a faint trace of his name in ink further up the tie.'

She looked towards the middle of the tie where it narrowed and saw the faint outline of Patrick Thorpe. She had put that on ages ago, and then she had bought tags because she thought it looked better, and nicer, especially on his shirts. She had marked all his things. She said slowly, 'It was planted; it was planted by Tim Brooks.'

'I can understand you wanting to think that, Mrs. Thorpe, but if that was his intention he was more likely to leave the tag on, don't you think? However, the little girl happened to come by the tie when she was struggling with . . . one of the boys.'

Cissie lowered herself into a chair, and she closed her eyes before saying, 'Was she . . . ?' She didn't finish the question, but with lowered head she said, 'What are you going to do now?'

'We would like you to come down to the station with us.'

She looked slowly towards her son. His eyes were staring out of his white face as he stood gripping the back of a chair. His gaze held hers and screamed at her for protection, and she said to herself, 'Oh my God! Oh my God!' Aloud she said quietly, 'Go and wash your face and hands.'

It was some seconds before he released his grip on the chair; then he turned from them, and he staggered as he went towards the bathroom.

She looked at the plain-clothes man again and said, 'Was the child harmed?'

'Yes, she had been interfered with.'

She dropped her head deeply on her chest and groaned aloud; then quickly she raised her face to the two men and her voice was strong and firm again, even hard, as she said, 'If Christ himself came down this minute and told me my Pat had anything to do with it I wouldn't believe Him, and I'll prove it to you. He couldn't have done it, he wouldn't.'

'Well,' said the plain-clothes man, non-committally, 'we'll be very pleased for you to prove it.'

* * *

It was five o'clock when Cissie returned home. For the second time that day she unlocked the door; but now, pushing Pat roughly into the hall, she said, 'Now you stay there and don't move until I come back.'

'But Mam, Mam' – he was crying bitterly – 'where are you goin'?'

'It doesn't matter. Just you stay there.' Turning from him she locked the door and ran down the stairs, to be met at the second-flight by Miss O'Neill.

'Is there anything wrong, Cissie? Anything wrong?' she asked.

'No, nothing, nothing, Maggie.' She didn't stop, and Maggie called after her, 'Are you sure. I'm only too willing to help. You know that, Cissie. Anything, anything.'

Out in the street, Cissie hurried across the road and ran towards the bus that had stopped round the corner. Five minutes later she alighted almost opposite Mr. Bolton's greengrocer's shop. This was her second visit here in the last hour.

As she went into the shop Mr. Bolton turned surprised eyes towards her, then moved his shoulders impatiently as he handed a customer her change. Not looking in Cissie's direction he called across the shop to another customer, 'What can I get you, missus?' then went fussily on attending to the order.

Cissie was standing near the potato bin when he came to fill the scoop, and he said to her under his breath, 'Look, I don't want to get mixed up in this.'

'Well, you're going to be whether you like it or not, Mr. Bolton.' She, too, was speaking under her breath.

His words came hissing from the side of his mouth now. 'Don't you take that attitude with me.'

'Then you speak the truth and there'll be no need for attitudes.'

The three customers in the shop were giving them their attention and Mr. Bolton banged the scales and blew out bags and clashed the till with a minimum of talk, until there was no one left in the shop but Cissie and himself. Then confronting her, he said, 'Look. I told them all I'm goin' to tell them, or you. Kids come round here lookin' for jobs. I set them on when they're fourteen and not under.'

'You're a liar and you know it.'

'You prove it, missus. You prove it.'

'You know what could happen to my boy just because you're afraid of being pulled over the coals for employing children under age?'

'Look.' He turned his hands, palm upwards, towards her. 'It'll blow over. He was in this scrape. It isn't the first time that kids have had a bit of a lark together, and it won't be the last. And likely she asked for it. They all ask for it the day. If you saw what I see at times outside the back of this shop your hair would stand on end. And them still at school, I tell you it's done all the time.'

'It isn't done, not by my son. I don't care how many do it or who does it, but he didn't do it. He wasn't with them. He was in this shop at the time that child was attacked, and you know it.'

'Look, I said I saw him out there knocking around among the boxes. There's a back way around here. All the kids come the back way and mess around. "Can I weigh up your taties, Mr. Bolton?" they say. "Do you want any rounds made, Mr. Bolton?" they say. "I'll do so-and-so for a bob," they say.'

'You gave my Pat three bob this morning. You don't give lads three bob for nothing. He was out here early on; he left the house just after eight. Where was he from then until dinner-time? He's been coming here week after week.'

'They all come week after week. He's just one of the rest.'

'You're a stinking liar. And, by God, I'll make you prove it if it's the last thing I do.' Her teeth were clenched, her eyes black with anger.

'You'll have a job.' He squinted at her and his mouth moved into a crooked smile. 'As I said to the polis, when they were all here a while ago, he could have been here an' he couldn't have been here. They looked out the back for themselves and what did they see? Half-a-dozen kids among the boxes and the refuse out there.'

'My Pat didn't get as far as the boxes and the refuse, he was in there' – she pointed to a small room to the side of him – 'where you do the orders. I'm going to get a solicitor, Mr. Bolton. And you know something? You might be sorry you didn't just speak the simple truth and admit that Pat was here between nine this morning and one. If you'd said you saw him between twelve and one that would have been enough, but no, you wouldn't say anything because they might start asking questions and you'd be out of a few bob. Well, Mr. Bolton, lots of things come to light once people start using a rake. So remember that.'

She turned from his grim face and walked out of the shop down the street and into the main thoroughfare. The sun was still shining, people were busy shopping, everybody seemed to be smiling and happy, and here was she on the point of losing her son, the only thing she had in life that she cared about. What could they do to him if they proved they were right? An approved school. And then? and then? She stoood stockstill, unaware of the buffeting of the crowd. She must have help. She had told him, Mr. Bolton, she'd get a solicitor, and she would, yes. Mr. Emmerson. Yes, Mr. Emmerson, he would help her. Without looking right or left she stepped on to the road, almost under the wheels of a car, and made her way to a phone box.

When she had got the number from the directory she lifted the phone and inserted the four pennies, and when a woman's voice said 'Felburn 289', she pressed the button, wetted her lips and said, 'Can I speak to Mr. Emmerson?'

There was a considerable pause before the voice came again, saying. 'Who's speaking?'

'I'm Mrs. Thorpe. I would like to speak with Mr. Emmerson, please.'

'I'm afraid Mr. Emmerson is busy. Could I give him a message?'

'I'm sorry, no. This is important, very important. Would you tell him it's me, Mrs. Thorpe? I'm sure he'll see me . . . speak to me.'

Again there came a pause, and then Cissie heard the receiver being laid down. She heard the faint sound of footsteps receding away, and it was a while later when John's voice came to her saying, 'Yes. John Emmerson here.'

'Oh, Mr. Emmerson, I'm sorry to trouble you.'

'That's all right, Mrs. Thorpe, quite all right. Is there anything wrong?' His voice sounded different.

'Yes. I'm in great trouble. It's about Pat, Mr. Emmerson. Do you think I could see you?'

'Pat? Something's happened to him . . . an accident?'

'No, not that . . . much worse. Could . . . could I see you?'

'Yes, yes, of course I'll come round right away.'

'Oh, thank you. Thank you, Mr. Emmerson. Good-bye.'

'Good-bye.'

When John turned from the telephone table he saw Ann

standing in the lounge doorway. There was a curious look on her face and he felt obliged to give her an explanation of the call, so he said, 'I've got to go out for a little while. It's a client, she's in a little trouble.'

As he went up the stairs he was aware that she was still standing in the doorway watching him, and it recalled to his mind that first night he had returned from Cissie's, when they had all stood watching him going up the stairs. He hadn't felt guilty that night, but he did today. There were times when he wished she knew about his visits to Cissie's. There was one way to enlighten her and that was to tell her, yet he knew he would never be able to bring himself to it. She would never understand his need of a person like Cissie, and it was as well that she didn't, for otherwise the personal affront to her would be terrible, and he had no desire to hurt her further.

Up in the bathroom, he washed himself, combed his hair, drew his fingers down his nose, then along each side of his upper lip and was ready to go . . . go to Cissie's, to see her twice in one day. He thought of it as going to Cissie's. He never called her anything but Mrs. Thorpe, but he never thought of her other than as Cissie.

He found himself almost running down the stairs, not quickly like Laurie did, but at a much faster pace than usual. As he stood in the lobby putting on his hat and coat his attention was brought to the glazed door and to the outline of Ann standing in the middle of the hall. She was apparently looking towards the closed door. This fact made him uneasy; she had been acting rather strangely of late. She came down to breakfast every morning now, and time and again in the evening he would look up to find her eyes on him. He had thought, just after Christmas, that perhaps she wanted to talk, and he had made a strong effort to open up a conversation with her, something that he had given up attempting many years ago. But apparently her attitude hadn't changed; she wanted nothing from him, not even small talk, except when they were in company, or in the presence of Mrs. Stringer, when appearances had to be kept up.

Having to reverse the car out of the garage, which was to the side of the house, he swung it round at right angles to the front door, looking in his mirror to take care that he didn't hit the

Part II

Laurie

CHAPTER ONE

THE IMPOSSIBLE

Ann was lying in bed, and Laurie was sitting by her side holding her hand. He had been holding it only a few minutes when, with an impatient movement, she withdrew it from his grasp and, pulling out of her closed fist a fine lawn handkerchief, she began to straighten it out on the silk coverlet, tugging at the lace edge and forming the whole into a small square.

He watched her in silence, nipping at his lower lip as he did so; then he closed his eyes, as if thinking deeply, before saying with gentle insistence, 'Now look, dear, you've got to tell me what's troubling you. I've never seen you like this before.'

She didn't answer straightaway, and when she did it was as if she was repeating a lesson. 'I've told you, I'm feeling run down. I had that cold and it's left me feeling run down. There's nothing more to it than that. Surely I can stay in bed for a couple of days.'

Laurie rose from the chair and walked to the window and looked down into the garden on to the groups of tulips, daffodils, and narcissi, and as he stood there he heard Valerie's car come on to the drive. He could not see it but he knew the sound of the engine and the way she skidded on the shingle when she drew to a stop. Turning now, he walked back to the bed and, his voice still soft, he said, 'I may as well tell you I went to see the doctor today.'

'You what!' She gathered the handkerchief again into a ball. 'You had no right to do that.'

'Someone's got to do it, and if I don't, apparently no one else will.'

'Don't say that.' Her tone was so sharp that it caused his eyes to widen and his chin to move upwards. He was surprised that his inference that his father wouldn't trouble should have roused her, and now, his own tone sharp, he said, 'The doctor told me you haven't got a cold, you are suffering from nerves. And that didn't surprise me, but what did surprise me was that he inferred you're worrying about something, and you won't be any better until you air it. He tells me it's been going on for months.'

She was staring at him almost, unbelievably, in hostility, he imagined. Going quickly round the bed, he took his seat again, and, gripping her hands, whispered, 'Oh, my dear, I'm worried about you. You've never been like this before, you've always been so calm, reasonable. What is it? Look, you can surely tell me? What is it?'

Her head was bowed, her eyes tightly closed, and her lips were trembling as she replied, 'It's nothing, Laurie, nothing. Believe me. I'm just run down.' She moved her head slowly. Then raising it, she looked him in the face and smiled, a stiff, small smile. 'I'm not getting any younger and I suppose I'm going through what is known as . . . as the difficult period in a woman's life.'

He stared back at her. Perhaps. Yes, it could be that. But he should imagine that she had started that some years ago. He also should imagine that anyone of his mother's type would have taken such a thing in her dignified, reserved stride.

There was a sound of quick, soft footsteps on the stairs now, and when she turned her head towards the door he said, 'It's Val; she's bringing her work round tonight. I've got a pile, too. We thought we'd get at it downstairs.'

She made no comment, and when a tap came on the door he called, 'Come in,' and rose to his feet.

Valerie smiled at him and he at her; then she moved towards the bed, saying, 'Hello, Aunt Ann. How are you feeling today?'

'Much better, Valerie, thank you.' The tone was polite.

Valerie now said, 'It's been a marvellous day; it's a pity you couldn't get out. Are you thinking about getting up tomorrow?'

'I may.' Ann now looked towards Laurie and said, 'When you go down will you ask Mrs. Stringer to come up; I'd like to see her.'

The request was also a dismissal. 'All right, I'll do that.' He put his arm around Valerie's shoulder and moved her towards the door, where she, half-turning towards the bed, said, 'You'll likely want to get to sleep, so I won't disturb you again. Good night, Aunt Ann.'

'Good night, Valerie.'

They went down the stairs in silence, but as he opened the study door for her he said, 'I won't be a minute. I'll just tell Mrs. Stringer.'

When he returned to the room Valerie was lighting a cigarette, and she handed her case to him. He lit his before either of them spoke again. And then, as she often did when she meant business, Valerie spoke enigmatically. She said, 'Something should be done.'

'Something should be done? About what?'

'Your mother, of course.'

'Well, I know. I went to the doctor today.'

'What did he say?'

He pushed his hand through his hair and paused before answering her, wondering the while if he should tell her what the doctor had said.

'Well, what did he say?'

'He said he thinks she's got something on her mind, something worrying her.'

She dropped her head back on her shoulders and puffed the smoke towards the ceiling. 'You're telling me,' she said.

'What do you mean?'

'Now look, Laurie.' She flicked the cigarette ash towards a tray and took no notice when it fell on to some papers on the long desk. 'These evasive tactics of yours annoy me to say the least. You always play so dumb about your mother.'

'What do you mean, play so dumb?' His annoyance was evident.

'Just what I say.' She leant towards him, speaking under her breath. 'You must be blind if you don't know what's going on. I said to Mother tonight, damn it all somebody should do something, promises or no promises, and I said I was going to tell you.'

He got to his feet, looking at her while he stubbed his cigarette out.

'Well, tell me,' he said quietly.

Valerie drew in a long breath that brought her shoulders up; then when they had subsided she said, 'Do you mean to say you haven't noticed anything in the atmosphere of this house since Christmas?'

He could say to her 'Nothing more than usual', although when he came to think of it there had been a difference, and it could be summed up by the statement that his father had talked more and his mother had talked less. Odd that, but that is how it could be summed up. But it meant nothing. The situation in the house had been the same as it always was, but only he knew that, not Valerie, or her old nosey father, or her mother, even if she was his mother's dearest friend.

'There's no way to give you this, Laurie, but straight; your armour needs to be attacked with an axe. Either you know, and you're covering up, or you're absolutely stone blind to the fact that your mother is ill because your father's keeping another woman.'

It was some seconds before he cried, 'Father's what! What did you say?' He leant towards her as if he hadn't heard aright.

'Just what I said. Sit down before you fall down.' She pushed him in the chest with the tips of her fingers and he sat down.

'Do you remember Christmas night when your father went all jolly? Do you remember when he told us about the bull, the bull in the Argentine. He had told it twice and he laughed like I'd never heard him laugh before. And do you remember your mother sitting like a statue most of the night? You don't remember, you just didn't take it in did you, the unusualness of your father telling jokes. My father used to say it would take a landmine to move your father in any way, and that night he was laughing, and causing laughter, and the landmine was a woman, the one that saw to him the night he was taken ill. You do remember the night when he came back with his collar and tie loose, the night that he forgot to turn up for the dinner, don't you? And father was right about him that night, too. . . . He was blotto.'

'Hold your hand a minute, hold your hand a minute.' His face was turned from her, almost buried in his shoulder, and he was punching the air with his clenched fist. 'This is all surmise; you're just looking for one thing to explain another. It's all guess work.'

'You listen to me.' She pulled at his arm and brought him round to face her. 'It was on Christmas night that mother, up in the bedroom here, asked Aunt Ann why she wasn't wearing the Chanel perfume, and your mother asked her what she was talking about. And then it all came out. You see Millie – you know our Millie. Well, she lives with a woman named Miss O'Neill. They live on the first floor in number ten Greystone Buildings, and she, this Miss O'Neill, happened to be in Danes' when your father was buying a bottle of Chanel which cost nearly ten pounds. So she tells Millie that she saw your father buying the perfume, and Millie says to mother in all innocence that she knows what Mrs. Emmerson's going to get for her Christmas box. A bottle of scent, a great big bottle of Chanel. Naturally mother asked Aunt Ann about the scent, and your mother was so taken off her guard that she gave herself away and she made mother swear that she wouldn't tell father or me. And she didn't at first, not until she started pumping Millie and learned that your father visited Mrs. Cissie Thorpe at least once a week, on a Saturday morning. Mrs. Cissie Thorpe is a typist and has Saturday mornings off. They thought nothing of it the first time, because he came to thank her for looking after him the night he took ill. But when it becomes a regular habit . . . well they are only human, as Millie says, and they start talking and prying. Miss O'Neill, who happens to be off on Saturday mornings too, goes upstairs to visit her friend and happens to find your father there, and the funny part about it is he hasn't come up the stairs to get to the top flat. Nor did he leave by the stairway, so they could only surmise he came over the roof. If they wanted any more proof, the old couple underneath this lady's flat gave the show away, because, not only had the old man been up there and seen your father but they could hear them talking on a Saturday morning, and, as the old lady said, they stopped going up because they didn't like to disturb them. . . . Ha, ha.'

Valerie now dropped her bantering tone, and, getting up and putting her arms around Laurie, she said, 'I'm sorry. Don't take it like that. But I just had to tell you, and in such a way as to make you believe it, because you know' – she pulled him tightly towards her now – 'you just will not face up to things, you pretend you don't see them.'

Laurie wiped the moisture from his upper lip, then asked quietly, 'What did you say her name was?'

'A Mrs. Thorpe. Millie calls her Cissie, and by the sound of it she's a right Cissie at that. There's a commercial traveller who lives on the ground floor; he's a regular visitor. And at one time, as far as I can understand, young Holloway – you know the wholesaler in the market, his son used to visit her.'

'I can't believe it.' He shook his head slowly and spoke as if to himself. 'Him running a woman? It's impossible. Of all people, him!'

'Yes, my reactions were the same when I first heard it, because there's no getting away from the fact that he's one of the most inane creatures. . . . I'm sorry, Laurie, but I can't think it possible that he's your father. Oh, I know he is, you look alike, that's the odd thing about it. You've got all his features, but thank God they don't make you look like him. Yet it isn't his looks so much as his manner that makes him so utterly watery. . . . Then the latest is that the woman's in trouble . . .'

'You mean . . .?'

'Oh no. No, not as far I know anyway. Not that way, no. It's her boy. He's been in the courts before – he was up before father – and now he's coming up for interfering with a girl, and him only ten. I tell you they're a real bad lot. But I wouldn't like to be that kid when he comes before my dear papa next week, for he feels very strongly about this business and if he can strike a blow in the defence of Aunt Ann he certainly will. As he said, there's more ways of killing a cat than drowning it.'

Laurie got to his feet, pressing her gently aside. He didn't heed what she was saying about the woman's son. He was thinking of his mother lying upstairs, on the verge of a nervous breakdown. That's what the doctor said. 'You must persuade her to get away, take a long holiday,' he had said. 'Is there any trouble at home? I mean. ...' and before the doctor had finished he had assured him there was no trouble like that, none whatever. 'Then get your father to take her away on a holiday, a sea trip. That might do the trick. Get her away from the house and all her present associates, this often works wonders.'

Get his father to take her on a sea voyage! He was walking blindly to the door when Valerie said, 'Where are you going?'

He turned back towards her and sat down. The numbness, the shock, was wearing off, but taking its place was a feeling of anger, of rage. It began to burn inside him as if a fire had suddenly been lit. The evidence of his feelings was pouring down his face in sweat, and it was as if Valerie's voice was coming from another room when she said, 'Now look, don't let it disturb you like that.' When she wiped his forehead he pushed her hands roughly aside, saying, 'Stop it. Don't do that,' and she stood back from him, her voice huffy now. 'Well, you needn't take it out of me. Don't be like that with me. I told you because I thought it was for the best.'

'Well, you should have told me earlier, months ago when you first knew about it.'

'My mother had promised.'

'And she kept her promise, didn't she?'

'Now look. Don't take it out of me, Laurie. I'm telling you.'

Instead of her tone giving him warning, it only increased his anger, and he rounded on her, crying, 'If she knows' – he thumbed towards the ceiling – 'that your father knows and you know, she'll go mad. Why couldn't Aunt May have kept it to herself, or told me on the quiet?'

'Look.' Her voice became cool, reasonable. 'My father is a magistrate, he's used to keeping secrets.'

'Huh!'

'Now don't use that tone when speaking of Father, Laurie.'

'Well, don't make him sound infallible because he's a magistrate; you said only a minute ago that he was going to take it out of that boy, that woman's boy who ever he is, for something he hasn't done.'

'The boy has done something. He helped to interfere with a girl. Isn't that something?'

'But your father won't be judging him for that, he'll be judging him because his daughter's future father-in-law has slipped up.'

She took a step backwards and her pert face became stiff, and she surveyed him with cold eyes for a full minute before she said, 'You're an ungrateful sod.'

She said the word sod in such a way that it was deprived of some of its coarseness, but nevertheless it caused the muscles of his face to twitch. She often used that word sod and he didn't like it, and she knew he didn't like it. She now grabbed up the papers that she had placed on the desk and stalked towards the door, saying, 'I'll see you when you're in a better frame of mind.'

He heard her pause in the hall to pick up her coat, but he made no effort to follow her. He sat bent forward, his hands between his knees. The feeling of rage was increasing in him. His father would be the laughing stock of the town; they'd all be a laughing stock. But if this had been going on for months, as it must have been, his father supposedly didn't mind being a laughing stock. Nor, apparently, did he mind jeopardizing his position in the town, but the contemplation of such an eventuality was driving his mother to the verge of a mental breakdown.

That his mother should be thrown over for some loose piece and become the object of pity to her friends was unbearable to him. There were those who would say, 'Poor Ann,' but who would glory in her downfall, and among those who would derive private satisfaction from the situation he included her dear, dear friend, Aunt May. It was very odd, but at this moment, this particular moment, he loathed the Wilcox family more than he did his father, and that was saying a great deal. And this did not come as a revelation, it was something he had been trying to disregard for a long time. But now he was facing it.

He sat on in the same position, waiting, listening for his father coming in. He felt sick at the thought of seeing him. He'd want to hit him; he pictured himself pushing his father's big flabby body up against the wall and slapping out right and left at his pale face. How in the name of God had he the nerve to go after a woman....

When seven o'clock came John hadn't come in; nor yet when the clock reached half-past. During the last half-hour Laurie had walked between the lounge, the study, the dining-room and the kitchen a countless number of times, finally ending up in the kitchen.

'What is it, Mr. Laurie?' asked Mrs. Stringer. 'Are you worried about Madam?'

'No, Stringy. Look.' Turning to her with an impulsive movement he said, 'I know you should be off but can you stay a little while longer?'

'Yes. Long as you like.'

'I have to go out and I don't want to leave Mother alone. I may be only half-an-hour, but it might be a little longer.'

'Don't hurry. Don't matter what time you get back as long as you run me home.'

'I'll do that, Stringy. Thanks.'

Without bothering to don a hat or take up his light overcoat, he hurried out through the side door into the garage. Getting into his mother's car, he drove into the town, finally bringing the car to a stop opposite number eight Greystone Buildings.

Afterwards he remembered that apart from wanting to confront his father and hit out at him, there was in him a deep curiosity to see what type of woman it was who had fallen for the big lump of inanity.

Getting out of the car he looked towards the door of number eight. It was locked. That squashed any possibility of his father still being in his office. He walked now towards number ten. In the hall he saw the names of the tenants. Mrs. Cecilia Thorpe's was at the top of the list. As he mounted the stairs his nostrils twitched with distaste against the mixed odours of cooking, and when he came to the last flight he paused for a moment, looking upwards, then went swiftly to the top. Without hesitation he rang the bell.

'Yes?' She looked surprised as if she had been expecting someone she knew.

He looked at the woman. But she didn't look a woman, more like a young girl. She had long sandy-coloured hair tied back from her shoulders; she had dark brown eyes, was tall, and extremely thin.

'Yes, what is it?'

'I'm Laurance Emmerson. I would like to see my father.'

His tone expressed his deep hostility and she appeared to stretch herself upwards before it as she anwered, 'Mr. Emmerson isn't here.'

'I'm afraid I don't believe you. Tell him I want to see him.'

Her mouth dropped open, then snapped shut again.

'I've told you he's not here. Come in and see for yourself.' She pulled the door wide. 'And what's more, Mr. Emmerson, I don't like your tone.'

He stood still, glaring at her. That's who she had expected. Well, he had got this far and he would wait too. He passed her, and she closed the door behind him with a bang that vibrated through the flat. 'Go on in. Go on in. Search.'

He moved into the room, just within the doorway, and then stood stock still. And what he saw proved to him how right Valerie was. He could see for himself she was a type and she was certainly living in style. You didn't collect this sort of stuff on a typist's salary.

She pushed past him and walked towards the middle of the room before she turned to face him, and from there she said, 'I know what you're thinking, Mr. Emmerson, but you're wrong, quite wrong.'

For answer he said, 'You're expecting my father?'

'Yes, I'm expecting him.'

'Then I'll wait.'

'Do, but let me tell you something. And get this clear. You're on the wrong track. I'm not going to say I don't know why you're here, I do, but you're on the wrong track. . . .' She turned abruptly from him, and looking towards a door at the far side of the room and to a boy standing with his back to it, she said, 'Go back to bed, and stay there.' When she turned to him again he said, but under his breath, 'Do you deny that my father visits you?'

'No, I don't. There's no point in denying it, everybody in the house knows it. You can't keep anything secret in flats not even if you want to, and I can assure you neither I nor your father went out of our way to keep anything secret. . . . Yes, he visits me. What of it?'

'And I suppose you talk art.' His tone, still low, was an insult in itself, and it brought the colour rushing into her pale face.

'Now look, I'm warning you. You be careful, because you're going to be sorry for what you're saying.'

He walked farther into the room now, looking around him, his stare insolent. He looked at the card tables flanking the window, then at the small baby grand, its lid closed now. Then he turned and without invitation seated himself, and looking up at her he said, still quietly. 'I know your type, and this set up, a sort of unbaited trap, until they get inside. . . .'

Cissie put her hand to her throat. She wetted her lips and closed her eyes for a second before she ground out, 'If . . . if you weren't his son I'd call Mr. Glazier up and have him throw you out.'

'Mr. Glazier?' He nodded at her. 'He's the one in the bottom flat, isn't he? I've heard about him.'

'Oh my God!' Her hand still to her throat, she turned from him and walked across the room and looked down into the street for some minutes before she said, 'Mr. Emmerson, I'm in trouble, I'm very worried over my son. Your father's seeing into it for me. I'm expecting him up any minute. . . . Now,' she turned to him, 'if I swear to you that you are wrong, will you go? I don't want any disturbance. He'll . . . he'll explain it to you.' She made the characteristic wide sweep with her hand. 'But there's really no explaining to do, nothing, nothing.' She joined her hands now in front of her and walked slowly towards him. 'Your father comes here. We have a cup of coffee, we talk. . . .' She suited her step to each word, her body swaying slightly as if to a rhythm. 'He likes music, and furniture, and . . .'

'You needn't press it. What do you take me for? Do I look green?'

'Stop it! Stop it!' Her voice coming as a scream startled him. And at that moment, there came sounds from the hallway, like a small door closing then quick footsteps and when he turned there stood his father in the doorway.

He rose to his feet and looked at this big now florid-looking man for his father's face was suffused with a deep red, almost purple tinge. It was evident that he had received a severe shock and was trying to rally against it.

'What are you doing here?'

It didn't sound like his father's voice. It had a strength about it that he didn't associate with the man before him. But here he was seeing a different man to the one he saw at home. Of course, this house was where he led his different life. He had been clever, he had used two distinct personalities. They said he was good in court, he wasn't a solicitor for nothing. This kind of thing had likely been going on for years. It explained too why this undeniably attractive piece should fall for him.

He watched him come forward into the room, slowly, heavily. He watched him ignore himself and go towards her. He saw him look at her with a look he had never seen on his face before, tender, loving, with a sort of mute adoration. When he heard him say softly to her, 'I'm sorry about this, very sorry,' and she answer 'I've tried to explain', it was too much. And his wrath burst from him, uncontrolled for the moment. His voice filling the room, he yelled at them, 'You're sorry. You're both sorry about being found out. But what about my mother? I suppose its news to you that she's on the verge of a nervous breakdown?' He was glaring at his father. 'I went to see the doctor today; you couldn't, you were otherwise engaged. The doctor told me she'd something on her mind, something worrying her. She'd been like it for weeks. Is it news to you that she's known about your carrying-on all the time?'

John opened his mouth to speak but found he couldn't. There was a racing feeling underneath his ribs. His brain was racing too. Ann had known about this? No, no, she couldn't. She would have said something, something mild, slightly sarcastic, telling him that she valued her good name, her position in the town. But that is all she would have said, because that was the only way it would have affected her. Yet if she had known, why hadn't she spoken of it? The racing feeling accelerated, bringing with it a pain, a pain so sharp that it brought his shoulders down. He was still looking at Laurie, trying to say something. The last thing he remembered was Cissie's arms going round him, and her voice spiralling upwards, crying, 'Oh, Mr. Emmerson. Oh, Mr. Emmerson.'

'See what you've done. See what you've done.' She was kneeling on the floor supporting John's head on her knees. Laurie, too, was on the floor, kneeling at his father's side looking into the lifeless face.

'You've killed him. You've killed him.'

'Be quiet!' He tore at his father's waistcoat and put his head down to his chest. Then looking up at her, he said, 'He's not dead.'

'It isn't your fault.' She poked her face at him as she spoke, and then, the tears bursting from her eyes and spilling down her face, she cried, 'You! You!' and after gulping two or three times she shouted at him, 'Don't sit there like a dummy, go and get a doctor.'

Obediently he scrambled to his feet. His own face was white and drawn and he felt a fear within him. Although his father's heart was beating, he looked dead; he might die at any minute. She was shouting at him. 'There's a doctor round in Cromwell Road, a few doors down. Bell, Doctor Bell. Go and get him.'

He took the stairs two at a time, almost overbalancing an old man who was coming up. He ran into the street and down Cromwell Road, and stopped at the door with the plate on it.

The woman who answered the door said, 'The doctor has finished surgery.'

He gabbled at her that his father had had a heart attack in Greystone Buildings. Reluctantly she went and brought the doctor, who as soon as he saw Laurie said, 'Oh, hello. What's the trouble? You're young Emmerson, aren't you?'

'Yes, yes, Doctor; my father's had a heart attack.'

'Where is he? In his office?'

'No, next door, in one of the flats.'

'I'll be with you directly.'

It was just a matter of minutes later when the doctor, following Laurie at some distance up the stairs, puffed his way into the room. Cissie was still in the same position, still holding John's head on her knees.

'Put him down,' said the doctor quietly, 'and get a pillow.'

A short while later the doctor looked up from the floor towards Laurie and said, 'Ring for an ambulance. Mention my name and tell them to be smart about it.'

Fear had entirely replaced his anger now, and once again he was dashing down the stairs, only to stop in the street and wonder where he would find a phone box. And then he remembered having seen one round near the garages at the back of the building.

After he had made the call he stood in the box and leant his elbow on the top of the directory and rested his head on his hand for a moment. What had he done? WHAT HAD HE DONE? What had possessed him to go to her house? He should have waited. Oh yes, now he knew he should have waited. When it was too late to alter anything he knew he should have waited.

He walked slowly back to the house and up the stairs. His father was still lifeless on the floor. The doctor was standing near the head of the couch looking down at him. The girl was standing near his father's feet, her hands joined tightly under her chin as if she were praying. As he walked into the room the doctor was saying to her, 'How did it happen? Anything to cause it? Was it sudden?'

She looked up, not at the doctor, but towards him, and after two gasping breaths that sounded like a child sobbing, she said, 'Nothing. It was sudden.'

The doctor now turned and looked at him and asked, 'You got through?'

He nodded his head but didn't speak.

'Has he had these attacks before?'

'I don't know,' he said. 'No.'

'Yes, he has; he's had them before.'

The doctor turned slowly round towards Cissie. He didn't know who she was, only that she wasn't Mrs. Emmerson, but she seemed to know more about the man on the floor there than the son did. There was something fishy here. 'How many?' he said.

'I know of one, a bad one, but . . . but not like this.'

'How long ago?'

She considered a moment, then said, 'Last November.'

The doctor raised his brows, looked down towards the floor again, then turning sharply towards the window said, 'That's them now. . . .'

When John had been placed on the stretcher the doctor followed the bearers out of the flat, and Laurie followed him. At least he followed him into the hall, but there he paused and looked back towards Cissie, where she was standing in the middle of the room. And he watched her press her lips together and fling her head from side to side before crying under her breath, 'You! You!'

CHAPTER TWO

THE REASON

It was turned twelve when Laurie brought his mother home from the hospital. His father had regained consciousness but the doctor thought it unwise that she should see him, such was the state she was in.

Since earlier in the evening, when he had dashed from the hospital back to the house and told her what had happened, at least that his father had had a heart attack and had been taken to hospital, she, too, had seemed on the point of collapse. During the time they had sat in the waiting-room she had hardly spoken. In fact, during the first two hours of waiting she had sat in a coma of dumb misery, and it wasn't until towards eleven o'clock, when the door had opened and that woman had come in, that she had come to life.

He had walked towards the straight grey-coated figure and under his breath had said, 'What do you want here?' She had looked past him towards his mother, and he had turned and seen the recognition in his mother's face. Then she had said, 'You know why I'm here. I came to inquire about your father.' There was dignity about her bearing, a quietness about her tone that maddened him, that made him want to go for her, expose her for what she was. What he would have done had the night nurse not come in at that moment he didn't know, but he glared at her as she said to the nurse, 'Can you tell me how Mr. Emmerson is, please?' And having been told there was as yet no change in John's condition, she had then looked back at him with one long, penetrating, disdainful stare before leaving the waiting-room.

It was after the nurse had gone that his mother had spoken for the first time. 'How did she know he was ill?' she said.

When he hadn't answered she had turned on him, her voice

deep and harsh in her throat, and said, 'Well?'

He had sat down in a chair before saying. 'It happened at her house.'

'And you were there?'

He moved his head downwards once.

'Why? Why were you there?'

'Mother.' He had appealed to her under his breath, 'Don't let's go into it here. Wait till we get home. Please.'

And now they were home.

He opened the front door for her and she stormed past him. The calm reserved woman was gone. Her fingers were moving agitatedly, her head was jerking all the while, first to one side and then to the other. She tore off her coat as she was crossing the hall; she flung her bag on to the table and her hat after it; and then she went into the lounge.

He followed her slowly, wondering what the outcome of this was to be. He had never seen her het up like this, never imagined her letting herself get into this state.

'Well now!' she turned on him. 'Tell me. Tell me about it; explain how you managed to be with him when this happened?'

'Look, Mother, sit down and calm yourself.' He went towards her, his hands outstretched, but she backed away from him. She had never moved away from him in her life before, but now it was as if she didn't want him to touch her.

'I want the truth. Do you hear? I want the truth.'

'All right then.' He found himself shouting back at her. 'I'll give you the truth. You know what's been going on for a long time.'

'What do you mean?'

'You asked for the truth, didn't you?'

When she didn't make any reply to this he said, 'I didn't know about anything until this evening, when Val told me.'

'Val? What does she know? She knows nothing.' All her body was jangling, her hands, her head, her legs, as if she was about to go into a dance.

'Aunt May knew, didn't she? Well, could Aunt May keep anything? Everybody knew he was having an affair with—'

'He wasn't having an affair.' Her voice was thin, the words pinging as if off stretched wires. For a second her body became still, and she remained poised, her head half turned to him, and when he looked away from her and said slowly, as if tired by her gullibility, 'Oh, my God, Mother,' she screamed at him. 'He wasn't having an affair. He wasn't! He wasn't, I tell you.'

'All right, all right.' Again he was shouting back at her. 'If you want to look at it like that, he wasn't having an affair. He was just visiting this girl but he wasn't having an affair.'

'That's right, that's right.'

'Look, be your age. What are you getting all worked up about if you think he wasn't having an affair?'

'He wasn't having an affair. I tell you he wasn't. HE WASN'T.' Her voice rose to a screech, and now to his amazement he saw her grip her hair on both sides of her head. He saw her face become contorted, her mouth open wide as if gasping for air, and then on a loud cry the tears gushed from her eyes and her nostrils, and the saliva ran from her mouth. Then, almost bringing him from the floor, she let out one piercing scream after another. After a moment's hesitation he had her by the shoulders, shaking her, shouting, 'Give over, Mother. Stop it! Stop it!' He tried to draw her into his arms to smother her cries but she fought him, struggling and pushing at him.

'Stop it!' he begged her. 'Don't scream like that; they'll hear you down the road.'

When she opened her mouth for yet another scream, he screwed up his face, paused a moment, stepped back from her, then struck her with the flat of his hand. The blow did not knock her off her feet, but like a deflating balloon she subsided on to the couch.

Gasping and sobbing now, she lay back staring up at him, and he, panting as if he had been in a fight, stood looking down at her. He had heard that slapping the face was an effective cure for hysterics, but had he been told he would ever use it on his mother he would have sneered at the ridiculousness of such a suggestion.

'I'm sorry.' Although he sounded sorry he did not sit beside her or take her hand, or show her any comfort; this wasn't, he felt, the time for softness. He went towards a chair and sat down beside a little table a distance from her, and he waited, not speaking until her breathing returned somewhat to normal.

But when at last she spoke to him, her tone calm, saying, 'He wasn't having an affair with her,' he thought, Oh my God is she going to start all that again? But he said nothing, he just let her go on.

'Don't look at me like that, Laurie. I'm telling you, your father couldn't have an affair with ... with anyone ... anyone.'

'What! Do you mean he's ...?' He didn't say impotent, but it was as if he had, for she shook her head. Then she pulled herself a little way up on the couch, and with both hands she smoothed her hair back from her brow, stroked down the front of her dress, then turned towards the high stone fireplace and said, 'We were only married a week when he was called up. I fell with you right away.' He felt surprise at her using this natural kind of expression. 'You father did three months' training before being sent to a unit. The second day at this new place they were handling some ammunition in a shed and it exploded. Seven of the men were killed outright, about ten others injured. ... The bottom of your father's stomach was shattered. ...'

He felt something jump within him, like a live thing. It leaped from his groins up through his stomach and into his throat and checked his breathing.

'He was in hospital for nine months. He tried to take his life twice during that time, and they sent him to an asylum.' Her voice was unemotional.

Almighty God! He never went to church; he didn't think about religion in any way, it was mostly bunkum; yet in this moment he cried to something outside himself, something that understood pain, the strange pain he was experiencing now, and the years, the eternities of pain suffered by the man he had despised.

'You were a year old before he saw you. By that time I knew that you were all I had, or would ever have, of comfort. He saw that I was wrapped up in you. Sometimes I thought he was glad that this was so; other times I knew that he suffered, and I couldn't do anything about it. And the years went on and on. He had his work and I ... I had you.'

He sat staring at her with the strangest emotion coursing through him. This elegant but now slightly dishevelled woman was his mother. He had always loved her, championed her, adored her, but in this telling moment no vestige of these feelings remained. Yet there was feeling in him for her, but what was it? Hate? No! No! No! How could he hate her? Did he despise her? How could he despise her? All this reversal of feeling was ridiculous and would pass. But at this moment he knew that if she were to touch him he would shrink from her hands, because whether she had intended to or not she had made him despise the man who was his father. From as far back as he could remember, and without saying a word against him, she had held him up as something as pulpable as unleavened dough, something lukewarm, spineless, inane, until her picture of him had become fixed in his mind. She had said she'd had only himself, and with her every breath she had secured him to her while alienating him from the man who was of no use to her.

With a feeling now that seared him he conjured up the picture of his father, the big flabby-fleshed blinking man, the eunuch hiding behind the fixed smile. God! God! He had the unusual desire to lay his head on his arms and cry. He knew now with a certainty that if his father were to die remorse would gnaw at him for the rest of his days. He turned his head slowly and looked at the woman who in the past few minutes had shattered his emotions, the emotions that she had guided, and he said to her, 'If you knew that nothing could happen between them why have you made all this fuss?'

Unmoved, he watched her as she closed her eyes and bit on her lip before saying, 'You don't understand. I couldn't expect you to. But . . . but lately, this last year or so, not just since I knew I was going to lose you. No, no,' she moved her head emphatically, 'before that. I felt . . . I felt. Oh! I can't explain.' She dropped her chin on to her chest. 'Perhaps it was remorse for the way I had treated him, for having shut him out. I don't know. I only know that for some time I've wanted to get near him, to take that awful lost look from out of his eyes. It had been there for years, but somehow I noticed it more of late. And then . . . then at Christmas when I got the first inkling of this business, I . . . I knew it was too late. I knew I had lost him. I think I knew from the very minute it started. He had never sought companionship of any kind from man or woman;

then this ... this thing I could have had, that would have been far more lasting than anything created by sex, this thing that was there for my taking, and which I scorned, and belittled him even further by doing so, he gave to someone else.'

Her lips parted and he saw her tongue wobbling in the dark cavity of her mouth, and for a moment he thought she was going to lose control again. But she didn't. She snapped her mouth closed, pressed her fingers against her lips, then said, 'I told you you wouldn't understand. I don't expect you to, because I can't understand it all myself. If anyone had told me three or four years ago that I would be jealous of him, that I would be nearly driven mad with the thought of him being happy in another woman's company, I would have laughed. Yes, even two years ago I would have laughed. I'd never had a normal married life, so what was there left to be jealous about. But even so I've gone through hell. I've been terrified of anyone finding out, terrified at the humiliation, of people feeling sorry for me. But now, funny, it doesn't matter any more what they know. I feel he's going to die, and I'll remember that the only happiness he's had in the last twenty-six years is what that cheap-looking girl has given him. For he has been happy lately. That's what's been so hard to bear; I've known he's been happy. There's been a lightness about him and he's tried in vain to hide it. Just last week I heard him singing softly to himself in the bathroom. It was like a knife being driven through me.'

She became quiet, one hand was resting on her lap, the other lying palm upwards on the seat of the sofa. He sat staring at her unable to go to her, or even to offer her a scrap of comfort, for there was nothing left in him for her. With her confession she had scraped him bare of sympathy; she herself had smashed the picture of a beautiful, not quite-of-this earth creature tied by law to a bloodless individual.

He saw her now like a leech sucking all his affection from him, leaving nothing that could be spared for the man who had created him, and whom he had needed, yes needed. . . . And now, because the despised, crippled creature had found comfort – other than physical. And there was the rub, other than physical – with someone else, she suddenly realized that she wanted him, that she needed him. After twenty-six years of isolation, of freezing him out, she had thawed towards him, only to find it was too late.

Yet, he now asked himself, was he blameless in this matter? Couldn't he, as he grew older, have made some kind of effort to look at his father through his own eyes? Why hadn't he stopped to think of what others saw in him. Men like Arnold Ransome and Michael Boyd; they both held him in high esteem. And they weren't the only ones. . . . But no, he had only allowed himself to see what she saw. He was, in a way, as much to blame as she. Strip out the childhood, when he hadn't much say in the matter, and come to these last few years . . . even at this late stage, he could have given this man a form of companionship, the rare form that exists between a grown son and his father.

When he saw her rise from the couch he made no move towards her. She said softly, 'I'm going up.' When she stood looking at his averted face and added, 'You're blaming me, aren't you? You're shocked.'

He, too, rose to his feet, and with his eyes averted from hers, he said. 'It's no use apportioning blame now, but to tell you the truth I do feel a bit shocked. I . . . I feel he's had a rotten deal all through.'

The force of her stare brought his eyes to her, and he saw that she looked tired and ill, and even old. Her chicness had gone; that calm, suave veneer was stripped from her; she looked more like an ordinary woman than ever he had seen her before. Yet the change evoked no softness in him. He would need time he knew before any such feeling would return; he was still stunned by her cold-blooded, diabolical treatment of a human being, whom, and this was a telling point, she had made feed, clothe and house her in style for years.

She left the room without speaking again, and when he heard her muted footsteps overhead he looked up towards the ceiling. Woman were vicious, cruel. If such a thing was to happen to him, say, if tomorrow morning he went out and was hit by a car and his sex life was finished, how would Val react? Say they were married, how would she react? In exactly the same way as his mother had reacted. He nodded his head in affirmation. Only Val would go a step farther; she would either divorce him or get her satisfaction elsewhere; she wouldn't starve of the thing she needed most.

Slowly he rose to his feet and went out of the room and up the stairs. As he crossed the landing he looked towards his father's room and a feeling of remorse, so weighty that he bowed his head under it, descended on him. And when he reached his room he did not switch on the light but groped his way towards the bed and dropped on to it and, his hands clutching at the pillow, brought it pressing hard against his mouth.

* * *

At half-past eight the next morning the Wilcox family came en masse to the house. Ann was up. She had been downstairs since six o'clock, when she had phoned the hospital. And now James and May were closeted with her in the lounge, while Valerie was having it out with Laurie in the study.

Laurie stood with his hands on the desk leaning slightly forward, letting her go on as she had for the last few minutes.

'... And when would you have told us? Tonight? Tomorrow? Can you imagine what we felt like when Millie came in and told us he was in hospital ... had been picked up from that woman's place and that you were there? Why did you have to go? At least why didn't you tell me you were going?'

Laurie turned his head to the side and did not speak, and Valerie continued, 'Father's furious. He says you're a damn fool and should have minded your own business and—'

'And what do you say?' His voice sounded patient, cool. His head was still turned from her.

'Well, if you want to know, I say the same. It's bad enough your father's name being bandied round the town in connection with her without you going out of your way to give it more publicity. And Millie says you were fighting with her. Miss O'Neill heard you. The whole place was raised. Are you mad?'

Now he turned on her, his voice no longer quiet, his lips squaring away from his teeth. 'Yes, I'm mad. But I'll be madder if you don't shut up. And another thing I'd like you to remember is that your father might be my boss at work but he had no say about what I do in my own time. As yet I can go where I like, talk to whom I like. Yes, and row with whom I like. . . . As yet I can even go into Bog's End and stay the night at Bella Pickford's and enjoy all she has to offer. As yet I can do all that, and don't you forget it.' He was now pressing his finger into her chest. But she did not move away. Her cool gaze appraising him, she said, 'Yes, yes, you can do all that. As for Bella Pickford, I've no doubt you're well acquainted with her.'

'No doubt,' he said, making a deep obeisance with his head. 'No doubt.'

After glaring at each other for a moment longer he turned towards the desk and began to gather up some papers. And now, her voice almost soft, she said, 'Oh, Laurie, I'm sorry. But you must admit it's shattering. Even if we weren't going to be married, our families have been close for years and this happens, and you don't let us know . . . we've got to hear it through the daily woman.'

'And by all accounts she gave you a graphic description of the events. She's missed her vocation, that one; she should have been a reporter.'

'There wouldn't have been any need for us to learn the news from Millie if you had acted like an ordinary human being. . . . But look. Let's stop this bickering and tell me, what's she like?'

'What's who like?' He turned his head towards her, but kept his eyes averted.

'That tart up in the flats.'

Looking fully at her now he said quietly, 'From outside appearances she looks no more like a tart than you do.' He did not know if this was his real opinion of the woman or he was saying it to annoy Val. He was still so churned up inside from what he had learned last night that he couldn't think straight.

'I beg your pardon.'

'You asked me what she looked like and I've told you.'

'Thank you. Well, for the present moment let's skip appearances. What did you say to her?' She was striving to control her rising temper.

'I can't remember.'

'You can't remember what you said to her? You went to tell

her to lay off your father and you can't remember?'

'No, I can't remember. I can only remember what she said to me. . . .'

At this point there came the sound of a door banging, then James Wilcox's voice, crying, 'Where are you, Laurie? You there, Val?' The study door was thrust open now and the little man bristled in.

'Ah, there you are. Now I've just had a talk with your mother. I've told her to leave everything to me.'

'And what did she say to that?'

'She said the same as all women do, that she can manage her own affairs. But you know how far that takes them. . . . Well now, about this piece you saw last night, this so-called Mrs. Thorpe. What was your impression of her?'

Laurie looked at his future father-in-law, wetted his lips, told himself to count ten, but got no further than five before saying, 'My impression of her was that she was an extra-ordinarily good-looking woman, with tastes beyond the usual, and somebody not easily frightened.'

James Wilcox screwed up his small eyes and surveyed Laurie through his pin-point vision, then looking towards his daughter he said, 'You two been having a row?'

When neither of them spoke he went on, 'Well, that's neither here nor there, there's something much more important to be tackled at the present moment. Now, Laurie.' He pointed his hand, fingers held stiffly together, gun-fashion towards him. 'If your father gets better there's a strong possibility that he'll carry on with this game. Who knows; he might even want a divorce. Once these Thorpe types get their claws on a decent man he hasn't got a chance. Well now.' He pushed out his little chest. 'It's fortunate, as I see it, that her boy's in trouble. Yes, I say fortunate, and I mean fortunate.' He bounced his head towards Laurie. 'I've had them before me on another occasion, and on this one I intend to make the town so hot for that lady that she'll be glad to go somewhere else to cool off.'

'Are you going to try the boy or her?'

'What do you mean?'

'Just what I say. Before the boy comes up you've already decided on your verdict. Is that right?'

'Now look here, Laurie; I want none of your altruistic

theories. I know my job as a magistrate; I know the types I have to deal with in this town, and I act accordingly. And I don't need any lessons in justice.'

'No?'

'NO! And don't forget who you're talking to.'

'Father.' Valerie took hold of his arm, and when he turned towards her she said, 'Leave this to me, will you? Please.'

'Huh!' The sound that Laurie made brought their attention to him. They watched him push papers into his despatch case, lock it, then walk past them into the hall.

'Where do you think you're going?'

'I'm going to the office.' Laurie was now putting on his coat. 'You have reminded me more than once in the past that unpunctuality keeps a man's feet on the first rung of the ladder. Isn't that so?' He picked up his hat and walked out, ignoring Valerie's voice, high and sharp, saying, 'Laurie!'

He would not use his mother's car, as he sometimes did. His father's he had never used, and he would not have used it today had it been here, but it was still where he had garaged it last night, in the stables behind the office.

Having reached the road he did not immediately board a bus but walked to the nearest telephone box, and from there phoned the hospital.

There was little change, the sister said, but he was holding his own. And yes, he could visit him at any time. After replacing the receiver he stood looking down at it. Somebody should be with him, sitting with him. Blast old Wilcox and his job. Blast the lot of them. He picked up the receiver again, put another four pennies in the box and gave his own number. When Mrs. Stringer answered he said, 'Tell Mother I want to speak to her for a moment,' then asked, 'Is Mrs. Wilcox still there?'

'Yes, Mr. Laurie.' Mrs. Stringer's voice was very low.

'Then just tell Mother she's wanted on the phone. Will you do that?'

'Yes, Mr. Laurie.'

A few seconds later he heard his mother's agitated tone saying, 'Yes? yes?'

'It's me . . . Laurie. I just wanted to know if you were going straight to the hospital. If not, I'll go and sit with him.' There was a short pause before she answered. 'I'm going straight along now.'

'All right; I'll come in at dinner time.'

'Very well.'

'Good-bye.'

'Good-bye.'

They were like strangers.

* * *

Laurie's office was one of four small rooms going off a dark corridor; the other three being occupied by two typists and James Wilcox's private secretary.

The door of James Wilcox's office was directly opposite the corridor, and although he was a bustling man, noisy in speech and manner, it was rarely he banged his door, and so the staff, in their cubby holes, seldom had any indication of the boss's arrival. But this morning was different; the boss's door banged and almost instantly the bell rang in his secretary's room. A minute later the secretary knocked on Laurie's door, and on being told to enter she came in, closed the door swiftly behind her and hissed, 'His nibs wants you. Hair's standing on end. Did you hear his door banging?'

Laurie had worked with Miss Patterson for years; there were no secrets between them with regard to their opinion of the boss.

'O.K., Patty.' Laurie nodded to her, and she swiftly departed. He did not immediately follow her but stood gnawing at his lip, asking himself what line he was going to take if the old fellow became impossible. Tell him to stick his job. No, he couldn't do that; there was Val. Val! How he wished he could push the last year back. This thought propelled him out of the room.

He went along the corridor, knocked at the door, and entered the office, there to be met by James Wilcox's back. He knew quite a lot about that back, having had to gaze at it on many occasions: the hands joined over the buttocks, the short legs astride, the shoulders hunched high, cupping the head. It always meant trouble. An odd thought came to him as he stared at it. He was glad he had never called this man 'Uncle'. It had been quite easy to say 'Aunty May' but something had stuck in his gullet at the thought of calling James Wilcox 'Uncle'.

'Well now, Laurie.' The voice was studiously polite. 'We've got to have a little private discussion, haven't we?' This was delivered as Mr. Wilcox turned his body slowly about and walked to his desk. Then sitting down, he pointed to the chair opposite.

After a moment's hesitation, Laurie seated himself and, his eyes unblinking, he watched James Wilcox go into action.

'Now,' the shoulders, still hunched, were bent over the table and the finger was wagging with ominous slowness, 'don't you remind me that I've always said it's bad business to bring your private woes into the office. There are exceptional circumstances, and I consider this business comes under that heading, so we'll start from there, eh? Valerie tells me you've been awkward in more ways than one lately. Now, now.' The finger beat became more rapid. 'If my daughter can't talk to me who is she going to talk to? Anyway, we're soon to be one family, and such being the case there should be no secrets between us. . . . Well, well, I won't go as far as that because every man has his secrets.' The wisdom of this statement brought his head down in a deep sweep, and when it rose again he continued, 'But about the simple fact of letting us know your father had collapsed. Such a thing as this doesn't come under the heading of secrets but of ordinary human behaviour. Then going off to that woman's house and not saying a word. And see what it brought about? Your father wouldn't be where he is this minute if you hadn't bulldozed in there. These things can always be handled better by finesse. It's no use using the bull at a gap tactics with women on the side, women like this Thorpe piece. Legality is what you want there; they're frightened of the law. They're all loud-mouthed, big noises until you mention the law, and then they come cringeing. I've seen it over and over again. Now, that said I'm going a step further.' Mr. Wilcox's body swayed backwards and forwards between his chair and the desk. 'As I said this morning it's ten to one, if your father recovers, this thing will go on, and it could lead to divorce. And we're not having that, are we?' He did not wait for an answer but continued. 'So . . . I want you to promise not to interfere in any way. Leave this business to me, and don't go near this woman, or speak to her. That's vitally important.'

'What made you think I'm going to?' The words were rapped out.

On this occasion Mr. Wilcox did not take umbrage at Laurie's tone, but said evenly. 'You went last night, didn't you?'

'I had my reasons.'

'You could have your reasons again, but I'm warning you.' The finger was once more in slow operation. 'You leave this to me. Don't go near the woman. Those types are dynamite.'

Looking across the desk into this little man's face, Laurie had an overwhelming desire to take the flat of his hand and push it back, not strike it, just push the face as far back as possible. A blow, being a spontaneous action, could be said to have some dignity attached to it, but what he wanted to do to this man was something that would carry with it the insignia of indignity. He had a mental picture of pushing him slowly backwards, his head going down and his feet coming up – he could see him lying in a ludicrous heap on the floor. It came to him, with no touch of humour, that since last night he had for the first time lived up to his looks. He had wanted to hit his father, he had actually slapped his mother, and now it was all he could do not to put his desire into action and lay hands on his boss.

He rose to his feet and said coolly, 'I don't think my father would want you to deal with this matter, sir.' The insolence attached to the sir wasn't lost on James Wilcox.

'Now look here, my boy.' He was on his feet, his head wagging like a golliwog's. 'Don't you take that tone with me, I'm warning you. And anyway, you've no say in this matter, it's your mother who will decide what's to be done. I don't know why I'm talking to you.'

'I think my mother's answer will be the same as mine; she won't wish you to interfere in my father's affairs.'

'You'll go too far.' Mr. Wilcox put his hand to the back of his neck and flexed it, as if trying to relax the muscles, and as he did this he kept on talking. 'You forget yourself, you're not being wise, in fact I would say very unwise. No man who wants to rise in this world bites at the hand that is stretched out to help him, so to speak. I tell you, you can go too far, too far.'

'Is that all, sir?'

James Wilcox, his face bright red now and choked with his

indignation, swung round, walked to the window, put his hands behind his back and placed his feet in the straddled position. It was as if he hadn't moved since Laurie had entered the room.

Back in his own office, Laurie sat with his head resting on his hands. He wouldn't be able to stick it, he wouldn't. He had known for a long time things were coming to a head. To be married to Val, to have the families even closer, to come in here each morning and see him; to have a partnership dangled on the end of a long, long pole before his nose, it's shortening depending entirely on his subservience to the little man's whims. He just couldn't do it. But how was he going to get out of it?

He knew now that what he had felt for Val wasn't love, never had been. Perhaps, if from the beginning she hadn't continually and blatantly extracted from him all he had to give, he might have felt differently. He didn't know, he just didn't know. His head pressed harder on his hands. He was in a mess and he couldn't see how he was going to get out of it.

CHAPTER THREE

FATHER AND SON

JOHN looked at his son sitting at the side of the bed and he was pleased he was there; he seemed to be part of the great stillness that was filling him. This stillness that he mustn't disturb, a stillness wherein his heart was beating faintly. He was strangely at peace in this stillness; except for one thing, one little niggling thought, that would keep drifting to the forefront of his mind, then drift away again. It always drifted away when they gave him his pills, but it was some time now since he'd had them and the niggling thought was back, and with it the gentle urge to do something about it. And he felt that Laurie could help him.

He remembered thinking earlier in the day that if he had known that his imminent death would have brought his son closer to him he would have done something about it a long time ago. He did not have to ponder, or reason, to recognize that the young man who sat evening after evening by his side was not the same person with whom he had lived for years; this man was his son, he could feel it; after all these years he could feel it. The bastion that had grown up between them, mounting as the years mounted, was no longer there. It had vanished. It was as if it had never been. Yet it had been; he had watched its erection brick by brick. Oh yes, it had been. But now it was no more. But about this thing? He moved his hand slowly on the coverlet towards Laurie, and as slowly he said, 'Laurie, will you do something for me?'

'Yes, Father, anything. Tell me.' Laurie leaned towards him.

'Mrs. Thorpe. She's . . . she's in trouble. . . . The boy's case is coming up. I . . . I was seeing to it, but . . . but Arnold won't talk business. I . . . I want you to go to her, get her to tell you everything about . . . about Bolton . . . the greengrocer.'

Laurie stared back at his father. The last thing on earth he wanted to do was to come face to face with that woman again. Doubtless she was all they said she was, but with regards to the situation between her and his father they had been wrong. Everybody had been wrong, but only his mother and himself and the two concerned would ever know. ... That was a thought. Did the woman know? It wasn't likely. Then if she didn't, why ...?

'Will you go ... Laurie?'

'Yes. Don't worry, I'll ... I'll see to it.'

John's hand came on his, and the fingers made a slight pressure. 'Thank you. Thank you. ... Bolton, he's the man. He's ... he's frightened. You see ... Mrs. Thorpe. She'll ... she'll explain.'

'All right, all right. Don't worry. Now don't worry; I understand.'

He watched his father pull at the air, dragging it into his chest, and he held his hand tightly as he said, 'Leave it to me; everything will be all right, don't worry.'

'Laurie?'

'Yes, Father?'

'She's ... she's a good woman. Very, very good.'

He had to lower his eyes.

'There was nothing ... nothing between us to ... to hurt your mother.'

'I know.'

They were looking at each other.

'Don't worry. I know. I know all about it.' His voice was gentle, as if he were speaking to a child, a sorrowing child, trying to convince it he understood all its unspoken problems.

John's head pressed back deeper into the pillow, as if to put more distance between his face and that of his son's, to get him into focus. ... So that was it. Ann had told him. It wasn't because he had nearly died, or was dying, it was because he knew. God, after all these years. But ... but what did it matter? If it had created this feeling between them, if it had brought them together at last, what did it matter? In a way he felt it lightened the shame of his inadequacy; it took some of the weight of the burden from him. ... But there were others. ...

John's hand began plucking agitatedly at Laurie now. 'You won't . . . you won't let that go any further? You wouldn't . . . tell?'

'No! No!' The syllables came rumbling up from his throat like a torrent from an underground passage, so powerful was the denial of any idea of betrayal of the knowledge that he possessed, and John was convinced and his agitation subsided.

To convince his father still further, Laurie said, with a half-smile on his face, 'You've never liked the Wilcoxes' ménage have you, Father? Well, I'm going to let you into a secret, neither have I.'

There was a crinkling on John's face that tended towards a smile, and a light in the back of his eyes that spoke of his amusement, but there was also bewilderment in his look.

'And . . . and there's something more.' Laurie paused. 'I can't go on with the marriage, Father.' He paused again, watching his father's face, then exclaimed, 'Oh . . . oh, I'm sorry. I shouldn't have mentioned it. Don't let it disturb you.'

There came a pressure on his hand now while they stared at each other. Then John said quietly, 'I'm glad.'

'You are?'

'Yes, she – she wasn't for you, never.'

'Keep it dark, won't you? You see, she doesn't know yet – I mean Val. And I wouldn't want to upset Mother. It'll all come out in good time and then . . . oh boy, the fireworks. I . . . I must admit I've got cold feet. I haven't got a notion of how I'm going to do it. . . . I – I shouldn't have told you. I'd no intention when I came in.' He lifted one hand expressively. 'But . . . but I thought you'd understand, and I felt I must tell someone.'

Again the pressure on his fingers. Then John said, 'It won't be easy . . . they'll put you through the mill.' He gasped and began pulling at the air again.

'You've talked too much. It's my fault. Lie quiet now, lie quiet. No more talking.' Laurie smoothed the side of the pillow.

They stayed for some time in silence, until John, his words more spaced, said, 'Don't . . . wait for . . . for your mother coming. Go and see . . . Cis . . . Mrs. Thorpe now. Will you?'

'Yes.'

'Now?'

'Yes.'

'It'll . . . it'll rest my mind.'

'Don't worry. I'll see to everything.' He stood up. 'I'll look in in the morning and tell you how things have gone.'

John nodded slowly. Then reaching out his hands, he caught at Laurie's, muttering, 'Thanks. Thanks for everything . . . everything, Laurie.'

The gratitude, the humility in his father's tone was too much for him. He turned swiftly and went out of the room, down the corridor that housed the private patients, into the main vestibule, out into the street and along to where his father's car was parked. Yesterday his father had said, 'Use her, don't let her rot.' He had put it as if asking a favour.

He sat in the car now making no attempt to move off. He felt uneasy to say the least. What would he say to her? How would he begin? Would he wait until it was dark before he went? All those nosey-parkers on the stairs, especially dear Mrs. Orchard and dear Miss O'Neill, private eyes of the Wilcoxes. Well, what was he going to do? He just couldn't sit here indefinitely. If he went home Val would descend on him; she would be on the watch as she had been for the past three nights.

He beat a tattoo on the wheel with his fingers, then pursed his lips into a whistle, but made no sound. Aw, he might as well go and get it over with. But God, how he hated facing her again. Talk about crawling in the dust; she'd make him do that all right.

Outside Greystone Buildings he parked in front of his father's office, in exactly the same spot he had left his mother's car five evenings ago, then walked to number ten. Making his tread as soft as possible, he mounted the stairs and made the journey without meeting anyone. And for the second time he rang the bell of Flat Four.

When the door opened there stood the boy he had caught a glimpse of the other evening. He looked down into the big-eyed, pale face, with the mop of fair hair topping it. Michelangelo's angels could have been designed from such a face. And this was the boy who was accused of interfering with a little girl. But didn't all little boys interfere with little girls, and mostly by invitation? And the little girls, as they grew up, didn't alter much, except to get worse. He could hear Val saying, 'What's the matter? Don't you want it?' IT. IT. It wasn't only the infringement on the male prerogative that got him down, it was the crudity of the approach. Where that was concerned education meant damn all; a low type pro would have more delicacy at times than Val had. He wondered where she got it from. Her mother? The old man? How could you tell by how people looked. Val, he supposed, would even look prim as she faced the girls in class. The thought of the girls recalled his attention to the boy again, although he hadn't taken his eyes from him. 'Is your mother in?' he said.

'Yes.' The boy didn't move.

'Who is it?' He heard her steps coming across the room.

She stopped at the doorway leading into the hall and looked at him; then came hurrying forward and pushed the boy backwards before saying, 'What do you want?'

'I want to talk to you.'

'I've got nothing to say to you. Now get away; I want no more trouble with you.'

He felt the colour draining from his face. 'My father sent me,' he said quietly.

He watched her concern. He watched her wet her lips, look round to where her son was, then grudgingly, 'Come in.'

In the room she walked swiftly towards the fireplace. Then turning to him, she said, 'Well?'

He was standing some distance from her, to the side of the couch, his hat in his hand. He felt utterly nonplussed. He looked from her towards the boy who was standing as if he were looking out of the window, then said quietly, 'My father's worried about . . .' He inclined his head towards Pat. 'He tells me he was taking the case. He wasn't able to explain it all to me; he wondered if you might give me the details. Something about a greengrocer, a Mr. Bolton.'

He stood looking at her, watching her rapid breathing. Her body was swaying slightly from side to side and she was moving her hands in long stroking movements up and down her hips, the whole attitude showing her extreme agitation, and it came over in her voice as she said, 'I don't see what you can do. Mr. Ransome's dealing with it.'

'Mam. Mam.' The boy turned and came towards her, his voice as agitated as hers. 'He said he had written to him. That's all, that's all, Mam. It's no good just writin' to Mr. Bolton, he'll just write back. I told you, I told you. You've got to go to him. I told you.'

'I've been to him, haven't I? I've been to him twice. You know what he said, if I went to him again, I . . .' She closed her eyes for a moment, shook her head, then pushed at the boy, saying, 'Go on, get yourself out and leave this to me.'

The boy looked from her to Laurie. Then, his head drooping, he walked listlessly across the room and out into the hall. But the moment she heard the flat door opening she was running across the room, calling, 'Don't go away, just round the block mind. Be back here in ten minutes. Do you hear?'

There was no answer to this, and then she returned to the room, and as she walked past him, said, 'I've left the door open; there's nothing you can do.'

'Is it any use saying I'm sorry.'

'No, it's no use saying you're sorry.' She rounded on him, her voice bitter. 'You come into my house and insult me, you show me up in front of all my neighbours, but worst of all, you cause your father to have a heart attack, and then you think you can get over it by saying you're sorry. You don't know the meaning of being sorry for anything, not your crowd.' She began to move about the room, throwing her words at him. 'You're so cock-sure about everything, you're of the chosen few. You've been set up in the world, you've got a position in the town, and because of it you think you can kick people around. Have a good address, belong to the right societies and clubs, and you're infallible. You can carry on how you like but nobody can point a finger at you; they can't come into your house and insult you. . . . Oh no, because you are the right people.'

He followed her movements as she upbraided him, and he was reminded of his mother the other night, only he didn't think this girl would lose her head. He said quietly, 'You're wrong; you've got it all wrong.'

'Am I?' She was confronting him squarely now, standing still. 'Look, I've been in business for years and I've met your type. You said you knew my type, well, I know yours. I meet them all the time, and they're ten-a-penny little upstarts. They're in their jobs because of their father's money, or their mother's money, or because they've got friends at court. If they had to rely on their own brains they'd be on the dole, half of them . . . three-quarters of them, and I'm telling you.'

'Did you think that way about my father?' There was an edge to his voice now.

'No, I didn't. Your father's different, a different breed altogether to you and your kind. Your father's a solicitor, I know, but in his mind he's still a simple man, living in the farmhouse where he was born. Besides, your father's a lost, lonely man, and he's out of his element; there's nothing brash about him. He needs ordinary things, ordinary people. He's lonely . . . lonely.' There were tears in her voice now, and in the back of her eyes, and she swallowed twice before she went on, 'I've never met anybody in my life so alone, so lonely, as that man. And there's a cause for it; there must be a cause for it. I didn't know what it was, but after having seen you and your mother, it isn't far to seek.'

'Thank you. Do you feel better?'

Her eyes widened, her mouth opened, and she gulped before she said, 'There you go, expert at the cool, smart answer. It puts everything and everybody in their place, doesn't it?'

'Look,' he said, 'forget personalities for a moment. You say you liked my father, then ease his mind by letting me do something about this business.'

'You can do nothing more than is being done at the moment, and as much as I would like to please your father I don't want any help from you, is that final?'

'Yes,' he said; 'I think it is.' He was staring at her and she at him. Then, only because he couldn't stand the pained look in the depth of her eyes, he looked away from her and around the room. It was a wrong move, as he found out when she cried at him. 'Go on and ask me how I came by all this.'

He screwed up his face in question but made no comment, and she went on, 'But there's no need, is there? You know how I've got all this stuff. It's the men I have, dozens of them. At times they queue up on the stairs. That's what you think, don't you?'

'Please don't talk rot.'

'Rot, you say? I'm talking rot? When you entered this house the other night you treated me as if I were a prostitute from Bog's End. Rot! Now look.' She put out her arm at full stretch, the hand vertical. 'Don't say any more. I don't want to hear your excuses, I just want you to go. And I'll thank you not to come back here. Is that clear?'

Slowly he turned his head to the side and looked towards the floor, and as slowly he turned round and walked out. As she had said, the door was open.

As he neared the first landing he heard a door click closed and it wasn't the one he had just come through. He realized that the private eyes were on duty, but the knowledge aroused no ire, for he felt numb. It was a humiliating numbness. He'd been given the treatment he had wanted to hand out to Wilcox. Metaphorically he was lying on the floor in a heap, and the indignity of it was weighing heavily on him. Wilcox had dressed him down, but that was different, very different.

He was getting into the car when he heard someone say 'Psst! Psst!' and looking to the corner round which led to the back of the buildings, he saw the boy beckoning. He paused a full minute before going to him, and when he did the boy put out his hand and pulled him into the shadow of the wall, and looking up at him he said, 'She's not going to let you, is she?'

'You mean help?'

He nodded.

'No; she doesn't want me to help.'

The boy now rubbed the nails of his thumb and first finger up and down the sides of his front tooth; then sticking his four fingers in his mouth he bit on them hard before looking up at Laurie again and saying, 'I didn't do it, I swear. I swear I know nothin' about it.'

'That's the truth?'

'Yes, it's the truth. Oh yes, it's the truth.'

'Come here.' Laurie drew him further up the alleyway that led to the garages, and when they stopped he stared hard into the boy's face before saying. 'Tell me exactly what happened on that Saturday morning.'

'Well, it was like this.' Pat sucked in his lips, swallowed and went on, 'I go to Mr. Bolton's every Saturday to help make up the orders, taties and things. I get there on nine and I leave about one, and then I go to a café near the market where I meet me mam and help her carry the groceries back. I've been doin' it for a long time like that. Mr. Bolton sometimes gives me two bob and sometimes three, depending, but I keep out of the way in the back 'cos I'm not supposed to work 'cos I'm just on ten, see, and he can't set them on until they're fourteen, an' he tells me to keep out in the back an' if anybody comes, strange like, to make on an' just play about like I was one of the lads come scrounging for bruised fruit in the boxes outside. It's near the dump you know, the car dump. You know where it is?'

'Yes.' Laurie nodded.

'Well, on Saturday mornin' I finished the orders an' I said to Mr. Bolton are there any more and he said no, and I said it's five to one and he gave me three bob, and as I went down the street I remember the Town Hall clock striking one. Then I was passing the dump and Barrie Rice, a boy I know, and Tim Brooks, another boy, he's older than me, nearly fourteen, came running down the side, dodging like, and Tim Brooks grabbed me by the shoulder and pulls me with him, and I say, "Leave over! leave over! What's up with you?" and he pulls me beyond a car, and I thought they were having a game, or being chased by the other gang or somethin'. An' I said again, "What's up?" an' I said I had to go because me mam was waitin' but Tim Brooks, he kept hold of me and he made Barrie do the same, though Barrie told him to let me go. Then they pulled me to the dugout, that's a place beyond Tollington's factory, and they wouldn't let me out, at least Tim Brooks wouldn't. And he kept saying to me, "You're in this, Pat Thorpe. You're in this." An' I got frightened 'cos he had got me into trouble afore. You see he used to lead a gang I was in, an' one day he swopped me a ball-pen and a key case for some medals I had, and then he swore he never did and that I had pinched them from Smith's. When the gang went round on Saturday they had a sort of game to see who could pinch most from Woolworth's, or Smith's, or Craig's, but I never did 'cos of me mam. But he said I did, and he said I never gave him no medals. Well, anyway, there I was in the dugout, and then the polis came, an' I didn't know what it was all about and I told them, but he said – Tim Brooks, that is – he said I was just playing dumb and I was in it, and then the polis said was this my tie, and he said didn't I tell you so. He said that to the polis. An' it was my tie, but I hadn't worn it, I'd lost it last week, with me pullover; it'd been swiped when I had stripped for gym. Then the polis asked Barrie Rice had I been with them an' he said yes. He's frightened of Tim Brooks, an' he had to say yes. . . . An' that's the truth, mister, that's the truth. I would have never have done such a thing, I wouldn't hurt me mam; 'cos she was upset the last time and frightened. I wouldn't upset her again. Anyway I'd never do a thing like they said.'

When he hung his head Laurie said, 'Were you wearing a tie when the police spoke to you?'

'No, just an open-necked shirt.'

'Where does this Barrie Rice live?'

'In Portland Street, number four.'

'And your mother's been to see Mr. Bolton?'

'Yes. She's been twice, but he takes no notice of her because she's a woman.' He moved his head slowly as he repeated, 'She's a woman, you see.' This statement conveyed his opinion of why his mother had failed to make any impression on Mr. Bolton.

As Laurie looked down on the boy he saw him standing in front of old Wilcox. He heard the magistrate's voice leading off, his holier-than-thou attitude well to the fore. 'You and your kind are a menace to our community and I intend to make an example of you. You are depraved and the only hope for you is strict supervision. I am assured that this would never have happened if you'd had the proper parental control. . . .' At this point he saw her face as Wilcox carried out his intention of making the town too hot for her.

'Where's his shop?' he said.

'Cox Road.'

'Does he employ anybody else?'

'No. Not now. He used to have bigger lads, but he got wrong once about something that happened in the shop. I don't know what it was, but after he didn't have any help for a long time.'

'Well now, listen,' said Laurie. 'You go upstairs and look after your mother. Don't tell her you've seen me or told me anything, understand?'

'Yes.' He nodded.

'And I'll see what I can do.'

'Thanks. Thanks, Mister.' He went to move away. Then turning and looking up into Laurie's face, he said, soberly, 'Me mam isn't bad, she isn't. She isn't a bad woman. She's good. I'm in the house all the time. Me mam isn't bad.'

God! this was dreadful, terrible. Laurie's gaze dropped towards the ground. Then raising his eyes again to the boy's face, he said softly, 'You go on thinking that way about your mother.'

'But it's the truth.' The nervousness had disappeared from the lad's voice, there was a touch of aggressiveness in it now. 'Everybody likes me mam. She's jolly, she's happy, at least she was . . . and funny, fun to be with I mean. Except this last week, and this business, and since Mr. Emmerson took bad. She likes Mr. Emmerson. But she's good. She could get married the morrow but she doesn't want to. Ted, Mr. Glazier, him that lives at the bottom, he's getting a divorce and wants to marry her but she told him no, I heard her. He's going to live down south, but she doesn't want to marry anybody, ever. And nobody ever stays in our house at night. . . . She's good.'

Ten years old and defending his mother. 'Nobody ever stays in our house at night.' He bent down until his face was on a level with Pat's. 'Don't worry about it. I believe your mother's good, I do. Go on now; go on, keep her company.' He pushed him away gently, then said, 'Wait. Where am I likely to find you if I want you?'

'I go to Remington Road School.'

'Very good, Pat.' He reached out and touched the boy's shoulder. 'If I need you I'll come there after school.'

Pat nodded solemnly, then walked into the street, and when Laurie reached the pavement he saw him entering the flats.

He got into his car, drove down to Cox Road, and there drew up opposite the greengrocer's shop. It was closed, and he sat in the car looking across at it. It was a double-fronted shop and had been newly painted, as had the windows above it. These were nicely curtained and looked like a flat. To the right side of the shop window was a door painted a vivid red, the private door to the flat, he supposed. It could be that Mr. Bolton lived above his shop.

He got out of the car and crossed the road, and after a moment's hesitation he rang the bell. The door opened slowly, but no one confronted him until a voice from the top of the stairway shouted, 'Yes, what is it?'

He put his head back and looked up to see a woman with her hand on a pulley.

'Does Mr. Bolton live here?'

'Yes, who wants him?'

'I wonder if I could have a word with him?'

'He's busy bookin'.'

'Well, I wouldn't keep him a minute.'

'Who is it?' A man had now joined the woman, and he bent forward and looked down the stairs as he asked, 'What you want?'

'I . . . I just wanted to have a word with you about the boy, Pat Thorpe.'

He watched the woman move back on the landing as she said under her breath, 'I knew it was about that, I knew. You tell him where to go to.'

'Look.' The man bent his knees and heaved further forward, but made no attempt to come down the stairs. 'I'm havin' nothin' more to say about that little nipper. What I'd to say I've said to the polis.'

Laurie stepped into the passageway and looked up to the man. 'You still mean to say you didn't employ him on that particular Saturday morning?'

'Not on that particuar Saturday mornin', or on any other mornin'. I've got me work cut out to keep the little bastards out of the back shop, thieves and scroungers the lot of them.'

Laurie let a moment elapse before he said, 'You remember the boy, Pat Thorpe, don't you?'

'Aye, I remember him all right because I was always tellin' him where to go to. And look . . . I don't know who you are, and I don't bloody well care, so get goin' an' shut the door behind you.'

Laurie kept Mr. Bolton under narrow scrutiny for another few seconds, then he turned around and closed the door after him.

As he drove away he thought: Types. My God! the types,

and he was a liar. His short acquaintance with him had convinced him of that.

Bolton. Bolton. The name kept repeating itself in his mind. Bolton. Bolton. He had an orderly mind for names, he rarely ever forgot a name. Bolton. Bolton. Was he on their books? Not on his. He didn't do any work for anyone of that name. But he had seen the name Bolton on a file somewhere. Now where would he have seen that, except in the office? Bolton. Bolton. There came a little click, Bolton. Wilcox. That's where he had seen Bolton's name, in the old man's files. He had a number of clients whom he attended to himself. He couldn't remember how long it was since he had seen the name, definitely before the old man started locking things away. It could have been years ago, and Bolton could have transferred his business elsewhere, but there was a chance he hadn't. There came another click in his mind which told him he was sure he hadn't. He was in the Wilcoxes' dining-room, where every week-end, summer and winter, was displayed a great bowl of fruit. James was so fond of fruit, he could hear May Wilcox remarking, and he had thought more than once that they spent a lot on fruit, and this had seemed out of line with Aunt May's cheese-paring budget. The only time she went to town with regards to food was for the 'dinners-at-eight'. Of course, he could be barking up the wrong tree. It could all be surmise, wishful thinking. But anyway he'd look into it tomorrow. Long shots sometimes paid off.

And now for this Barrie Rice's abode.

When he reached number four Portland Street, he hesitated before getting out of the car, because, standing at the open door, her arms folded on the top of her stomach, was a woman of more than ample proportions. Moreover, she was in loud conversation with another woman. She might or might not be the boy's mother, but he felt chary of approaching her. Still, as he had stopped the car and was now under scrutiny from the two women he thought it best to make the approach.

Stepping across the pavement, he addressed himself to the large woman, saying, 'I'm looking for a Mrs. Rice.'

'I'm Mrs. Rice.' The arms still remained folded.

'I wonder if I could have a word with your son, Barrie?'

'You from the the polis?'

'No, I'm not from the police.'

'Then you can't have no word with him.'

'Well, you see I'm from a firm of solicitors.'

'Thompson and Curry, they're the solicitors we've got. You one of them?'

'No, no, we're not that firm.'

'Well, then, Mister, whatever you want to know you'd better go and ask the polis, that's my answer to you. What you want to know you go and ask the polis.' Mrs. Rice nodded at him, then to her friend, and without more ado he turned round, got into the car and drove away. He knew when he was beaten.

* * *

When he came downstairs before half past six the following morning he wasn't surprised to find his mother already up. She had been down before him every morning since his father had taken ill. He wondered if she slept at all, but he didn't inquire. The wall that had stood between his father and himself hadn't fallen into disuse; it had re-erected itself now between him and her.

When they spoke to each other it was quietly, as if each were considering the other's feelings. It seemed strange when he remembered that he hadn't touched her or held her hand for days, nor had he kissed her good-bye, which had been the usual morning procedure. Could the tie that had held them together be severed so completely?

Although he wasn't due at the office until nine o'clock he left the house at eight-fifteen, and scooted down the avenue as if the devil was after him, part of the evasive tactics that he knew only too well must soon come to an end.

Thursday was court day and consequently a day when there was a slackening of routine and nerves in the office, but this morning he felt no benefit from this. For one thing he had a thick head, having had a session at the club last night in order to evade going home and being waylaid by Valerie. He had even driven up Handley's rutted lane and come into the avenue by the top way. And then there was the Bolton business. If it wasn't that today was the only time he'd get the chance to investigate the files he would have left it over.

He heard the girls come in; then a few minutes later when he heard Miss Patterson's firm tread along the corridor he went out of his office and followed her into her room.

'Can I have a word with you, Pattie?' he said.

'Yes, of course, but let me get my things off.' She laughed coyly at him over her shoulder; then patting her greying hair into place she said, 'You're here bright and early. And it Thursday an' all. Now, what is it? By the way, you look tired; you been on the tiles?'

'Well, not exactly on the tiles, Pattie. Just indulged a little last night.'

'Oh, naughty boy. You won't be able to do that much longer.'

He slanted his eyes at her, and she giggled. Then he said, 'I want your help, Pattie. I want a little information. First of all can you tell me if the old man does Bolton's, the greengrocer's accounts?'

'Bolton's? Yes. He's done them for years. His stuff came in only last week.'

'Do you think I could have a look through them?'

'I don't see why not. But . . . but wait.' She flapped her hand at him. It was another coy movement. 'He might have them locked away, he does with some of them. I don't do all the work on all of them you know. I couldn't, could I? Just the working out of the fees and covering letters and such.'

'Will you have a look?'

'Yes, yes, I'll do that. But what do you want to know?'

'Just a little thing.'

'It won't cause trouble?' She looked apprehensively up at him.

'Oh, no, no.' He shook his head at her. 'And I won't keep it long. If you could bring it into my office, it would be better, for who knows he may pop in and I wouldn't want him to find me along there.'

'Oh, my, no.' She laughed her high thin laugh. 'We don't want any high jinks on a Thursday, do we? All right.' She winked at him. 'I'll go along in a minute and have a look for it.'

'Thanks, Pattie.' He smiled at her warmly, then went out.

Back in his office he sat thinking. Since he had been first articled to this firm certain names had become synonymous to him with success, or failure. Year after year he had watched the rise or fall of the businesses to which these names were attached. When he qualified Wilcox had handed over to him a number of clients, and with time the number had risen, but he had always been aware that there were, on the books, names about which he knew nothing. Bulky parcels would arrive addressed to 'Mr. Laurance Emmerson', and underneath 'James Wilcox, Chartered Accountants'. And bulky packets would arrive addressed to 'James Wilcox, Esq., Chartered Accountants', and marked 'Private'.

He didn't think the old man was up to any fiddle; he was too wily for that. But there were many things an accountant could do to lighten a client's burden, such as not asking too many questions, while praying that the tax inspector would be of like mind. And there were always ways of being paid in kind; it went on all the time. Still, it wasn't with the idea of getting anything on old Wilcox that he wanted to see Bolton's file. It was simply with the hope that he'd get a clearer picture of Bolton and perhaps in some way get a handle with which he could turn the truth out of the greengrocer. The whole thing was just a hunch, but he had always believed in hunches; and a hunch might make all the difference to the fate of that boy. He hadn't been able to get him out of his mind. Nor had he been able to get the woman out of his mind. The more he had drunk last night the more clearly he had seen her as he had left her in that room.

The door suddenly opening, Miss Patterson tripped in, whispering, 'Here they are. He's never touched them yet. But mind you, if I hear him come in I'll give you a buzz, and you make them scarce.' She nodded, as one conspirator to another.

'Thanks. Thanks, Pattie, I won't keep them long. Thanks.' He smiled at her, and she tripped out.

Knowledgeably, he sorted out the contents of the large packet. Under the heading of 'replacements' was the price of a new van, and set against it was what had been deducted for the old one. There'd been alterations done to the shop which amounted to £200; the bills were there all signed. There was a thick sheaf of wholesalers' weekly receipts. Then there was a book marked 'Wages'. The first knowledge he gained from this was that the greengrocer paid his wife ten pounds a week for serving in the shop. Fair enough; she would have to pay tax on it. Then under a heading of 'Casual Labour' was 'Van driver: Saturdays 1 p.m. to 6 p.m. £2.15.0.' Beneath this was given the year's total. Then below this there was a statement that brought Laurie's teeth on to his bottom lip. 'Two boys packing orders: Saturday 9 a.m. till 1 p.m. 30*s*; and under this, too, was given the year's total . . . '£78'.

He was still biting his lip but smiling as he put the papers back into the envelope. Funny about this hunch. Damn funny.

He took the envelope back into Miss Patterson's office, and, placing it on her desk, said, 'Put that back where it belongs, Pattie. And remember, you never gave me that envelope, I must have gone into the office and got it myself.'

'There's not going to be trouble about this, Mr. Emmerson, now is there?' She poked her face up to him.

'Not for you, Pattie, not for you.' He grinned broadly at her. 'Just remember you know nothing at all about it.'

'Oh, I'll remember that all right. He'd go mad if he knew I'd . . . Oh, I'll remember that all right.'

'You do, Pattie. And thanks, thanks.'

Back in the office again he got through to Arnold Ransome, and the first thing Arnold said was, 'How's your father?'

'Oh, much improved this morning, Arnold; the sister seemed very pleased with him.'

'Good, good. Oh, I'm glad to hear that. I got a shock when I saw him on Tuesday night.'

'He's worried about this Thorpe case, Arnold. You know, the little boy from the flats next door.'

'Yes, I know, I know. I'm dealing with it; there's no need to trouble him further with it.'

'Have you seen the greengrocer?'

'No, I've written to him.'

'He's a wily type, Arnold, and he's a liar. I believe the boy when he said he worked there. Father was on to something and I've taken it from there.' He lowered his voice. 'This fellow Bolton told the police that he never employed any boys, yet on his income tax returns he's got down thirty shillings every week for two boys working from nine till one on a Saturday.'

'Are you sure of this, Laurie?'

'I've just seen it with my own eyes.'

'Oh, oh.' Laurie could imagine Arnold tapping the desk with his fingers. Then his voice came again, saying, 'That's all very well but one's got to prove it in court, and we'd have to get old man Wilcox to show the statement, and I can't see him doing that; he would consider his client's affairs as being private. And another thing, he's got his teeth in this case, and you know why, Laurie?'

'Yes, I know why all right.'

There was a short silence, then, 'I can't see it's much use really,' said Arnold.

'You mean that?'

'Yes. Yes, I do. If this fellow sticks out and says he doesn't employ anyone, and we've got to bring proof that he has done, it's going to take time.'

'But it could be done?'

'Oh yes, of course it could be done, but by that time the boy will be wherever old Wilcox decides to put him, for I can't see us getting a remand on such slender evidence, which after all will be merely hearsay if we can't produce his tax returns. And about that we'd have to be very careful, for he – the greengrocer – could turn the tables on us.'

'I see what you mean.'

'Of course the case can always be reopened.'

'Yes, yes. It comes up a week today, doesn't it?'

'The preliminary hearing, yes. Wilcox tried to push things through for today but the little girl is still suffering from shock and the mother said she couldn't appear, so it was put back for a week.'

'Well, that's something. Thanks, Arnold.'

'You've got a point, Laurie; I'm not saying you haven't. I must give it some thought; and given time it might alter the whole case. In fact I'm sure it will. But it's time, it's time we want. ... And Laurie. This is going to upset Wilcox, you understand that?'

'Yes, I understand.'

There was a pause. Then: 'Oh well, as long as you understand. Good-bye, Laurie.'

'Good-bye, Arnold.'

He sat looking down at the desk. The law was meticulous, finicky, and slow. Arnold said it was time they wanted, and in the meantime Mr. James Wilcox, J.P., would see that that little fellow got time in an appropriate place, and he would scathe the mother not only by this act, but with his public censure of her. As he'd said, he'd make this place so hot for her she'd have to find some place to cool off.

At dinner time he had lunch in the town as he had done all the week, then he went on to the hospital, and it was as he was going in the main entrance that he saw Cissie coming out. They passed in the open doorway and she looked through him and beyond him, not flicking an eyelid in recognition.

As soon as he entered his father's room he knew that she hadn't been there, for he was lying as he always was now, propped up against the pillows, calm, quiet, almost serene, and he didn't think that if he had seen her he would be like this. She had likely been to the desk to inquire.

'How are you?' He sat down by the bed.

'Oh, better, much better. Your ... your mother's just gone.'

'Just gone?'

'Well, about a quarter of an hour ago. Did ... did you do what I asked?'

'Yes, yes, Father, I saw her.'

'And she told you all about it?'

'Yes. Yes. She told me everything.'

'Did you see the boy?'

'Yes, I saw Pat.'

'No, no.' John shook his head. 'The Rice boy.'

'No, but I will.'

'And Bolton?'

'I'm seeing him tonight.' He did not mention his fruitless visit last night.

'Bolton's crafty, Laurie, and he's a bad lot. He's been cautioned about employing boys under age. Also, something much more serious with regards to them; it wasn't proved absolutely. They are frightened of him around there. Anyway that's ... that's why he won't come into the open about Pat.'

Laurie leant towards him. 'He'll come into the open now if I know anything.'

'Yes?'

'I think I've got him where I want him. Just you wait. I'll

likely have news for you tomorrow. Just leave it till then.'

John smiled. It was the most his face had stretched in days. Then, the smile sliding away, he said, 'She'll die if that boy's taken away from her. He's all she's got. And the boy's innocent. I'd swear my life on it.' He raised his hands and his lips twisted slightly, 'For what it's worth.'

'It's worth a lot yet, you'll see. Just take things easy.'

'You think so?'

'I do.'

'You know, Laurie, it doesn't matter much.'

'Oh, don't say that, please.' Without embarrassment he took up the pale limp hand and held it firmly, thinking as he did so how strange it was that he should feel so intensely for this man now, and that the feeling should contain so much remorse and guilt, for up till a week ago he would have said that he had done nothing in his life to elicit these levelling emotions, for he was no better or no worse than any of his contemporaries. And what did that mean? He suddenly thought of Val and Tony Clark, and all the others before him. She had started early, he knew that. And then himself and Susan Lumley, and Betty Fuller, and Kitty Frost. His faculty for remembering names took him back down the years to the first one, Henrietta Jacobson. She was fifteen and he was thirteen. She had terrified him. She chased him for weeks; then raped him, and his fear fled. Girls were easy after that, too easy, but they all seemed the same, always rushing things, always pressing, demanding, usurping the male prerogative. And Val had beaten them all at this. At times she had sickened him. You could have too much of a good thing. . . . Oh yes, he had learnt that early. He had also learnt that it had nothing whatever to do with love. This thought brought his attention back to his father. His mother was right. What his father felt for Mrs. Thorpe was likely something bigger than any feeling that stemmed from the sex urge.

As he looked at him, there was added to his emotions yet another, and it surprised him most of all, and after a moment he discarded it with an inward deprecating laugh. Jealous of his father. Jealous of this man he had despised for so long. What was happening to him anyway? He was getting so damned mixed up he'd soon have to see a psychiatrist.

'Have you told Val yet?' asked John.

'What? Oh that. No. No. I'm jibbing.'

'The longer you put it off the harder it will be. Are you sure you want to break it off?'

'I'm not sure about many things, but I'm sure of that. Oh yes, I'm sure of that.'

They looked at each other, their faces straight, no smile between them. 'That's all right then,' said John softly. 'And I would get it over.'

CHAPTER FOUR

MR. BOLTON

IT was just turned five o'clock when Laurie entered Mr. Bolton's shop, and the greengrocer turned from sorting some fruit in a box and said, 'Yes, sir, what can I . . .?' His voice trailed away and the set smile left his face, and he ended, 'You again. Now I've told you.' The last words were drawn out and took the shape of a threat.

'Yes I know, but now I've got something to tell you, Mr. Bolton. Would you like us to talk quietly, or otherwise? It's all the same to me.'

There was something in Laurie's voice that stayed Mr. Bolton's next remark, but he stared fixedly at him for some time before saying, 'Come in here, and make it snappy.'

He pushed a door open and let Laurie pass him; then going to the stairs that led out of the packing-room, he shouted, 'Gladys. Shop.'

Almost immediately Mrs. Bolton came down the stairs, to stop dead the moment she saw Laurie. She cast an apprehensive glance at her husband, and he said, 'See to things; I won't be a minute. And I mean a minute. . . . Well now, spit it out.'

'You told me last night,' said Laurie, coming straight to the point, 'that you never employ boys. You also told this to the police. That right?'

'Right.'

'You're lying, Mr. Bolton.'

'Now, I've warned you, chum.' Mr. Bolton did some contortions with his face. He widened his eyes; he thrust out his lips seemingly in an effort to meet his nose. The whole effect was comical, but there was no one to laugh at it.

'You have your returns done by James Wilcox, do you not?'

Laurie now watched the face slowly iron out, leaving the mouth dropping slightly. 'In your returns there is an item. To quote: Paid to two boys for casual work Saturday mornings, 30s.; Total for year £78. Right, Mr. Bolton?'

'You bloody sneaking bastard.'

'I would save your breath, Mr. Bolton. You haven't heard it all yet; but I think that's enough to be going on with. It'll be enough anyway for the magistrate whether he be Mr. Wilcox or not.'

'Who the hell are you anyway? And wait till old Wilcox finds out about this.'

'I happen to be his accountant.'

'Well you won't be that much longer, laddie; he'll skin you alive. You open your mouth about this and he'll skin you alive.'

'Why should he? He's not to know that you're fiddling your returns. He's checked them in good faith hasn't he, Mr. Bolton? You've got signed receipts, one from your casual driver?' This last was a shot in the dark, but he saw it had struck home.

'You're a smart bloody Alec, aren't you? But wait till I tell old Wilcox.'

'I shouldn't worry too much about old Wilcox if I were you,' said Laurie with aggravating coolness. 'It's the police I should worry about. But anyway you won't tell Mr. Wilcox that I've been here.'

'Won't I, begod!'

'No, you won't. I'm going to make a deal with you, Mr. Bolton. I'd much rather go straight to the police and tell them you've been lying about the Thorpe boy and show them your returns to prove it, but it won't suit my purpose. This is what I want you to do, Mr. Bolton. I want you to go to the police, you yourself, and tell them you made a mistake. Tell them that you were rushed that particular Saturday morning, but now you remember that you did employ Patrick Thorpe, up till one o'clock. Therefore he couldn't have been with that gang of boys when they attacked the little girl. And for once you'll be speaking the truth. They mightn't be too lenient with you, as this isn't your first offence in this and other directions, is it, Mr. Bolton?'

Mr. Bolton gulped. He gulped three times before he said, 'I'll see you in hell's flames burnin' afore I do.'

'It's up to you. You'll likely get fined and a strong reprimand, but that would be a flea-bite to what the tax inspector will do to you, because there's not only the case of the casual labour on a Saturday, is there, Mr. Bolton?'

This was another shot in the dark, based on the fact that if a man fiddled in one way he was more than likely to do it in other ways.

That his second blind shot had found its target was evident when the greengrocer, after grinding his teeth and wiping the sweat from his brow with the back of his hand, growled out, 'You're a dirty blackmailing swine.'

'What?' It sounded like a polite inquiry.

'I'll not do it.' Bolton's voice rumbled deep in his throat. 'I'll not be got over by a bloody young punk like you.'

'I wouldn't speak too hastily, Mr. Bolton. I'll give you twenty-fours hours to think it over. Talk it over with your wife; women have a way of seeing these things sensibly. One warning though. Speak a word of this to Mr. Wilcox and I don't hold my hand. I'll go straight to the police and I'll kill all your birds with one stone, and I wouldn't be a bit surprised if you'd have to sell up all this' – he waved his hand about the room – 'to pacify those dreadful Inland Revenue people. And don't think that you can tell Wilcox about this visit and he'd keep his mouth shut. He couldn't; you see I know him very well; he's shortly to become my father-in-law.'

He now felt a desire to laugh as he saw the surprise on Bolton's face. 'You can get me at my office any time tomorrow. Ask for me personally, Mr. Laurance Emmerson.'

As he went through the shop he fully expected some heavy implement to hit him on the back of the head. He was shaking slightly when he started up the car, and he fumbled at the gears before he got her going. He was smiling to himself, but nervously, and when he had travelled some distance he pulled in to the side of the road and, leaning back against the seat, wiped his face with his handkerchief. He had started something, and if it went the way he thought it would the boy would be all right. But what about himself?

In the shop he had been not a little proud of the way he handled the man; cool, tough, James Bond fashion. But the play-acting was over. He had to face the fact that he had made an enemy of Bolton and he'd have to look out.

CHAPTER FIVE

VAL

'HE'S a lot better.'

They were having their evening meal. There were only the two of them, but everything was set as usual. He glanced up at her and swallowed the food in his mouth, then said, 'Yes.'

'Laurie.'

'Yes, Mother.'

'I feel we should talk.' She laid down her knife and fork. 'You've turned a complete somersault in a week.'

'What do you mean?'

'You know what I mean, dear.' She shook her head at him. 'Your father was all wrong before and I was all right; now he's all right and I'm all wrong. You know, there's never any real black or any real white.'

'I'm sorry if you see it like that.'

'You know it's true, and I . . . I never thought that when I told you the truth that it would turn you against me. I – I don't think I would have told you if I'd known it would have come between us.'

'It hasn't, it hasn't.' He stopped eating and leant towards her, trying to convince her, and himself as well.

'I'd like to think that but I can't, Laurie. But anyway, what – what I want to say now is that perhaps we could start from here. Everything's in the open now, there's nothing more to hide, or at least from ourselves, and – and it would be nice if we could get along on a sort of friendly footing until you . . . you were married.'

He watched her breaking some bread, her eyes cast down towards it, and he said, 'I'm not going to be married.'

'You're not . . . you mean? Oh, Laurie.'

For the first time in days he took her hand, saying, 'Don't be upset, please.'

'I'm not, I'm not, not for me. But why?'

'Oh, so many reasons. I just can't stand the old fellow. And Aunty May either, for that matter. Oh, I know.' He lifted one shoulder. 'I wouldn't be marrying them but . . . but they're all bound up together, and we've done nothing but fight for months now.'

'They say that isn't unusual with an engaged couple, although your father and I—' She bowed her head and he passed over the allusion quickly by saying, 'But this is different. They're not just rows we've had or differences of opinion, it's our whole outlook.' He paused. She still had her head bent when he ended, 'I'm sorry.'

'Oh, don't mind me, Laurie.' She was looking up at him, her expression tender and understanding. And there was relief in it too, and he saw this.

'You never really liked her, did you? Val, I mean.'

'No, Laurie, I didn't. But . . . but that doesn't mean that I'm glad about it, because, well, because I think you should marry.' She raised her eyebrows. 'That might seem strange coming from me, but I feel now that you should marry, and, and get away from us both.'

They stared at each other, she waiting for a comment on her last remark, but he didn't get it. Instead, he said, 'You know, for days now, weeks in fact, I've been longing to be a free agent again, to come and go as I please without having to clock in at Syracuse, either by tooting the car horn, or waving, or stopping. It's odd the few times you can pass that house without somebody seeing you.'

He had risen now and was standing at the french window of the morning room, looking out into the garden, when she asked guardedly, 'Is there anyone else, Laurie?'

Slowly he turned towards her. 'Anyone else? No, no. Good Lord, haven't you been listening? I've just told you I want to be free. And who else could there be?'

'But you've left it so late and May will go mad. Then there's your father. You'd better not tell him.'

'He knows.'

'Oh, Laurie.'

'It did him good. It acted like an injection on him.'

'You really mean . . .' She nodded her head, then said, 'Yes, yes, I suppose it would. He's never had any room for them.' She paused awhile before adding softly, 'There'll be trouble, Laurie; I doubt if Val will take this quietly . . . or James.'

'I doubt it too. But I've got to go through with it, or through with the other, and the other is for life, and I know I just couldn't stick it.'

He moved from the window now, saying, 'Are you going to the hospital— I can run you there and look in on him; then I've got some business to do and I can pick you up later, any time you like.'

'That would be nice, yes.' She sounded grateful that he wanted to go with her to the hospital. . . .

Ten minutes later she stood dressed in the hall and he said to her wryly, 'I hope we can break through the lines.' She turned an inquiring glance towards him, then gave a small laugh. 'Oh, yes, yes. Oh, Laurie.' She shook her head.

But they passed Syracuse without seeing any of the Wilcox family. They got out of the car in the hospital foreground, crossed through the hall, went up the private corridor to No. 7 and Laurie, pushing the door open, went to hold it for her, to allow her to pass in, but the next minute he had let the door swing closed almost in her face, and, taking her arm, hurried her back along the corridor, round to the side of the entrance hall and into the waiting room.

The room was empty, and he stood facing her now, holding her by her shoulders, saying, 'It means nothing. It doesn't mean anything, I tell you. He told me, and she told me. It means nothing.' He watched her close her eyes and press her lips tightly together.

'Let me sit down,' she said. When she was seated he gripped her hands in his, saying, 'It looks bad, but she could just have been saying good-bye to him. Anything. Anything.'

'Yes, yes.' She moved her head slowly, but he knew she didn't believe that the woman kissing her husband was saying good-bye to him, more like setting a seal on the future.

'Stay there,' he said. When he reached the hall it was to see Cissie leaving by the main door and he glared after her; then, returning to the waiting room, he said, 'It's all right. Now listen. Don't let him know you saw anything. If they heard the door open they would think it was a nurse. They didn't see me. I tell you it's all right, take my word for it. Come on, come on.' He touched her chin with the old tenderness. 'Don't let him see you're upset, it would make him worse.'

She was dry-eyed, but she breathed deeply before saying, 'I'm all right. Are you coming in?'

'No, I'll see him when I get back. As I said, I have some business to do. How long do you want to stay?'

'An hour or so. It doesn't matter; don't hurry.' Her voice was flat, dead sounding.

He left her at the corridor, squeezing her arm before parting from her. He felt something of the old feeling for her; he was also deeply indignant on her behalf.

He had intended to go to that one's flat in any case to tell her what had taken place with regard to Bolton. He had waived, in his mind, what her reception of him might be, thinking only of easing her worry over the boy, and now he was so blazing angry inside he could slap her from here to hell. He could see the picture of her; bending over the bed, her arms around his father, her loose towy hair hanging like a sheath covering their faces. He could hear her again as she went for him the other night, defending herself, putting on the innocent act, making him feel an out-and-out swine. . . . Wait till he saw her.

When he arrived at Greystone Buildings he knew that she couldn't have reached home yet, not by bus, and that suited him. He would act as a reception committee for her. He went up the stairs, not bothering to step softly now. He didn't care about the private eye, or who saw him. He felt a hatred of her, cheap little get-up that she was. Good woman! Of course his father would want to think of her as good, he was ripe for being gulled. Well, she wouldn't gull him. He would make it plain that his mother would fight her every inch of the way; and if she were to win there wouldn't be much money left in the kitty for her. This fact, he felt, would be the main deterrent.

When he reached the top landing the door was open and the boy was standing there.

'I thought at first it was me mam,' he said. 'She's out.' He looked up at Laurie.

'I know, I would like to wait for her.'

'Come on in.' The boy left the door open and followed him into the long room, and as he did so he said eagerly, 'Did you see anybody? I mean Mrs. Rice or Mr. Bolton? Did you do anything?'

As he stared down into the boy's face, he thought, old Wilcox was right where she was concerned. Perhaps after all he did know about her kind and how to deal with them.

'Well did you?'

'Oh, yes, yes, I saw them both. Not the boy, the boy's mother, Mrs. Rice. She wasn't very communicative, I mean helpful, but I think it's going to be all right. I saw Mr. Bolton. I'll . . . I'll know by tomorrow for sure.'

'You mean . . . you mean he'll tell the truth?'

'I hope so, but you mustn't say anything about this to anyone, you understand?' His anger didn't touch on the boy. He still felt sorry for him.

'Oh, yes, yes, Mister. Oh, yes.'

'Do you think your mother will be long?'

'No, she should be back at any minute. She was just going to the hospital to see . . . to see your father.'

'She wasn't going any place else?'

'No. No, she told me to stay put, not leave the house an' she'd be back directly. Won't you sit down?' The boy made the same movement as Cissie did, his arm extended towards the couch by way of invitation.

'No, I like walking about.'

And he walked about, looking from one piece of furniture to the other. She had invested her money all right.

When he came to the piano he said to the boy, 'Do you play?' He wasn't interested whether he played or not, but the boy was standing watching him with a set look on his face.

'I'm learnin', I've just been at it a year, but me mam plays lovely, she can play anything, all the hard stuff. Beethoven and Bach.'

She could play more than Beethoven and Bach if he knew anything about her.

They both heard her on the landing. The door closed and neither of them moved.

Cissie came into the room and stood just in the doorway. She looked from her son to Laurie, then kept her eyes on him. As she threw down her bag and took off her coat she still kept her gaze tightly on him. Then without looking at Pat she said, as she had done last night, 'Go into your room.'

'But, Mam, Mr. Emmerson . . . Mr. Emmerson's got news.'

'Go into your room, Pat.'

The boy went slowly into the bedroom, and not until he had closed the door did she come forward. Snapping her eyes from him, she went to the fireplace, switched on the electric fire, kicked the pouffe to the side with her long pointed shoe, then sitting down and endeavouring to pull her skirts over her knees, she said coolly. 'Why don't you start? I'm waiting.'

When he didn't speak but continued to glare at her, she said, 'I'm surprised you're stumped. I'll give you a lead, shall I? I'm a bitch. I'm all the things you think I am. You've just had proof of it, haven't you? You came into your father's room, and found him in my arms and me kissing him.' When she saw his eyelids flicker she went on, 'Oh, yes, yes I knew it was you and your mother. You weren't quick enough in closing the door. And you know something else? I'm not going to give you any explanation.'

To say the wind was taken out of his sails was putting it mildly, but the anger in him was intensified. 'What do you hope to get out of it?' he said. 'If you think that my father would ever leave my mother for you you're vastly mistaken.'

'Am I? Well now, Mr. Know-all, I'll tell you something. If I had wanted to I could have made your father leave your mother weeks ago, months ago, like that.' She raised her little finger slowly upwards.

He said disdainfully, 'You're suffering under a great delusion, woman. There are things you don't know about my father. If you did you'd know that your cause was absolutely hopeless.'

'There's nothing, Mr. Emmerson, that I don't know about your father. NOTHING. NOTHING. You understand? You don't want me to explain further, do you?'

He felt the blood draining from his face. His father had told her that. There had been so much between them that he could tell her that.

'You don't want me to go on, do you?' She rose abruptly

from the pouffe and went to a cabinet in the corner of the room and dragged the doors open, took out a bottle of whisky and a syphon, put a dash of whisky into a gill glass, then squirted in a long drag of soda, almost filling it to the top, and with the glass in her hand she walked back across the room, saying, 'I won't offer you a drink because I might be tempted to put something in it.'

'Your type's good at one other thing, and that's cheap prattle.' He sent the words at her with his upper lip pulled back in a sneer, and the next minute he was gasping and spluttering as the contents of the glass enveloped him. He had taken it full in the face. Some had gone into his mouth and was causing him to choke; the rest had drenched his collar and shirt, the front of his head, and was running down his face.

His eyes were stinging, and when he squeezed the liquid from them and blinked hard he saw her standing immobile, one hand pressed tightly across her mouth, the other hand still holding the empty glass. She was no longer looking fierce, her expression was now one of amazement as if she had seen someone else do this. Then he saw the glass drop to the floor and watch her long body crumple as she threw herself on to the couch, and as he listened to her sobbing he went on slowly wiping his face down with his hand.

He was still standing in the same place when the boy rushed past him and to the couch, crying, 'Oh, Mam, Mam.'

He took a handkerchief out of his pocket and began drying his face as he continued to look at her. The sound of her crying was a strange sound, not high and hysterical but a deep strangled sound, more like the sound a man would make, or like someone not used to crying. The boy, too, was crying, talking through his wide open mouth. 'Oh, Mam, Mam, give over. Oh, don't cry, Mam, don't cry.'

Then quite suddenly the boy was standing in front of him, his attitude threatening, the tears spilling from his chin like rain. He was shouting, 'My mam's good, she is. She's good, she is.'

Perhaps it was the sound of her son's championing of her that brought Cissie up from the couch. Groping blindly towards Pat she pulled him away from Laurie, and pushed him before her to the bedroom, and there she said, 'It's all right. It's all right. Go on in. I won't be a minute, stay there.' She closed the bedroom door; then came slowly back across the room, crying still, and as she came near him, her head bowed now, she said, 'I'm sorry I did that.'

'Can I have a towel?'

Without lifting her head she went to the kitchen, and returning with a towel she handed it to him.

He put his sodden handkerchief in his pocket, and wiped his face and neck, the front of his hair, then rubbed down his coat and waistcoat.

She stood away from him now but looking towards him, the shuddering sobs shaking her body, and after a time she said, 'Why had you to come? There's always trouble.'

'I . . . I had news for you about the boy. I thought it might ease your mind.'

He was amazed at his change of attitude. His anger had gone, seemingly washed away on the wave of whisky and soda. He said, 'I think I can make Bolton tell the truth. I'll know by tomorrow anyway.'

She swallowed deeply, her eyes widening as she looked at him. Then she whispered, 'You can?'

He nodded, still amazed at himself as he said, 'Whichever way he turns, I've got him. I don't think you need to worry any more.'

'And . . . and you came to tell me that?'

'Well . . .' he closed his eyes and turned his head to the side for a moment. 'That was primarily my intention, and on the way I dropped my mother off at the hospital.'

Now she lowered her eyes from his face and said contritely, 'I was saying good-bye to your father. It was the first time I had kissed him. The first time that there had been any endearment between us, but . . . but he had been talking, telling me about . . . about his life. About the war and what happened to him, and he told it to me for a purpose, and I loved him in that moment more than I have ever loved anyone in my life. And . . . and I can tell you now, quite quietly, that . . . that if he'd asked me to stay with him and it was for his happiness I would have done it, but he didn't. He's – he's got a sense of responsibility to your mother. And I'll also say this to you now, she's not worth it. A woman . . .' She gulped in her throat, and there was the dry harsh sobbing sound again. 'A woman who could live with a man for years and years, twenty-six years, and make him as lonely as your father is, isn't up to much, not in my opinion.'

He looked down towards his feet as he repeated the words his mother had said to him earlier on, 'There's nothing really white, and nothing really black, in any of us.'

'Oh, it's all very well saying that, but I think her treatment of him was a subtle form of cruelty. Not that he's ever said a word against her, he's hardly spoken of her till this morning, and then it was kindly, but I know women, as I know men, and he didn't have to tell me what had put that look in his face. It had puzzled me since I first met him, but not anymore.'

'Your boy said a moment ago you were a good woman; I can say the same of my mother. She's a good woman.'

'It all depends on what you mean by good.'

They were talking quietly now, as if they were discussing something abstract. When they both stopped speaking and the room became filled with a silence that yelled at them, he wanted to get out, away from her, but he remained still and watched her go to the fireplace again and stand with her foot on the raised hearth, her hand on the mantelpiece. She stood like this some time before she asked quietly, 'How did you get Mr. Bolton round?'

'I would rather you didn't ask.'

After a moment she said, 'Well, it doesn't matter how you did it as long as you did it. And . . . and believe me . . .' There was another pause before she finished, 'I'm grateful.' She half turned her head towards him now. 'It mightn't appear so . . . but what's just happened is another thing, isn't it? Nothing to do with Pat and the court business.'

Solemnly he agreed with her, saying, 'Yes, another thing entirely. I'll be going now.'

She turned from the fire and went towards him. Her face had a deep look of sadness on it, and her tone was laden with remorse. 'I'm truly sorry; I've never done anything like that before.'

'There's always a first time for everything. That's what they say, isn't it?' At the back of his mind he thought he couldn't have made a more trite remark if he had tried. 'Good-bye,' he said.

'Good-bye.' She inclined her head towards him but didn't move. He went out of the room and let himself out of the flat and drove back to the hospital.

When he went into the room he saw his father talking in his slow, laboured fashion to his mother. He had hold of her hand and seemed to be trying to impress something on her.

He felt awkward as he said, 'How are you?'

'Oh, I'm feeling well today, quite well,' said John. He smiled at Laurie. 'I was telling your mother I'll be home in a week or two.'

Ann exchanged a glance with Laurie as she said, 'The doctor advises a sea voyage; we were just talking about it.'

'Oh, that would be fine,' said Laurie. 'The very thing to put you on your feet.' They talked a little more; then Laurie said his good-byes and went towards the door. He did not wait to see if they kissed or not.

In the car they said little, but once they were alone in the lounge he said to her, 'It's all right, you've got no need to worry.'

'What do you mean?'

'I've seen her. It – it was . . . Well, she was saying good-bye to him and – and that was the first time it had ever happened – I mean anything like that between them.'

'Laurie! You haven't been to that woman again? But why?' There was a note of fear in her voice.

'Her boy's in trouble. Father was taking the case. Arnold took it over and was going about it in a legal way, naturally, but you can't deal legally with men like Bolton. . . . Oh.' He raised his hand. 'Forget all about that, that's got nothing to do with you; only I can assure you,' he took her hands in his now, 'you've got nothing to worry about. Do you know what she said? She said Father loved you. . . . There.' It was easy to stretch 'responsibility' to 'love' and it did no harm. What was vital at the moment was she needed reassurance and comfort.

'How did she know?' The note of fear was now replaced by one of indignation.

'I don't know, but that's what she said.' As he looked at her walking away from him, pulling at her handkerchief, he thought she was an entirely different creature from the mother he had known a week ago. The lady with the cool façade and slight hauteur of manner was gone, and the woman in her place was more human, more, he would say, of a woman.

'Now everything's going to be all right. Don't you worry any more, just take things as they come, eh?' He was speaking to her back, and at that moment the front door bell rang, and he knew that particular ring. When she turned towards him he said, 'Out of the mouth of babes. Take things as they come, I said.'

She came to him and caught at his hand. 'Go gently with her. It's an awful thing for a girl.' She shook her head slowly from side to side. 'I didn't tell you but she was over last night, Mrs. Stringer left a message.'

'I'll be in the study,' he said, then went quickly out and across the hall and into the room where the battle was to take place.

Awful thing for a girl. Valerie was no girl. His mother was still living in this century; Valerie was a twenty-sixty-four female if ever there was one. She was an Amazon, a five-foot-three Amazon, and his maleness resented being dominated by an Amazon of any size. He heard his mother say, 'He's in the study, Valerie,' and her voice was gentle.

Then Valerie came in. He was sitting at his desk as if he had been there for some time; he had a pen in his hand and he looked up at her as she stopped with her back to the closed door. She returned his scrutiny and, to his surprise, she smiled at him before saying, 'I'm going to make no reference to Mohammed and the mountain.' She moved towards him now. 'Been busy?'

'Yes. Yes.'

'Girls!' she began abruptly. 'Oh, how I get sick of the sight of girls. Beseeching eyes, moist lips, groping minds.' She flung herself into the leather chair and stretched out her shapely legs. Then looking at him out of the corner of her eyes, she said, 'You'd never believe it but one's got a pash on me; she brought me a box of chocolates today. It's half mother-instinct I think. She's sixteen and already five foot seven.' She laughed.

At this point he knew he was expected to make some witty quip, and when he didn't and she made no comment on his blank reception of this biological tid-bit, he knew she was working to a set plan. She had likely talked it over with her mother and been advised to play it cool so to speak. Not that Aunt May would have used that term, and not that Valerie needed any advice, tactical or otherwise. She was the kind that walked the road she had mapped out, and stepped over the corpses in her way. She didn't believe in by-roads.

'Feel like going out?'

'Not tonight.'

'Well, I don't much either. I could have brought my work up but I've had a bellyful today.'

He rubbed his hand across his brow, then leant his elbow on the desk and supported his head with his finger tips. This was going to be harder than he thought, damnable in fact.

'Oh, I forgot to tell you. We've got another wedding present. My cousin from Bromwich; you know, in the electric business. A toaster. I bet it was a throw-out. I'd also like to bet we'll get half-a-dozen before we finish.'

He did not raise his head.

'Did you hear what I said, Laurie?'

He knew by her tone that her control was slipping. It was going to be as difficult for her to follow the path of mediation as it was for himself to do what he had to do.

'Yes, I heard what you said.'

'Well, why the hell don't you answer?' She was on her feet looking down at him now. 'I came round here fully prepared to forget the last few days because I knew you were worried about your father and all this rotten business, but what meets me? A blank wall, and I don't take to blank walls, Laurie. Now, look ... whatever's on your mind, spit it out and let's get it over with.'

He placed his forearms on the desk and joined his hands together and looked at her for a long moment before saying, 'I can't go through with this, Val.' He moved his head in small jerks. 'I just can't go through with it.'

He felt an overwhelming sense of pity for her as he watched her rear up with the shock, stretching herself to the limit of her height. And he felt himself to be something so low it could have crawled out of a sewer when, placing her two hands flat on the table, she leant towards him, opened her mouth twice, then said, below her breath, 'Are you telling me, really sitting there telling me you can't go through with it? You mean, our marrying?'

He bit hard on his lip, then gave her a small nod.

Slowly she straightened up and from the top of her brow to where the curve of her small full breasts disappeared behind the square neck of her dress her flesh looked stiff and cold. 'You're telling me quite calmly that it's off?'

'I don't feel calm about it, Val, I feel damned awful.'

'Really! Well, it's nice to know you are a little troubled. And now would you mind explaining why, at this stage of our acquaintance, you have decided that you are going to drop me?'

'Look, Val,' he moved his head desperately. 'I . . . I just don't think we're suited, we wouldn't make a go of it.'

She stepped back from the table and pressing her forearm into her waist she cupped her elbow in her hand and surveyed him for some time before she said, 'and you've just found that out?'

'No, no, I've got to be honest with you. . . .'

'Oh, yes, let's be honest, let's be honest. Go on. . . .'

'Please, Val, please. It's just that I should have told you sooner but I didn't want to hurt you.'

'You didn't want to hurt me! You leave it until now and you say you didn't want to hurt me. Six weeks' time, the date's fixed for the 12th July, remember? We're in the process of buying a house, we've got most of the furniture, and you can sit there calmly and tell me. . . .' She gulped as if overcome with the enormity of his nerve. Then in a slow ominous tone she went on, 'Oh, no, you don't, Laurie. You don't do this to me. You're not going to show me up before everyone in this town. Remember, I work in a girls' school. Seven hundred girls, a good proportion of them sixteen, seventeen and eighteen; you don't know girls in the horde, Laurie. But apart from that you're not doing this to me. I'll make you go through with this even if we get a divorce within three months. But you're not standing me up. . . . You're not standing me up.' Her body now snapped forward. Her hands again on the desk, she brought her face within an inch of his. 'We're getting married on the 12th of July.'

'You can't force me to marry you, Val.' He gave a short laugh, but there was no mirth in it, it was merely a gesture to hide his nervousness.

'Can't I? You don't know your Valerie. Our community wouldn't hold a man who jilted his girl on the eve of their marriage and her going to have his baby.'

She drew back from him and surveyed his gaping face with one long, long look; then she marched from the room.

After a moment he sat back in his chair and put his hands across his eyes.

CHAPTER SIX

MR. BOLTON REMEMBERS

IT was eleven o'clock the next morning when Mr. Bolton phoned Laurie. 'Is that Emmerson?' said the voice on the other end of the phone.

'Yes, this is Mr. Emmerson.'

'It's Bolton, here.'

There was a pause, during which Laurie remained silent.

'You can have it your way.'

Another pause.

'Well, I've said it, haven't I?'

'Have you been to the police?'

'No, not yet.'

'Well you can phone me again when you have; I'll be here till six o'clock.'

'Blast you!'

'The same to you, Mr. Bolton....'

It was just on half-past five when the phone rang, and picking it up, he expected to hear Bolton's voice, but it was a woman who said, 'I would like to speak to Mr. Emmerson.'

'Mr. Emmerson here,' he said.

'This, this is Mrs. Thorpe. ... I don't know how to begin but... but the police have been round, and Mr. Bolton's been to the station and said he's made a mistake and that Pat was with him until one o'clock on that Saturday.... Are you there?'

'Yes, yes, I'm here. I'm very glad.'

'They say this is a big factor in clearing him and ... and if the other boys would own up he'd be cleared altogether. There's no hope of Tim Brooks doing that but Barrie Rice could. I'm going round to see his mother now.'

'I doubt if you'll make any headway with her.'

'Oh. Why?'

'I called on her the other evening, she strikes me as another Mr. Bolton. I'd leave her to Mr. Ransome.'

There was such a long silence now that he was about to ask, 'Are you there?' when her voice came to him softly, saying, 'It was very kind of you. You've been so kind and . . . and after what happened last night, it makes me feel awful.'

'Think no more about it I'm . . . I'm sure everything will be all right now. Mr. Ransome will be getting in touch with you. I've had a word with him. He thinks even as things stand your boy'll be cleared.'

'Oh, thank you. Thank you. I . . . I would like to express my thanks more fully but I can't I – I don't know what to say.'

'There's no need to say anything.'

'Good-bye, Mr. Emmerson.'

'Good-bye, Mrs. Thorpe.'

So that was that. . . .

* * *

When he reached home Mrs. Stringer met him in the hall. 'Missis told me to tell you that she wouldn't be back till 'bout seven, Mr. Laurie, but Miss Valerie's in the lounge.'

'Thank you, Stringy.' His voice was level. He took off his hat and coat, dropped his case on to a chair, went into the cloakroom, washed his hands, took a long drink of cold water, then went into the lounge.

Valerie was sitting on the couch. Her face looked a little paler than usual, but that was the only change visible in her. There was no nervousness showing, no sign of hysteria. He closed the door firmly behind him and took a seat near the empty fireplace; then looking towards her, he said, 'Well?'

'I thought I'd pop in to tell you that the mistresses are wondering what to buy us for a wedding present. Miss Becker came and asked me today. I said I would consult you.'

He got up from the chair and walked the length of the room and into the dining section, and he stood with his stomach pressed against the back of a dining chair as he said, 'You're not going to have any baby, Val.'

'How can you prove that at this stage. Only I know if I'm going to have a baby or not. And if I wasn't going to have one you couldn't be blamed for not trying, could you?'

His back still to her, his face screwed up with distaste.

'I've said nothing about this to anyone, as you will have already gathered, because had I mentioned it to father you would have been eaten alive by now.'

He turned towards her, and over the distance he said, 'You can mention it to him as soon as you like, Val, the sooner the better, because more than ever now I know that I can't marry you.'

'What if I sue you for breach of promise. I could skin you alive, and I would you know, because if there's got to be publicity I would make it pay. I would rub your nose in the mud, and not only your nose.'

He moved swiftly towards her and, standing over her, said thickly, 'Do whatever you like, Val, whatever you like. But just get it into your head I'm not going to marry you.'

He had never seen Val in tears, or near to them. He didn't associate her with tears, but now they were in her eyes. But they were tears of rage, and the rage brought her springing up from the couch to stand close to him. Her voice full of venom, she cried at him, 'I could tear you to shreds. I could claw your face to pieces. Talk about your father being inane and gutless; you mightn't look like him outside but you're him inside, every inch of him. I could spit on you.'

He thought for a moment she was going to do just that, and he felt himself flinch and shrink inwardly as if from the ignominious assault. As he looked down at her he felt her hate coming at him like hot steam. He watched her turn about and move across the room. She went slowly as if her rage was weighing her down, and at the door she turned and looked at him once more, then from between her clenched teeth she said, 'You dirty sod. You weak-kneed dirty sod.'

When the banging of the front door reverberated through the house he went to the couch and sank on to it. Weak-kneed, dirty sod. Well, the sod had cleared the first hurdle, but by the end of the course there was no doubt he'd be in the mud, as she had said, and in ribbons. Weak-kneed dirty sod.

He was still sitting on the couch, his eyes closed, his head back, when his mother came in. 'What is it?' she asked quickly. 'Are you ill?'

'No.' He opened his eyes slowly. 'Val's been.'

'Oh! . . . Has she accepted things?'

'I don't know about accepting things. If she does what she threatens to do, and I haven't a doubt but she will, there'll not be much left of me by the time she's finished.'

'You'll survive, dear.' She sat down beside him. 'She can't kill you, nor can she take your credentials from you.'

'True, true.' He sighed. 'But she can strip me of every penny I have, and she knows what that is. She'll be totting up at this moment what Uncle Robert left me, plus what I've saved in the last few years. That's on the monetary side. On the moral side she'll make my name stink; she'll be the wronged, innocent girl and she'll play it to the finish. She threatens breach of promise and she'll make a three-act play out of her wrongs. I can see her doing it.'

'It may not come to that, but if it does it isn't the end of the world, and if you've got to leave your job, well there's plenty of others.'

'If?' He turned and looked at her. 'There's no if about that, that's a dead certainty from both sides. And with the pull he's got in this town I can't see me getting another.'

'Oh!' Her voice was high. 'There's Newcastle . . . dozens of places you could go to.'

'Yes, yes.' He smiled wearily at her, then asked, 'What about you and Aunt May? I'll break that up too.'

She rose from the couch, patting his hand as she did so, saying, 'It's been long overdue. I won't be sorry.'

'You're sure?'

'Absolutely. May has bored and irritated me alternately for years. . . . Now have you had anything to eat?'

'No,' he said. 'But I don't feel like anything.'

'You must eat, and it'll be all ready,' she said. 'I told Mrs. Stringer to set it in the morning room; I thought it would be more cosy than in there. Come along.' She waited for him to rise, then added, 'The Avenue won't hold May and me after this. I'm going to look for another house.'

He looked slightly startled. 'But there's been so much spent on this. And Father. . . .'

She cut him short by saying, 'Your father's always hated stucco walls, he'll be glad to change.'

As she followed her out he thought, She must have known

that when she had the place decorated. And there came back to his mind the Thorpe woman saying, 'I think her treatment of him was a subtle form of cruelty.' Like a door opening from a dark passage showing a lighted room, he knew why his father had been drawn to that woman. There was no cruelty in her, subtle or otherwise – she was kind. ... Yes, even if she had drowned him in whisky and soda! ...

Laurie left the hospital at about a quarter-to-nine. His father had looked extremely tired tonight. The sister said it was nothing unusual in cases like this; doubtless he would be much better tomorrow. Not till he was seated in the car did he decide to go to the club. The thought that he wasn't answerable for his movements to anyone brought a little relief to his worried mind. There was no use in trying to put a good face on the situation to himself for he knew there was trouble in front of him, and change, but the latter didn't matter. He had been tied to the town by his mother's need of him. But with her change of heart he was no longer absolutely necessary to her. This had been revealed clearly to him when she said: 'You should marry and get away from us both.' It was as if at last she was throwing him out of the nest. He felt no hurt at this, only relief. If he was honest, an overwhelming relief. He hadn't realized before how much the home ties had irked him. He had taken compensation from the standard of living under her management, but now he saw all her actions towards himself like local injections. He had been living under sedation for years. Well, it was over, finished. Many things were finished.

The Rover was almost jammed in between two other cars that hadn't been there when he parked, and he had to nose his way gently out, feeling as he did so that the fellow in front in the grey Ford could have helped him by driving a few yards forward, but apparently he was against co-operation.

He noticed, through his mirror, that the car moved away almost immediately after he had passed it. Example of the considerate driver, he commented to himself.

In the club he had a small whisky and a lager, and a long chat to Harry Belham, whom he hadn't seen for several months. It would be more correct to say that Harry Belham had a long chat with him. Harry was a keen fisherman, and an authority on fishing rights, river boards, and the crazy, mad, ignorant nincompoops who took their holidays in motor cruisers and sailing craft, and selected for their enjoyment all the best rivers in the land, so it wasn't until quarter-past ten that he left the club. His car was parked in the private car park by the side entrance. There were not more than half-a-dozen cars there, and as he went to insert the key into the lock of the Rover a voice behind him said, 'Have you a match, chum?' . . .

What he remembered later was turning round, then doubling straight up as a fist was rammed into his stomach, then being dragged up straight by the shoulders and another fist meeting him under the chin. As the world spun round, he felt himself choking, then slowly dropping to the ground as if he was floating down.

Following this he was vaguely aware of something sharp being repeatedly jabbed at his hip. The fact that it was the toe of a boot didn't get through to him until he felt the car stop. He hadn't realized he was in a car. There were hands grabbing his shoulders again and he was being hauled from the floor of the car, then pushed against something hard. Vaguely he became aware of his surroundings as he was pushed up against the wall, then the fists came at him from all sides, into his stomach, his chest, his face. . . . Oh, his face. Once more he was floating down and then there was nothing.

When he next regained consciousness he thought he was on a rack, for his arms were being dragged out of his body. Only faintly he realized he was being pulled along by his arms. And then he was on his feet, but they kept flopping against something. Flop, flop, flop, flop. As he groaned out a protest something hit him in the face and the blackness came down on him again and he sank into it as if never to return.

* * *

'Oh my God! Oh my God!' The words were swirling round his head as he crawled up through the layers of blackness towards the surface. 'Oh my God! Oh my God!' They kept repeating themselves over and over again. They were like rumblings heard through the dentist's gas. When with a gasp he thrust himself into the light and tried to open his eyes he groaned and joined his voice to the other one, crying, weakly,

'Oh! Oh! Pol-ice! Pol-ice!'

'It's all right, it's all right. Oh my God! Who's done this to you?'

'Help!'

'Try to drink this. Come on, come on.'

When the raw whisky reached his throat, he coughed and the effort caused excruciating pain in every part of his body. 'Oh God!' He spluttered into the whisky.

'Try, try to drink it all up.'

'Wh . . . where am I? What's?' He opened his eyes as wide as he could and saw her above him with that hair hanging down each side of her face. 'Wh-where?'

'Lie quiet. . . . Is that kettle not boiling yet? Bring the water, Pat.'

'It's here. It's here.'

The warm sponge on his face was soothing, but the rest of his body felt terrible, and he was going to be sick. He tried to push her away and retched, and she said, 'It's all right, it's all right.' She held his head and he turned on his side and vomited into the bowl on the floor at her knee. When he had finished she wiped his mouth and laid his head gently back on a cushion.

'Oh God!' He lay panting, trying to understand what had happened to him. Then looking at her he said with the simplicity of a child, 'Why?'

She shook her head. Her voice and her body were trembling. 'I don't know, I don't know.'

'How . . how did I get here?'

She gulped and blinked her wet eyes. 'I . . . I was in bed. The bell rang, and when I opened the door, there you were.'

He wanted to shake his head at her but he couldn't. It didn't make sense.

'You must have the doctor,' she said, 'you're in an awful state. Pat!' she called softly. 'Get your things on.'

A few minutes later, when the boy was standing by her side, and he said, 'Doctor Bell, Mam?' she answered, 'Yes, and be quick.'

At this point Laurie protested. 'Wait . . . a minute. Don't go. Not a doctor. I'll . . . I'll be all right. Help me up.'

With her arms about him she got him to his feet and on to

the couch, and as she did so she thought, first the father and then the son.

She pillowed his head, then knelt by his side and muttered coaxingly, 'Let me send for the doctor. You're in a bad way.'

'No, no. No fuss, only cau-se trouble . . . more. . . .' He was finding difficulty now in moving his lips. 'If . . . if I could get home'

'You could never get home like this.' She shook her head at him. 'You're in an awful state.'

'You drive?'

'Yes.'

'My car. . . . Don't know where it is. Would . . . ?' He looked towards Pat and she said, 'Go downstairs and see if Mr. Emmerson's car is by the garages.' She looked down on Laurie again and asked, 'Is it your father's?' and when he made a slight movement with his head, she said, 'It'll be a Rover. You know, a big blue one. Take the torch.'

When the boy had gone she said, 'You'll never get down the stairs.'

'You help me.'

She stared at him, all the pity in her body showing in her face. Then her head drooping, she murmured, 'Oh! oh!'

'Could . . . could you get me some black . . . black coffee?'

'Yes, yes.' She put out her hand and gently touched his distorted, swelling face; then she flew to the kitchen, but was back within seconds. And again by his side, she said, 'It won't be a minute.'

He put his hand to his thigh now and as he gasped she said, 'What is it?' He made a motion with his head that indicated he didn't know.

'Will you try to sit up and I'll get your coat off.' Again he made a motion with his hands to be left alone.

Then Pat came back hurrying into the room. He stood at the bottom of the couch and whispered hoarsely, 'There's no car there, Mam, and the garages are all locked up.'

Laurie looked at the boy as he tried to sort things out. He had to get home. He was in a bad way, and he was going to get worse, he knew that. He had to get home. He said to her now, 'Can . . . can you get word to . . . to my mother?'

'Yes,' she nodded swiftly. 'I'll get someone from downstairs to go and phone.'

He put out his hand, caught hers and groaned at the sudden movement. 'No, don't let this . . . this get about. Don't want any fuss. Pat . . . Pat could phone.'

'He can't use the phone, I'll go.'

Of a sudden he was fearful of being left alone, of dropping into that blackness again . . . or worse still, of someone coming at him again. His hand tightened as much as it could on hers, and he whispered, 'Don't . . . don't leave me.'

He watched a tenderness suddenly flood her face. She turned from him and spoke to her son. 'You know where Lime Avenue is, don't you?'

'Yes, Mam.'

'If you hurry you might get the last bus, the one that goes to the corner of Newton Road. . . . What's the number of your house?' she was bending over him.

'Seventy-four. Right-hand side. Near – near the top.'

'Seventy-four. Near the top,' she repeated to Pat. 'Go on now, and if you miss the bus run all the way; you can do it in quarter of an hour or less. That's a good boy. You're not frightened, are you?'

'No.'

'Go on then. . . . Wait a minute.' She went after him and led him towards the door. 'Ring the bell and ask for Mrs. Emmerson. See her yourself and tell her . . . tell her to come here. Tell her to bring the car. Tell her Mr. Emmerson is ill. All right?'

'All right, Mam.'

Laurie lay with his eyes closed. He heard her running towards the kitchen, then it seemed only a second later that she had her arm under his shoulders and was holding a cup to his lips. 'I've made it ready for drinking,' she said.

He took a sip, and then another, and then two long drinks, and she put the cup down and he lay back.

His mind was clearing a little. He was trying to think, think what had hit him, who had hit him, and why. There had been two of them, but he never saw their faces. Not even the face of the man who had asked for a light. Yes, that's how it had started, a man had asked for a light. That was the only time he'd heard anyone speak. No, no it wasn't. Some time after when they propped him up against the wall. One of them had said. . . . What had he said? . . . Tax collector. . . . Something about a tax collector. . . . 'That's one for the tax collector!' But he couldn't have said that, he was imagining it. It was because his head was going round and round. But no. No. 'Have you got a light, mister?' 'That's one for the tax collector. . . .' It had been the same voice. Bolton had promised him something and he had kept his promise.

'Bolton.' He wasn't conscious of speaking aloud.

'Who? Bolton? Bolton's done this? Yes, yes, of course. Oh my God!' And again she cried, 'Oh my God! . . . and all because of us.' She was touching his blackening, swelling face with her finger tips and he peered up at her through his fast-closing eyes. She was kind. His father said she was kind, and her son said she was good. She was also beautiful, in spite of that towy hair she was beautiful. 'Don't cry, don't cry,' he said.

She gasped out now between her catching breath, 'I . . . I never meant it. It was the last thing on earth I meant to do, but, but I've brought trouble to you both, both you and your father.'

He put his hand out. It touched her hair, but he could see nothing for the blackness was descending on him again, and without protest he was sinking into it. The last thing he remembered at this time was that she held his hand tight in both of hers and buried it between her breasts.

*   *   *

Pat caught the last bus. He was one of two passengers, and the conductor, looking at him, said, 'You're out late, sonny. What's your mother about?'

Pat said, 'There's someone ill; I'm taking a message.'

When he alighted from the bus, he ran up the lane leading to the avenue as if someone was after him; it was very dark in the lane and he was frightened. In the avenue he paused before numerous gates, peering at their numbers. When he came to No. 74 he ran swiftly along the shingled drive towards the house.

There was a car standing outside the front door, and a light shining in the porch, but before he had passed the car and entered the porch he heard the sound of an angry voice, like someone fighting, he thought, which was very puzzling to him, for people that lived in houses like this didn't fight.

As he paused with his finger hovering over the bell he heard a man's voice say, 'I'm waiting. If it's two o'clock in the morning when he comes I'll be here to greet him,' and a woman's voice, angry sounding too, replied, 'If John were here you wouldn't act like this.'

'Oh, don't make me laugh, Ann. John! John! You faced up to the fact years ago just how much spunk John had, so don't come that over me now.'

'Shut up you! Shut up. . . .'

It was a row. They were really rowing in there. The surprise jerked his finger on to the bell, and almost immediately he heard the sound of the woman's voice, high now, crying, 'No, you won't, this happens to be my. . . .' Then the man's voice saying, 'Get out of my way, Ann.'

The next minute Pat was looking up into the red, angry face of a man he had seen before, and for a moment he was swamped with terror and had the desire to turn and flee. Although he knew that Mr. Bolton had told the truth and things looked better for him now, he knew that this was the man he'd have to go before next week. He had seen his face in nightmares during the past week, and it had looked just like it did now.

'What do you want?' Apparently the man did not recognize him, and Pat, looking at the woman who had come to the door, said in a small voice, 'Are you Mrs. Emmerson?'

'Yes, I'm Mrs. Emmerson.' He saw her put her fingers to her lips, and he glanced towards the little man again before saying, 'Me mam sent me. She said would you bring the car, Mr. . . . Mr. Emmerson's took bad.'

'W'what! Mr. Emmer. . . . You mean. . . . Who are you?'

'Pat . . . Pat Thorpe.'

'Thorpe?' James Wilcox almost screamed the name. 'Yes, yes, I thought I recognized you. Yes, of course, Thorpe. And your mother wants the car because Mr. Emmerson's taken bad? Well, well.' He turned on Ann, his fury almost lifting him from the ground. 'It's clear now. Oh, it's clear now. This is what you were trying to hide, and no wonder, father and son drinking from the same fountain.'

'How dare you! Be quiet.'

'Don't you tell me to be quiet, Ann, because I haven't started yet. . . . Bring the car, Mr. Emmerson's taken bad. . . . How bad is he, young man? Is he drunk?'

Pat moved his head back on his shoulders away from the red face, and he shook it slightly as he said, 'No, no he's not. He's been beaten up.'

'O . . . O . . . h!'

Pat looked quickly up at the woman as she groaned, then back towards the little man, who was standing straight now, his head wagging from side to side on his shoulders and a funny expression on his face, as he said, 'Beaten up? Well, well, now the situation is becoming interesting. Likely another of her gentlemen friends didn't take to the new arrangement.'

'My mam's got no gentlemen friends.' As Pat's fist shot out and caught James Wilcox in the thigh it was a question of who was the more surprised, he at the assault, or Pat at his own daring.

Ann now held Pat by the shoulders, pulling him to one side, and she was talking in a strangely quiet voice. 'Get out, James,' she was saying. 'And I'll thank you not to come back here again.'

'I'll be back again, Ann. Oh, I'll be back, if only once, for I mean to have my say to that white-livered son of yours. And he's finished, you understand, finished. Not only in my firm but in this town. And he may think that he can go farther afield and find a job, but he's mistaken. If I have to spend the rest of my life putting spokes in his wheel I'll count the time well spent. . . . As for you, young fellow, we'll meet later.'

Pat, wide-eyed, watched the little man almost throw himself out into the porch, so furiously did he move his body; then he watched the woman close the door, lean her back against it, cover her eyes with her hands for a moment and inhale deeply before she looked at him again. Then she took him by the arm and led him into a big white room, and staring down at him, she said, 'Tell me what this is about.'

He looked up into her face and said hesitantly, 'We . . . we were in bed, and there was a ring at the door and I heard me mam get up, and I waited. And then she told me to get up quick, and when I went into the room Mr. Emmerson was lying on the floor. She said she had found him outside the door on the landing.' He shook his head slowly at her now. 'His face was all battered, he's bad.'

He watched her hand go across her mouth again; then he said, 'Me mam wanted to send for our doctor but he said no, he wanted you, and to get home.'

Ann was still staring down into the boy's face. He was a good-looking boy; the mother was a good-looking woman; why was it she had come into their life? She had taken John from her. Yes, she had, although she was on a better footing with her husband than she had been since Laurie was born, she knew that she had lost part of him, and would never be able to retain it because it had been given to this boy's mother. And now her son had become involved with her. How had this come about? Why? They were leading people of the town, highly respected, and they had become involved with this cheap woman. Because she was cheap; you had only to look at her, her good looks couldn't hide it. Why was it that nice men were always attracted by cheap women?

'Aren't you going to come?'

'Yes, yes.' She put her hand across her brow, then said, 'I'll get a coat. Come along.'

A minute later he stood aside and watched her lock the front door. Then going to the garage, she beckoned him silently into the car beside her.

* * *

Within half-an-hour the car was back on the drive and Pat was once more seated beside 'the stiff lady' as he thought of her in his mind, while in the back seat were Mr. Emmerson and his mother, and without looking round he knew that his mother was trying to keep Mr. Emmerson up straight.

'Unlock the door.' The lady was thrusting a key into his hand and he scrambled out of the car and ran to the front door. After a moment of fumbling, the key turned and he pushed the door wide, just in time for them to pass, his mam on one side of Mr. Emmerson, the stiff lady on the other. Mr. Emmerson looked awful, like people, he imagined, when they were going to die. He took his eyes quickly from the blue-black distorted face, then from beneath lowered lids he watched them go slowly up the stairs, and when they had disappeared across the landing he stood with his back to the thick oak post from which the banisters started, and looked about him, and although he couldn't quite make it out he connected what he saw with the stiff lady.

Upstairs Ann went to lower Laurie into a chair, but he made a movement towards the bed, and when they sat him on the edge he fell sideways, and it was Cissie who lifted his feet up, shoes and all, on to the grey satin quilted cover.

'We should get him undressed.' She spoke under her breath as she looked at Ann Emmerson, and for the first time since their meeting Ann looked fully into her face. Her own expression had a startled quality about it as if Cissie had suggested something improper. 'I can manage quite well now, thank you.'

It was a curt dismissal, and Cissie felt the heat of indignation sweep over her body as she stared unblinkingly back into the cold, pale face, before her. She wanted to make some protest against all this woman's look was saying to her, but this was neither the time nor the place, so she turned swiftly about and went towards the door, only to be stopped as she opened it by a weak voice from the bed muttering, 'Cecilia.'

She turned her head quickly over her shoulder, thinking for a moment he was speaking to his mother. She couldn't remember anyone calling her Cecilia; no one had ever given her her correct name. She still thought he was addressing his mother until she saw his hand lifted towards her; then she went back to the bed. And she took his hand and held it, and when, through his distorted and broken lips, he muttered, 'Thanks, thanks,' the only thing she could do was to nod towards the two narrow slits which was all she could see of his eyes. Then she turned from him and passed the woman who was standing at the door.

Ann followed her down the stairs, and in the hall, in the manner of someone who knows her duty towards her inferiors, she said, 'I'll phone for a taxi to take you home.'

'There's no need, thank you very much, we can walk.'

Cissie's tone was bitter; and she added, as she held out her hand towards Pat, 'It's a doctor you want to phone for, and quick. And don't try to cover this up by not getting a doctor or you'll likely have something much more serious on your hands.'

Ann drew herself up and her flat chest took on shape as she exclaimed with chilling haughtiness, 'I don't need you to tell me where my duty lies, Mrs. Thorpe. And were there more serious consequences of tonight's business who, I ask, should be held responsible for them?'

Cissie was near the hall door now, and she turned quickly as she said, 'You, Mrs. Emmerson, you and no one else. If I hadn't known your husband I wouldn't have known your son, and I leave you to work out how I, a common individual, because that's how you consider me isn't it, came to be acquainted with a man in Mr. Emmerson's position. Just you work it out, Mrs. Emmerson. Good night.'

Pushing Pat before her she went out into the lobby, then through the front door and round the drive into the road, and when they had left the avenue and turned down the dark lane Pat stopped and, flinging his arms around her waist, pressed his head into her ribs, whimpering, 'Aw, don't cry. Ma, don't cry.'

Part III

Bread-and-cheese and Beer

CHAPTER ONE

THE PROPOSAL

JOHN came in through the lower gate from the field path and began to walk round the garden. It was the last time he would ever walk round this garden, and he asked himself if he was sorry, and the answer came: No. No, not at all.

Tomorrow they were starting on a three months' holiday, going first to Denmark, then round the Kattegat and up the Baltic to Finland. On the return journey they were leaving the boat at Stockholm and were staying there for a time. Ann had planned it all. She had been wonderful really, because neither he nor Laurie had been able to see to a thing. She had even done the whole business of the new house. He thought he was going to like the new house; it wasn't as big as this and it was more homely. She had discussed the decorations with him. Her taste had changed quite a lot, for she had suggested having patterned wallpaper. He would have further to travel back and forth to the office from the new house – it was more than three miles beyond the town boundary, and it was rather isolated, but he didn't mind that, not in the least. It was on a rise and had some splendid views; a most interesting feature was a piece of woodland with a stream at the bottom. All the garden had been set out in a natural way, mostly with shrubs, no stiff borders. Yes, he felt he was going to enjoy the new house, and there would be only the two of them. Would he enjoy that? Why not? He stopped in his walk. It would be like starting a new life. Everything was different now. Yes, quite different.

He moved on again; past the greenhouse and the potting shed, and through the arch in the privet hedge that separated the vegetable garden from the lawns and flower beds, and up the side path that led to the terrace that flanked the french windows of the dining-room.

There was a small rose pergola here that formed a wind break, and he sat down in the wrought-iron chair that stood beneath it and looked over the garden, but now without seeing it. The phrase, new life, had set his mind working, pushing queries out along paths that he didn't want to explore. For some time now he had kept telling himself to take things as they came, that everything would work out; the main thing was not to hurt anyone. It was odd, but he hadn't thought until recently that it was in his power to hurt anyone, but now he knew it was, and the possession of this power brought him no gratification.

To check his trend of thought he was about to rise from the chair when he heard a door open in the room at the other side of the pergola, and then Ann's voice speaking to Laurie. Again he was about to rise when the tail end of what she was saying kept him still. 'You can't evade it any more. There's not much time left.'

Then Laurie's voice answering her: 'There's nothing to discuss, nothing to talk about, I've told you. . . . Oh, for God's sake, Mother!'

'How can you say that when she's been on the phone this very minute?'

'Well, she didn't ask for me, did she?' The words were hissed.

'No, but she hoped you would answer.'

'Look, Mother.' Laurie's voice was patient sounding now. 'I was in a devil of a mess, as you know, when she found me. She's phoned three times in a month to find out how I am. I don't consider she's overdone it.'

'Stop hedging, Laurie. I'm going away tomorrow and I can't leave with my mind in this state; I've got to know what's between you and her. Can't you understand how I feel? First your father, and now you. . . . It's terrible to me, and disgusting. . . . Yes, disgusting.'

John was leaning forward, his forearm resting on the iron

table in front of him, his eyes riveted on a piece of grass growing between the slabs of the crazy paving on the terrace. The voices from the room became indistinct. He knew that Ann was still talking and Laurie answering her, but what they were saying he couldn't hear for the noise in his mind made by the whirling names: 'Laurie and Cissie, Laurie and Cissie.' He felt the beat of his heart quickening to the repetition of 'Laurie and Cissie. Laurie and Cissie.' And then he pressed his fist to his chest, saying to himself, 'Steady, steady.' And the noise in his head faded away and he heard Laurie speaking again, his tone low and harsh.

'I've ... I've seen the woman four times, and each time we've rowed, except the last time, when I was in no position to do anything, and from that you've got me living with her. You've convinced yourself that I've taken over where father left off, haven't you?'

Out on the terrace John's head drooped lower. 'Taken over where father left off.' Then he raised it slightly again as Ann said in a dull, flat tone, 'It was because of her that you gave up Val, wasn't it?'

'Oh my God! Now don't get me mad. Now look, I'm telling you, don't get me mad.'

'And don't treat me as a child, Laurie, asking me to believe that you've only seen her four times and that you fought with her. If that is so, well, all I can say is that your manner underwent a great change the night she helped to bring you home.'

'What do you mean?'

'You don't hold a woman's hand and call her Cecilia, and she doesn't cry over you after four meetings in which you fought all the time.'

'Cecilia? I held her hand and called her Cecilia? You must be bats. I didn't even know she was called Cecilia, I've never called her anything but Mrs. Thorpe.'

'Laurie, Laurie.' She was almost shouting now. 'Be quiet. I don't want to hear any more. If there was a doubt in my mind before over your association with the woman you have certainly dispelled it.'

'I . . . TELL . . . YOU . . . MOTHER . . . !'

'Please, please, Laurie, don't protest any more. I don't want to think of you as a liar too. But let me tell you this. Wilcox has ruined your career, that man Bolton has ruined your looks, but that woman will ruin your life. She's gone a good way already. And I'll say one more thing, one more thing ... you'll have to choose. I mean it, Laurie, I mean it. If you continue your association with her I never want to see you again. Do you understand what I'm saying? Don't think I will soften, for the very thought of her makes me physically sick.'

As the sound of a door closing came to John he pulled himself up from the chair, went hastily from the terrace along the side path, and through the arch in the privet once again, and going into the tool shed, he shut the door behind him and sat on an upturned crate.

'Cissie. Cissie.' He was saying her name aloud, his voice, sad and tender, was yet threaded with reproach. Slowly he rested his elbows on his knees and bowed his head over his hanging hands. He had been a fool, a fool. He could have had her and all she meant to life; gaiety, warmness, understanding and kindness. Yes, he could have had Cissie. He knew that morning she came to him in hospital that she was his for the asking, and because of this he had told her about himself. It had been quite easy to tell her, but he had not been prepared for the effect of the telling. When she had kissed him on the mouth he had wanted to hold her and never let her go. But he knew that he could not lay the burden of his deformity on her. He had watched Ann become crippled under it and he could not let the same thing happen to Cissie, although she would have known what she was taking on....

But Laurie had denied his mother's imputation. Perhaps he was right and there was nothing in it. How could there be seeing her only four times. But he himself had only seen her once, well twice, and it had happened to him. But he had been lonely and ripe for such an affair, if you could call the relationship between them, an affair. ... And he himself had sent Laurie to her, begged him to go.

He felt the old feeling of aloneness return, and it was more poignant now than at any time over the long bleak years, for then he'd had really nothing to lose, but during the last few months, whilst he had known Cissie, life had come back into his living, and when having lost her, as it were, he had found his son, he had thought that things usually balanced themselves out. . . . And now, before he had hardly found Laurie, he was to lose him too, for if there was anything in it, it would be as Ann said, Laurie would be cut off from them. She wouldn't bear to see him because of the girl, and he wouldn't dare to see him . . . because of the girl.

'Oh, there you are, dear. Why are you sitting in here? You are not feeling ill again?'

'No. No.' He pulled himself upwards and took the hand she held out to him, and as it gripped his firmly he thought what a sense of wonder it would have brought to him if it had been held out this time last year; but now between their hands would always be Cissie's; no matter what happened it would always be there. . . . No matter what happened.

* * *

At twelve o'clock the following morning Laurie stood on the quay and watched the boat move slowly from the dock. High up above his head on the first-class deck stood his mother and father. He did not raise his hand until his father raised his, and then he waved back. His mother did not wave until the boat was some distance from the quay, and then it was a small movement of her hand conveying over the distance to him her worry and anger. Her last words to him had been, 'You will go to your uncle's, won't you, Laurie? You'll go straight away, they're expecting you.'

And he had said, 'Yes, yes, of course,' knowing full well that he had no intention of going to his uncle's.

She had bent forward then and he had kissed her, and he had smiled at her and said, 'Now forget everything and have a good time.'

He had left her in the special suite which was filled with flowers, and going out on deck he had walked with his father to the gangway, and there for a moment they had stood facing each other. He had smiled at him too, and had been about to say what he had said to his mother, 'Now forget everything and have a good time,' when John muttered abruptly, 'I have something to say to you, Laurie, and we haven't much time. And please don't be offended.' John had glanced downwards for a moment before looking back into his face and adding under his breath, 'I happened to be on the verandah last night when you and your mother were talking.'

He had closed his eyes and brought his teeth down on to his lip. The attitude was one of striving for patience, but he could not keep the weariness from his voice as he said, 'Now look, Father, let me say this. . . .'

But John cut in on him, 'No, Laurie. No. Don't give me any reasons, just listen to me for a moment. What I want to say to you is, follow your heart. Do what you want to do. Don't, don't, I beg you, sacrifice yourself for anyone, not for your mother . . . or me. You'll get no thanks for it in the end and I've brought enough harm to you already.' His eyes had moved swiftly over the discoloured face.

'Father. Will you listen just a moment?' He had stood with his elbows pressed tight against his sides, his hands spread out in front of his chest, but John, ignoring the plea, went on, 'I know how you feel. I'm well aware of the fix you're in . . . I've been in it myself, so I know all about it. One thing I ask of you: give her a message from me, will you? Tell her . . . tell her that she's got to take happiness, grab it with both hands. Tell her I'm happy for her, will you; will you tell her that?'

He had remained silent as he returned his father's fixed stare. It was no good, it was no good protesting, one way or the other. The only thing to do was to let them think what they liked, only time would prove them wrong. But in the meantime they would both be as miserable as hell. Well, he had done his best. All the talking in the world wouldn't convince them. It was just one of those unbelievable things that happened; surmise became stamped with truth because he had apparently spoken her Christian name. He put out his hand, and John took it and held it fast for a moment.

'Get well,' he said.

'Don't worry, I'll be all right.' John smiled at him as he looked into his face. 'Good-bye, Laurie.'

'Good-bye, Father. Good-bye.'

He had turned away, then stopped as John's fingers touched his arm. 'You'll write and tell me how things go?'

He drooped his head slightly before half turning it over his shoulder and nodding. Then he was running down the gangway and on to the quay.

Their faces were now getting smaller. His father was waving all the time, his mother intermittently. Soon it was no use standing any longer. He turned slowly away and, going to his car, drove back to the house.

* * *

When he got into the hall Mrs. Stringer came from the kitchen, saying, 'Well, they got off then, Mr. Laurie?'

'Yes, Stringy.'

'Did they have a comfortable room?'

'Marvellous, almost as big as the lounge. Home from home.'

'You're jokin'.'

'I'm not. It's a fact. Bathroom, shower, the lot, and the place swamped with flowers.'

'Aw, how nice. I hope it will do them both good. . . . Well now, I've set your lunch in the breakfast-room, Mr. Laurie, and I've put all your clean things out on the bed ready for packin'.'

As she was talking he bent forward over the hall table and looked at his face in the oval mirror. Even after a month it hadn't fallen back into shape. He doubted if it ever would. He touched his left eyebrow with his fingers as he looked with a sideways motion at Mrs. Stringer through the glass and said, 'I won't be going tomorrow, Stringy.'

'Oh now, now, Mr. Laurie, it's all arranged; your uncle's expecting you and the missus was on the phone not ten minutes afore she left telling them what time you'd get there.'

'I'm going to ring them now, Stringy.'

'But why, Mr. Laurie?'

'I'll explain in a minute.' He nodded slowly towards her, then went and sat down on the gold-coloured cane chair near the telephone table and picked up the receiver.

'Hello,' he said after a moment. 'Is that Uncle Ron?'

'Yes, yes, they got away all right,' he answered. 'Splendid cabin. . . . They'll be living it up for weeks.'

The hearty voice from the other end of the line now asked, 'When you setting out? We're all waiting for you. The girls have got you booked up for the next three weeks, God help you.'

'Uncle.'

'Yes, Laurie.'
'Uncle, I'm sorry I won't be able to come.'
'What's that? Did I hear you say you won't be able to come? What's the matter, you haven't taken bad again, have you? Ann was on the phone to Susan first thing this morning telling her you'd be leaving in the morning. What's the matter? What's happened?'
'It's just this way, Uncle. I'm, I'm going into hospital; I believe I'm going to lose the sight of one eye.'
'God almighty! But your mother . . . why . . . ?'
'She didn't know. Neither of them knew. I didn't tell them. They wouldn't have gone, and everything was booked up, and Father needed to get away.'
'But an eye. Is it certain?'
'They think so. Anyway it won't matter, for I've hardly been able to see anything with it since I . . . I was hurt. It was a blow on the temple apparently that caused it.'
'Oh, lad, this is terrible. Look, do you want Susan to come down there and see to you.'
'No, no. You see, I'll be in hospital, and I don't know for how long.'
'Well this is a shock. I don't know what Susan's going to say, she's out at the moment. Oh, I am sorry about this, Laurie. And do you know something? I think you should have told your father.'
'It couldn't have helped, and I didn't want to give him any more worry at this stage.'
'No, no, I see your point. But oh my God, boy, I'm right sorry for you. ... Look, when it's over will you come through?'
'Yes, yes, I'd be glad to.'
'And you'll keep us informed?'
'Yes, I will, Uncle.'
'But what if you go to this new house? When is that going to take place?'
'Oh, not for another three weeks, and Stringy's here to see to things as usual. She's doing all the packing and going over there and putting things to rights. She'll have everything more than ship-shape by the time they come back. In the meantime, she's looking after me fine.'

'Laurie, I don't know what to say; you've knocked the wind completely out of my sails.'

'Oh, don't take it like that, Uncle, I feel I've been lucky; it could have been both of them.'

'Yes, yes, that's the way to look at it I suppose. But nevertheless it's a tragedy. I'll get your aunt to phone you as soon as she comes in, eh?'

'All right, Uncle.'

'Good-bye, lad.'

'Good-bye, Uncle.'

When he put the phone down he heard a small sound from the kitchen door and there stood Mrs. Stringer with her two hands cupping her face, her compact body swaying slightly from side to side.

'Oh, Mr. Laurie. Oh, Mr. Laurie.'

'Now, now, it's all right.'

'And for you to let them go and not tell them.'

'It's better this way, isn't it?' He put his arm around her shoulders and led her back into the kitchen, saying, 'There, there. Now don't you start howling.'

'Oh, Mr. Laurie.'

'Look,' he said; 'I'm hungry and I want some lunch. Come on.' He pushed her playfully towards the stove. 'Give me the dishes, I'll carry them in.'

As she handed him the vegetable dishes she looked up into his face and muttered again, 'Oh, Mr. Laurie. Oh, Mr. Laurie.'

A few minutes later, sitting in lonely state eating his lunch, he put his elbow on the table and rested his head on his hand, bringing his fingers as he did so over his left eye. Oh, Mr. Laurie. Oh, Mr. Laurie. It was funny what sympathy did to you. It probed the soft spots, the fear spots, and there were more than one of those under his skin at the present moment. The only way for him to tackle this thing was on the side, so-to speak, treat it as something unpleasant but necessary, that had to be done, like having a tooth out. There were two things he had to steer clear of, sympathy from others and resentment against the source and cause of his condition.

It was funny, the little things, the little decisions and actions that led up to losing an eye. That was the way to look at it . . .

philosophically, as if it had had to be and nothing he could have done would have prevented it. That was the only line to take.

It was as he finished his meal that he heard the doorbell ring and Stringy go to answer it; and then her voice, high and indignant, saying, 'The family's all gone, Mr. Wilcox. There's no one here, they've all gone.'

'All but one, Mrs. Stringer, and I'll thank you to get out of my way.'

Laurie rose to his feet and went to the morning-room door, and from there, looking across the hall, he said evenly, 'It's all right, Stringy. Let Mr. Wilcox in.'

James Wilcox came in, his step slow and heavy like that of a man twice his size. He kept his eyes on Laurie even while he passed him and went into the room, and there he continued to stare at him, seeming to derive satisfaction from what he saw.

During a long tense moment in which Laurie returned the older man's glare neither of them spoke. Then James Wilcox, clearing his throat, began, 'You knew I wouldn't let you get away with this, didn't you?'

'I've been expecting you.'

'Then you're not disappointed, are you? I thought I'd wait till they got off, so you wouldn't have any skirts to hide behind.'

As Laurie ground his teeth Wilcox went on, 'I blame her as much as anybody, she's spoilt you since you were born and she suckled you until you went into long pants....'

'I'm going to give you a warning, and take heed, I'm past taking anything more from you. Just another crack like that and I'll take you by the scruff of the neck and throw you out of the door.... And I mean it.'

'I would like to see you try it on, young man. Like all your breed you're gutless.' He tugged at his waistcoat and drew in a deep breath. 'Well, I came here to tell you what I think of you and to pass on two items of news that you'd better pay heed to. ... The first one is that my daughter has broken off her engagement to you.... You understand, SHE'S BROKEN OFF HER ENGAGEMENT TO YOU because of your carry-on with the Thorpe woman....'

'Oh. ... Oh no, you don't.' Laurie's face was scarlet, and

digging his index finger towards Wilcox's chest, he cried, 'You set that tale about and I'll have you up in court before you know where you are, and on the wrong side of the Bench this time.'

'Try it on, try it on, and we'll see who wins.' Mr. Wilcox's head was wagging as if on wires. 'It's public knowledge now that your father was visiting that woman for months, and now everyone knows that you were seeing her on the side too. It's a public scandal ... and, and my daughter finding this out wouldn't stand for it. That's the story, and you try to alter it in this town and see how far you get. It's also current news that one of her fancy men beat you up and deposited you on her doorstep.'

Laurie only just stopped himself from springing on the older man, but he moved towards him, and his fists clenched and held stiffly by his sides, he growled at him, 'Nobody's fancy man beat me up. It was Bolton's thugs who beat me up, and you know why. ... Or don't you?' He thrust his scarlet face down towards the now slightly surprised countenance of Mr. Wilcox. 'He had me beaten up because I exposed his little game. I went through his returns ... among your files, and found out he was doing some twisting, as you knew he'd been doing for years and shut your eyes to it. He said he had never engaged the Thorpe boy on a Saturday morning, but he'd been putting thirty shillings on his returns for employing two boys on a Saturday morning for years. I went and confronted him with it and forced his hand. I made him go to the police and clear the Thorpe boy. That's news to you, isn't it?'

'You! ... you went to my files and ... ?' Bubbles of saliva spurted from Mr. Wilcox's lips.

'Yes, I went through your files.'

'You. ... You mean to stand there and tell me ... ?'

'Yes, I mean to stand here and tell you, and if you hadn't anything to hide you wouldn't mind who went through your files.'

'The client's business is private, you know that.'

'But YOU have a section that is specially private, haven't you?' He paused for a telling moment before going on, 'So now I'm warning you. You drop this fancy man business or it isn't too late to do what I should have done the night I got this.' He pointed to his face.

Mr. Wilcox swallowed deeply. He was definitely flustered now as his voice showed. 'You've got no proof that it was Mr. Bolton who instigated th . . . that.'

'I've got all the proof I need.'

'Well, why didn't you use it? I can't see you having a trump card in your hand and not playing it.'

Laurie stared down into the mean little face, then he stepped back from him as if the proximity of this man was distasteful to him, as it was. And he said slowly, 'Yes, you would think that way because that's how you would have acted, isn't it? Well, I'll tell you now why I didn't play my card. It was because if I had accused Bolton I would have had to give my reasons for the attack, and I couldn't have done that without bringing up the matter of how the boy Thorpe was cleared and that would have involved you. Funny, isn't it, me considering you.'

'I need no consideration from you, young man; my business can stand scrutiny of the closest kind.' Mr. Wilcox was bristling again.

'Doubtless, doubtless, you would have been able to prove that you knew nothing about his little fiddles on the side, but you know and I know that Her Majesty's Inspector of Taxes has just got to get the tiniest inkling that there is some laxity with regard to the scrutiny of the returns of privileged clients and they're on to you; they'll watch you like a hawk until the day you retire.' Laurie wiped the sweat from around his mouth with his hand, then shook his head as he said, 'It's funny. As much as I hate your guts, and I'm telling you to your face I do, I didn't want to do this to you.'

Mr. Wilcox too wiped his face, but he did it with a large white handkerchief, and when he had finished he was smiling, a twisted, sarcastic smile. He spread his lips wide, revealing his neat dentures, as he said, 'A very noble way of putting it. But it would have been nearer the truth had you said that you held your hand because your conscience was troubling you concerning your treatment of Val and your association with that woman.'

'Look. I'll tell you once again, I had no association with . . . that woman, as you call her.' Laurie's whole attitude now was one of taut aggressiveness. 'But if I'd known as much the night

I got this,' he touched his cheek, 'as I do now I wouldn't have hesitated in taking the whole matter to the authorities. . . . But mind, as I've said, it isn't too late; so I'm warning you.' He again dug his finger towards Wilcox. 'You start any rumours going about fancy men and me having an affair with Mrs. Thorpe and I'll bring the whole matter into the open. . . . Now.' His voice dropped. 'You've had your say; you've acted, as you would put it, like a man . . . the little mean man that you are. Now get out.'

James Wilcox's lips met and were drawn in between his teeth. His portly body quivered; he tugged with both hands at the points of his waistcoat; he was about to go but he had to have one more shot. 'You're finished in this town, you know that, don't you?' He now lifted his body around almost with a jump and made for the door, and Laurie followed him. He followed him across the hall and he stood behind him as he fumbled with the latch of the front door. And when he had succeeded in opening it, Wilcox turned to him once again and, nodding towards his face, said under his breath, 'Well, whoever did that, they made a pretty mess of you, and I'm going to say now, and frankly, that I wish I'd had a hand in it.'

Laurie remained quite still, and his voice was deceptively calm when he replied, 'Thank you, your honour. And I'm sure that if you had I would have lost the sight of both eyes, instead of just one.'

In the moment that he paused before banging the door in Wilcox's face he saw the startled look of surprise spreading over it.

When he again entered the morning-room his body was shaking and he felt slightly sick. He stood for a moment with his hand to his head, before turning about and going into the dining-room and pouring himself out a stiff drink. . . . Her fancy man! He knew that all his brave talk about what he would do if Wilcox spread that rumour was mere wind, for it would already be in circulation – Val would have grabbed at the whole business as a face-saver. He wondered that old Wilcox had bothered to come and tell him. What he had really come for was to act the man, the enraged parent, and shout his mouth off.

His father had started something, hadn't he? The old feeling against him revived with a surge, swamping that more liberal one that had emerged during the past weeks. He walked back into the lounge and, standing before the high hearth, finished his drink at a gulp, then hurled the glass into the empty grate.

* * *

The same evening Laurie went to see his doctor, who told him that he would get him into the hospital towards the end of the following week. He'd had a report from the specialist, but he was afraid there was nothing to add to what he already knew. In the meantime he would give him a prescription for more drops. . . .

It was as he stood to the side of a partition of baby foods waiting for his prescription to be made up that he saw Cissie go up to the counter; and as he stood looking at her back he felt a galloping racing emotion within him that could have been fear. If there had been a door to the left of him he would have sidled out, but any move from where he stood must bring her attention to him, and so he stood still.

She was wearing a plastic mac over a brown suit, she was hatless and her long wet hair hung in separated strands on to her shoulders, and the undisciplined sight of it irritated him. He heard the assistant say to her, 'Will you take a seat, it'll be a few moments.' When she turned to where the seats were she was directly in front of him and as his own face reddened he watched hers light up. For a moment he saw her eyes shine with a warm brightness, as if she was seeing someone she had never expected to see again.

'How are you?' She was standing close to him, looking into his face and her eyes, after moving from one feature to the other, came to rest on the dilated pupil of his left eye.

'Fine,' he said; 'fine.'

'Sure?' Her face had suddenly dropped into straight solemn lines. 'You don't . . . I mean, it hasn't . . .?'

'Oh, this.' He patted one cheek and then the other. 'Oh, that'll disappear in time.' As he continued to look at her he thought she would never know the extent of the trouble she had caused him. Nevertheless, what little he knew of her, he gauged she was the kind of person who would not wittingly bring trouble on anybody. He believed now, as his father had impressed on him from the beginning, that she was kind. Whatever else she might be, she was kind. She had dropped her eyes from his and was standing to the side facing the counter now, and she said, 'I've got Pat in bed with a cold.'

'Oh, I'm sorry,' he said. Then: 'The other business was cleared up all right?'

'Oh, yes, yes.' She turned her head quickly towards him, nodding in small jerks. 'When Barry Rice knew that Pat could prove that he had been working all that morning he told the truth. He also told the names of the other two boys. . . . But you know all this, I suppose. Mr. Ransome would tell you all about it?'

'Your drops, sir.' The chemist handed Laurie a small wrapped bottle, and he thanked the man, pocketed the bottle and looked at Cissie with the intention of saying good-bye.

She had been looking at the bottle; now she was looking to the one side of his face and she asked under her breath, 'Is there anything wrong with it, your eye?'

'No, no.' He shook his head. 'At least nothing that can't be put right.'

'You're sure?' Her voice sounded anxious and he nodded again, 'Yes, perfectly sure. Good-night.' His accent was exaggerated, rebuffing.

'Good-night.'

Outside it was raining heavily and he paused for a moment in the shelter of the shop doorway looking towards his car parked against the kerb before hurrying to it and unlocking the door. Inside, he pushed in the ignition key and pressed the self starter, but then he sat back making no move towards the gears. 'Don't be a blasted fool. Get going.' It was as if the voice with no high-hat accent now was coming from the back seat, and his head drooped under the derisive condemnation of the tone. 'Get going,' it said again. 'For God's sake, man, have sense and don't prove them right.'

As he put his hand towards the gear lever she came out of the shop. She was on his right-hand side and he could see her without having to turn his head. He wound down the window and spoke to her across the pavement, saying, 'Get in.' There was impatience in his tone now, as if he were speaking to a wife who had been dawdling.

'What?' She came towards him, bending down until her face was level with his, and the rain from her hair splashed on to his shoulders. 'Get in,' he said; 'I'll run you home.'

'Oh, no. No, thanks, I can get the bus.' She backed away and straightened up, and he bent over the wheel and looked up at her and said again, 'Don't be silly. Come on, get in.' He leant away from her and opened the other door, and when he sat up again she was still standing on the pavement, and now she bent towards him again and hissed quickly under her breath, 'It would be silly, you know that. . . . But thanks all the same.'

'Look. Don't argue, get in. You're getting wet.'

He watched her turn her head to the side and look down at the grey shining pavement, then slowly raise her head again and look at him. 'You know what you're doing, don't you?' she said.

'I know what I'm doing. Get in.'

Once she had entered the car he didn't speak, but when she couldn't get the door locked he leant across her and flicked the handle into place, and he was aware as he did so that her body was pressing tightly against the seat away from contact with him, and he had the strongest desire to turn on her and say brutally, 'It's all right. It's all right. You've got nothing like that to fear from me; I should say not!'

They had covered some distance when her voice, tentative now, asked, 'How is your father?'

'When I saw him this morning he was in fine fettle. They left Newcastle for a three months' holiday, mostly by sea.'

'Oh, oh, I'm glad. That should do him good . . . the world of good.' Then she added, as if to make polite conversation, 'You should have a holiday yourself; I'm sure you could do with it.'

'Yes,' he said, swinging the wheel round as they took a corner. 'I feel I could do with a change. I'm going to Oxford shortly to stay with an uncle of mine. I don't suppose I'll come back here again.'

'You . . . you've left your job?' There was a high note of surprise in her voicc.

'Oh, yes. Yes, I've definitely left my job.'

She had her face full towards him and her words tumbled over one another. 'B . . . but I thought you were g-going to be married.'

He swung the wheel again. 'I was, but I am no longer.'

Her face still towards him, she asked in a frightened tone, 'All this business . . . me . . . am I anything to do with it?'

'Not a thing.' Glancing swiftly towards her he asked sharply, 'What makes you say that? Why should you? Why should you think you have anything to do with it?'

Even in the short glance he gave her he saw the blood rush to her face, and he added. 'Well, what I mean is, how could you?'

'I know that, I know that, I-know-all-about-that. But people's tongues . . . they say. . . .'

'Well, what do they say? What can they say in this case?'

'I know, I know.' Her voice was high and agitated. 'But some folks are wicked. They'll take your name away if it's the last thing you've got left; they'll not be satisfied till they've stripped you.' She stopped abruptly. Then hanging her head, she said, 'I didn't mean it, I wasn't referring to the other day or, or what you said, or anything.'

'I couldn't blame you if you were.'

He brought the car now to an abrupt stop outside the flats and immediately she fumbled with the door handle, and once more he had to lean across her to open it, and almost before he had released the handle she was standing in the road. The door still in her hand, she looked at him and her face was again showing concern. 'I hope you get on all right,' she said.

He did not answer her. With his hand still on the wheel he stared at her as she banged the door, but still not hard enough to close it, and for the last time he leant forward and adjusted the handle. As he started up the car he saw her enter the doorway, and she didn't turn round.

* * *

The following day he helped Mrs. Stringer to pack. From early morning until after tea he packed articles ranging from clothes to kitchen utensils. Then in a room that was already beginning to look unlived in, he had his evening meal, and later took Mrs. Stringer home. It was eight o'clock when he returned, and from then until eleven o'clock the time seemed longer than the whole of the day.

The pattern was almost the same the following day, and returning to the empty house after depositing Mrs. Stringer he had such a longing for company that he played with the idea of going to the club. But even while he did so he knew he wouldn't go because he was afraid to, afraid of the power of Wilcox's malice, afraid of someone making an excuse that he had to go and meet the girl friend, or that he was expected home, or had a business appointment, and so he sat and looked at the television. And as he looked he suddenly thought, If I never see her again, I'll never forget her. Then getting to his feet and switching off the set he said aloud, 'Blast her!'

* * *

It was half past eight when he got into the car and drove into the town and to the flats. He glanced at her name on the board in the hallway before he mounted the stairs: Mrs. Cecilia Thorpe. He did not go quietly up the stairs, and he hoped that someone would come out of their doorway, preferably Mrs. Orchard, but he met no one, and when he reached the top landing he immediately rang the bell.

When she opened the door he saw that she was startled and that his presence made her afraid.

She stood with the door in her hand blocking the entrance, and she said simply, 'Yes?'

'Aren't you going to ask me in?' His voice was as aggressive as his look.

She gulped in her long throat. 'What do you want?'

'I want to talk to you.'

She glanced behind her, and suspicion rose in him and he thought, Ah! Then she stood aside and he went past her, across the little hall into the long room. But there was no one to be seen.

The electric fire was reflecting on imitation logs. There were some magazines on the couch and the indent in the cushions where a head had been. He glanced about him, still expecting to see someone, and the reason for his interest wasn't lost on her. With a touch of harshness in her voice that dispelled the suggestion of fear she said, 'I'm on my own, except for Pat, and he's still in bed.'

'What makes you think I . . . ?'

'Oh, I know what you were thinking. Suspicion dies hard, doesn't it? Look . . . I don't want to be angry with you, I want to forget about everything, all I want is a quiet life. Why have you come here?'

'Because I'm lonely.' His voice was rough, coarse sounding.

'Lone . . . ? But what has that got to do with me?' She screwed up her face at him. 'Why come to me?'

'Because I think you owe me something.'

'Owe you something!'

'Yes, just that. You owe me something.' His manner changed. He threw his hat on to a chair and undid the buttons of his raincoat, and there was a hint of wry amusement in his voice as he went on, 'I'm out of a job, I'm estranged from my parents, I've lost my future wife, and my home has been sold over my head, and last but not least the town's so hot for me I'm having to leave it.'

She was gaping at him, her mouth and eyes stretched wide. Her whole body appeared to be swelling; her voice spiralled: 'And you're blaming me for all this?'

'Yes. Yes, everything.' One side of his lip curled inwards at the corner.

She joined her hands together and held them against her waist; her face tightened, and a wary, defensive look came into her eyes as she said quietly, 'And you expect me to do something about it?'

'Yes, just that.'

'And what, may I ask?'

'Oh well, I'll leave that to you.' He was grinning engagingly at her now.

'Get out!'

'Oh look. Look.' His manner changed completely and he put his hand out towards her. 'It was meant to be funny. I'm sorry.'

'Funny!' she cried. 'You can't get it out of your head that I'm loose, can you? You've just said it again. Things have happened to you and you're blaming me, and I've got to pay you, pay you in a way you think I pay most people. . . . It's true. It's true.' She wagged her hand quickly in front of her as if warding him off; yet he hadn't moved. 'You've only got to come here and say you're lonely and I'll comfort you like I've comforted others. That's what you think, don't you?'

'Listen to me a moment, just a moment, please. Why do we always get off on the wrong foot?'

'You call it the wrong foot! You say what you do, you make suggestions, and you call it—'

'Listen!' The word was a bark. Then bending his body towards her, he asked more quietly, 'May I sit down?'

'No, you can't.'

He bit on his lip. 'Well, it's going to be harder saying what I have to standing up.' He paused, staring into her hostile eyes. Then lowering his gaze from hers he began to talk. 'You see, I'm in a hell of a state inside; have been for the past month. It's all connected with you and I can't get it straight, and I don't know why. The last thing I meant to do was to insult you, yet I thought there was somebody here when I came in . . . I thought that because I feared that, and I found I was furious with you. Does that surprise you? Yet, believe me, the last thing I want to do is to upset you. Can you understand what I'm getting at? Why should I want to upset you when my main aim is . . . is to get you to like me?' The last words had dropped to a whisper, and in the silence that followed he saw her put her hand across her mouth, and the pressure of her thumb and fingers set the blood upwards and towards her eyes.

He said again, 'May I sit down, please? I feel a bit wobbly.'

When she gave neither her consent nor a refusal, he walked towards the couch and sat down on the far end of it, and looking towards her he said, with touching gentleness, 'Come and sit down and let me talk.'

As if under hypnotism, Cissie went to the couch and sat down, but at the extreme end, away from him.

Looking towards her, his voice still very low, he said, 'I was three weeks in the house without going out, and every minute of it, night and day, I couldn't get you out of my mind, and I didn't know why. I thought it was a sort of a delirium and it would pass, but it didn't. And then I tried to reason it out. The few times we have met we have fought. To all intents and purposes you had been having an affair with my father. . . . Please, please.' He put up his hand. 'Hear me out. Then as the days went on I realized why you attracted me and I didn't like it. It was because I've a great deal of my father in me. The things that attracted him appealed to me.

'All my life, right up until he took ill, I repudiated the thought that there was anything of him in me, any trait that I couldn't crush that is, and then, lying there with time to think, I discovered I liked the kind of people he liked; I wanted the same kind of things, the same kind of responses. The first words he ever said about you to me were that you were good and kind. I knew then that I wanted someone kind, warm and kind. This was the sort of person I needed. I must have known this even before I met you because that was one of the reasons why I gave up my fiancée. She wasn't a kind person, and I knew that one rarely grows to be kind, you must be born kind.'

He was now looking at her bowed head, and his voice had a touch of hoarseness to it as he went on, 'I gave up all idea of trying to see you; I felt that during our slight acquaintance you had brought sufficient havoc into my life to last me all my days; and then a few days ago I learnt that we were irrevocably linked together, at least in this town. Does it come as a surprise to you to know that we're supposed to be having an affair? That the reason why I was beaten up was that one of your admirers objected to our association?'

Her head was up and she was gaping at him now. 'It's a fact.' He nodded slowly. 'So much so that my parents believe it.'

'Your father?'

'Him most of all, I should say. He gave me a message for you a moment before he sailed. He said you had to take happiness, grab it with both hands. He said to tell you he was happy for you. Oh yes, he believed it.'

Again she had her hand across her mouth and her head was moving in utter bewilderment, and through her spread fingers she muttered, 'People are cruel, cruel. I don't mean your father ... but the things people say. And now—' her voice cracked, 'and now they'll believe they're right ... you coming here. They'll have seen you and ...'

'Does it matter very much?'

'Yes. Yes, it does.' Her tone was vehement. 'I don't want to be thought of like that. All my life I've had to fight it. People think I'm cheap. Oh, I know what they think, but I'm not, I'm not.' She poked her head towards him. 'I could have married over again if I'd wanted to, but I don't want to.'

'Why haven't you?'

'Because I swore I'd never marry again.'

There was a long pause before he asked, 'Were you so very happy with him that you couldn't bear to put anyone in his place?'

'Happy? Happy did you say?' Her lips were showing all her upper teeth, the twisted one at the side. 'I was seventeen when I married. He was twelve years older than me, and I had three dirty, filthy years with him. Dirty and filthy in every conceivable way. There are so many ways in which a man can be nasty, from his eating, to his sleeping. I was so very young in all ways when I married, but I was full of life, and I died for three years. But when he was killed – he was killed when his lorry went over the Low Town bridge – I came alive again. From that day I was reprieved. It was as if God had given me another chance. I had Pat. He was only a few months old; he was all I wanted; and I promised myself never again, never, never ... again. And then I met your father. ... He was so kind, so good....'

'Don't! Don't!' He pulled himself up abruptly and walked towards the electric fire and stood looking down at it.

'Well, you've been pouring yourself out, why not me?'

'Because I can't bear to hear you say it. It's another thing I've been fighting, the fact of him being so,' he substituted the word placid for inane, 'so placid yet having the power to attract you.' He turned round and came back to the couch and sat down nearer to her now, within an arm's length of her. 'Tell me something? Did I call you Cecilia the night you and mother brought me home?'

She made a little movement with her head, then said, 'Yes.'

'My mother said I did, but I couldn't believe her. I didn't even know that I knew your name.'

'No one's ever called me Cecilia before. Cissie's a bit common, I know, but I've always been Cissie. Cecilia's so starchy and that's not me.'

'I told my mother I didn't even know your name and she was

wild. It seemed to stamp me a liar in her eyes for good and all, but I didn't remember calling you by your first name. So it just goes to show; you must have hit me even before you drowned me in whisky.' As he smiled at her now she turned her face from him and said, 'Please don't go on because . . . because I don't want to take up with anybody.'

'But you would have with my father.' His tone was low, but not nasty.

She jumped to her feet and stood looking down at him. 'Don't keep on about that. That's over, but it won't stop me liking him I'll go on liking him as long as I live; he was something nice that happened in my life and I want to remember it just like that, something nice.'

'Other nice things could happen to you if you'd let them.'

'If I'd let them.' She bent her thin body towards him. 'Look, let's get this straight once and for all, and let's put it in plain language. You're lonely, and you want an affair . . . well, you've come to the wrong shop.'

'I don't want an affair.' He was on his feet facing her. 'Who's talking about an affair?'

'What else could you be talking about, we haven't met more than half-a-dozen times? We know nothing about each other, only that we go for each other like cat and dog. I've never in my life argued and fought with anybody like I have with you . . . no, not even my husband, because he didn't use words.'

Into the significant pause he said quietly, 'I'm asking you to marry me.'

She was no more surprised than himself when he heard the words. This was jumping the gun with a vengeance. He'd had no idea of saying such a thing . . . well, not yet. He'd just got out of one trap, so to speak. But this was different. There was no bait in this trap, of sex, or money, or promotion, or family ties. Then what was attracting him? Her. Just her. All of her. He wanted to have her belong to him. Have her near him all the time. See that light in her face that would mean she wanted him, that she cared what happened to him, like the night he lay on the floor with his head on her knees. He wanted to marry her. Yes, he wanted to marry her. As if he were the recipient of a revelation he felt himself uplifted by a great surge of feeling, and now he whispered softly, 'Say something.'

Slowly she sat down on the couch without taking her eyes from him. 'You're mad,' she said.

'Why? Tell me why.' He brought his face down to the level of hers.

'Oh,' she twisted her body back and forwards from the waist, 'there's a thousand reasons, but the main one is it wouldn't work . . . you in your position. . . .'

'I haven't any position. I'm one of the unemployed, and likely to be. . . . And look, don't belittle yourself so much. About your name and everything. You're doing it all the time in different ways. There's no difference between us.'

'No?' She raised her eyebrows at him. 'Say that to your mother. I'm as low down the social scale in your mother's eyes as a kitchen maid to the Colonel's lady. As for my name, the likes of her wouldn't give it to the cat.'

'You're talking rot. . . . Anyway, this doesn't concern my mother, because I know now that whatever happens I won't live at home again. The ties between my mother and me are broken, finally, so let's forget about her and her social status, which after all exists only in her own mind. . . . Let's forget about both of them, eh, and concentrate on us.'

She now turned her eyes from him and ran the fingers of both hands through her hair, lifting it from the scalp.

He sat slowly down on the couch again, his knees almost touching hers, and watched her as she repeatedly combed her hair with her fingers. And when she stopped she looked up at him and, her face now soft, as was her voice, she said, 'I couldn't. I'm sorry, I . . . I would have to care for somebody very much before I could marry him.'

He could only see her face with one eye, but she looked to him at this moment like a picture set in a deep frame, all toned down, soft and tender. He asked quietly, 'Could you like me?'

Her lips parted, and her eyelashes sent shadows across her cheeks as she lowered them. 'Oh, I could like you all right. I . . . I don't find it hard to like people, it . . . it's loving that's difficult.'

'Well, what about letting us start at the beginning: I'll put up with the liking.' He put out his hands and caught her fingers and, as if she were being burnt, she snatched them away and held her hand tightly pressed to her chest. Then pulling herself backwards and upwards away from him she said, 'No, no, it's no use, don't let's start anything. It's madness and it'd come to no good.'

'All right,' he said quietly, looking up at her, 'don't be alarmed, I was just suggesting that we could be friends.'

'It wouldn't work. You know it wouldn't.'

'I don't see why not.' He smiled wryly, sadly. 'We could discuss music – Pat told me you played beautifully – or antique furniture, you definitely know about that, or the latest book, or we could. . . . Oh, Cecilia, don't, don't cry like that, please. I'm sorry. I wasn't meaning anything. What have I said?' He rose and moved quietly to her, and he put his hands on her quivering shoulders and pleaded again, 'Aw, don't, don't cry like that. I'm sorry.' Gently now his arms went about her and for a second he held her pressed against him, and for a second her body relaxed against his, and while it did he buried his face in her tousled hair. And then it was over. By a thrust that nearly knocked him on to his back, they were apart, and she was standing half the length of the room from him. Her face streaming with tears, she was shaking her head violently, crying, 'No! No! No!'

'All right, all right,' he said. 'Don't distress yourself. I'll go.' He went slowly towards the chair and picked up his hat with a shaking hand. Then turning towards her, he asked quietly, 'May I come and see you again?' And immediately she answered with another violent shake of her head. 'No. No. Don't come back here . . . ever. I don't want to see you, understand. . . . I've had enough trouble. Don't come again. I'm telling you.'

When he went out of the flat and closed the door behind him she was still talking.

He started the car up immediately and drove fast through the town. As he went up the avenue the Wilcoxes' car was at the front of their drive, and from habit he almost tooted his horn.

Strangely, it was Val he was thinking of as he entered the house and what she must have felt like when he turned her down. He had said to her he was sorry, and he had been sorry for her, but he hadn't known what she felt like; he had a good idea now.

He took off his outdoor things, then looked in the hall mirror. He stood straight staring at himself. She had thrown him off her as if he were a reptile, as if bodily he was offensive to her. But he was a man; he looked a man, whereas his father looked like a big flabby . . . He swung away from the mirror and went into the lounge. And there, her voice in his head seemed to reverberate through the room, crying, 'It was as if God had given me another chance, and I promised myself never again, never, never again. . . . And then I met your father. He was so kind, so good. . . .' And on that alone she would have taken him, knowing he had nothing else to give her, nothing, she would have been satisfied with that as long as it was from him.

He thought again of the girls he had known before Val. How they had poured themselves over him and how he had tired of them, as he had tired of Val. . . . Perhaps if things had gone as he wished tonight the pattern would have been repeated. Unconsciously, he flung his arm out in a wide sweep rejecting the idea, then began to pace about the room. She was different from anyone he had ever known. And the point was, she wasn't a girl, she was a woman. She was older than him; he knew that, he worked it out from Pat's age. She could be three, nearly four years older. What of it? The feeling he had for her was different, new; he had never experienced anything like it before. If it was love it was not blind love, for there were things about her that annoyed him, irritated him. Her silly name for instance, Cissie; and that hair, like tow flopping all around her face. And the way she dressed; no sign of taste. Stiletto heels and her skirts up to her knees; it might be all right for some but she was too tall. Had his father picked these points out of her? Damn his father. He had started all this; because of him he was losing the sight of his eye. 'She's a good woman. She's worried about her boy. Go and see this Bolton chap.' And the result: half vision, and a deep craving to touch, hold, and possess Mrs. Cecilia Thorpe. Having seen her only half-a-dozen times, yet knowing from the start that she'd got into your blood like a disease and you'd die of her.

Did every man who met her feel like this? No, not like this; they couldn't. Only two men felt about her this way; he and his father, because under the skin they were one.

CHAPTER TWO

THE SEARCH

AFTER almost two weeks of rain and high winds which made people say, 'Well, we'll soon have winter on us, and autumn hardly started,' summer returned. For three days the sun shone. Women went back into sleeveless dresses. The leather jackets of youth were flung open, some showing bare chests. It was hotter than it had been all summer; in fact, hotter than it had been for years.

Cissie had been across the town to Holloway's new office. Being such a lovely day she had decided to walk both ways, but before she reached the main gate she was regretting not having taken a bus, for she had developed a skinned heel.

She was limping as she crossed the yard, and immediately she had passed into the small hall, from which a staircase led up to her office, she whipped off both her shoes and walked up the wooden stairway in her stockinged feet.

The door of her office was open, as was the window, and she lowered herself gratefully into her chair and, letting her head drop back on to her shoulders, sighed.

The clatter of typewriters came to her from the other office, where the three typists worked. Her adjusted ear told her that only two of the typewriters were busy; then only one. She heard the girls chattering, and then the other machine stopped and she heard Susan's voice saying, 'That's likely why she's been off colour lately; it's not like her to be snappy.'

Then Jean's voice. 'I've been here six years and I've never known her like she's been these past few weeks.'

Then Susan's voice again, low and disjointed: 'Well, I suppose being saddled with someone blind's no joke. Seems like retribution on him for doing the dirty on the Wilcox girl. Then she had Pat in that trouble, and although he got off she was worried to death. You remember?'

Cissie was standing now looking towards the wooden partition and frosted glass door that divided the two offices; then after a moment she moved swiftly and noiselessly forward and, pulling open the door, looked at the three girls.

Startled, they stared back at her.

'You were talking about me?' she said.

'Oh, Mrs. Thorpe, we didn't mean any . . . we . . .'

'It doesn't matter about that.' She wagged her two hands. 'It was me you were talking about, wasn't it?'

They glanced at one another now, and it was Susan who said sheepishly, 'Yes. Yes, we were.'

'About . . . about someone being blind?'

'Well, we didn't mean anything, Mrs. . . .'

Again she wagged her hands at them. 'That doesn't matter. Just tell me; was it Mr. Emmerson you were talking about being blind?'

'Yes.' Susan screwed her face up as she answered. 'We thought you . . . well.' Again the girls exchanged glances.

'Jean.' Cissie was bending over the middle desk, addressing herself pointedly to the eldest girl. 'What . . . what do you know about Mr. Emmerson being blind?'

'Well, it was just what I heard, Mrs. Thorpe. Well I thought you knew and that's why . . . well you've been a bit upset lately. And we were just saying. . . .'

'All right, all right.' Her tone was level and controlled as if she was talking to a child. 'It doesn't matter about that, only just tell me what you know.'

'Well, just that he had to go to hospital because he was losing his sight.'

Cissie straightened up and continued to stare at Jean; then she looked at the other two girls, and they looked back at her. They watched her turn slowly round and their eyes dropped to her stockinged feet as she went into her office and closed the door.

'Oh no! Oh no! Oh, my God. No.' She was sitting with her elbows on the desk now, her two hands pressing against her cheeks. 'Why hadn't he said? He must have known. That night he must have known; that's why he had come. He said he was lonely. Yes, he would have felt lonely . . . and frightened. If he had told her, would it have made any difference to her attitude?' As she read the answer in her mind she thought, if only he hadn't said that bit about discussing music and furniture, and books, and me thinking his father had said something and he was taking the mickey. But blind! Oh my God! Bolton . . . he should do time, he should, he should. But it was my fault, in the first place it was my fault. Ooh! . . . She thrust out her hand and grabbed the phone and dialled his number.

Within the next half-hour she dialled the number countless times before finally getting through to the exchange and being told that that particular number was no longer in use.

Hastily now she went to the first-aid box attached to the wall outside her office door, and, taking out a sticking plaster, applied it to her heel. Then, her shoes on again, she opened the communicating door, to be met immediately by three pairs of eyes, and, speaking to Jean, she said, 'Take my calls, Jean, will you? And if Mr. Holloway should come in tell him I had to go home, but I'll be back in the morning.'

'All right, Mrs. Thorpe.'

'Oh, and should he ask for the Williams contract it's in my desk drawer, I've just brought it back from the bottom office. But I don't suppose he'll call in today; it's just in case.'

'All right, Mrs. Thorpe, I'll see to it. Don't worry.'

After the door had closed on Cissie the three girls listened to her heels clicking down the wooden stairs before they spoke again, and then it was the youngest member of the group who, laying her hands flat on top of her typewriter, said breathlessly, 'Well, and would you believe that! I thought she was living with him. Everybody said they were, and that was why the Wilcox girl threw him over and he lost his job. And it must be all lies 'cos she didn't know. What do you make of it?'

For answer Jean contemplated her typewriter as she said, as if to herself, 'It could be lies an' all about her throwing his father over for him. Eeh! The stories that get about.'

* * *

Lime Avenue looked detached and aloof, much more so in the hot sunshine than it had done in the dark. The houses resting behind their green façade had a disdainful look. Cissie kept her glance directed ahead away from them as one does from the passengers when passing through a Pullman to get to the second-class. These houses, like the occupants of the Pullman, spoke of money, position. They didn't awe Cissie, but they were coupled in her mind with the cold white face of Ann Emmerson.

When she came to number 74 she stood staring at the board above the gate. It was like something desecrating the road, bringing it down to the ordinary level of commerce. 'For sale', it said in large letters. 'This desirable residence comprising. ...' She did not finish the description but, quickly pushing open the gate, she went round the drive and looked at the gaping windows. Quietly she walked all round the house, then out into the avenue again and down the lane that looked as if it was in the country, and out into the main road. She had noticed a telephone kiosk as she got off the bus, and she now hurried to it almost at a run.

He would be in the Newcastle Eye Infirmary.

She got the number from the directory and picked up the phone. 'Could you tell me which ward Mr. Emmerson's in, please?'

'Has he just come in?'

'I don't know.... No. Some time ago, a week or two.'

'Just a moment.'

As she waited she heard the familiar click of the switchboard and the murmur of two people talking.

'Are you there?'

'Yes.'

'I'm afraid Mr. Emmerson's left.'

'Oh!' She stared into the mouthpiece, wetted her lips, and then asked, 'Could you tell me the extent of his trouble ... his eye trouble?'

'I'm sorry I can't, but I can put you through to the sister.'

'If you would, please.'

After a moment a crisp tone said, 'Yes?'

'I was inquiring about a Mr. Emmerson, but I find he has left. Could you tell me how ... how bad his eyes are? Is ... is he blind?'

'No. Oh, no. He's losing the sight of one eye, but the other is quite all right.'

She drew in a long breath, then said, 'Do you think you could give me his address?'

There was a pause at the other end of the line, then the crisp voice said, 'Well. Well, just a moment.'

In her duty room Sister Price stood looking down at the telephone receiver lying on her desk. The request for a patient's address was rather unusual, but then Mr. Emmerson himself had been rather unusual. He was the first patient she'd had for many a long year who hadn't had one single visitor all during his stay, and people with eye troubles needed visitors. More than anyone else they needed human contacts. The last one in that position she seemed to remember had been an old tramp, and he had died in hospital. She had at times thought that Mr. Emmerson wouldn't have cared if he had died too, although there hadn't been anything physically wrong with him except the sight of the one eye, and when it could have been both eyes he should have considered himself lucky. Flicking over the pages of her admittance book she picked up the phone again and said, 'There are two addresses. The one on admittance was 74 Lime Avenue, Fellburn, but on his discharge he gave his address as Meadow Mere, Hill Lane, Bromford. Have you got that?'

'Yes, yes.' Cissie repeated the address, then said, 'Thank you. Thank you very much.'

Bromford was on yon side of the town, quite a way out.

She stood outside the box now considering what to do. She could likely get his number from the exchange as she had the name and address, but no, no, she would go there. But what would she say to him when she saw him? She walked slowly up the road towards the bus stop. She would know what to say when the time came. At present all she could think was: Thank God it's only the one eye.

In the market place she got on a bus that was going to Bromford. Half-an-hour later the conductor put her off at Hill Lane and, pointing up the steep winding path, he said, 'You can't miss it; there's only one house up there.'

Her heel was paining again and she felt inclined to limp, but she made herself walk straight. Then she reached the end of the lane and saw the house. It was a lovely house, small, low and white, with a verandah running along two sides of it.

She was shaking with nervousness, and sweating too when, leaning forward, she knocked on the open door. When she heard a man's heavy tread crossing bare boards in a room to the left of the hall, her heart began to pound against her ribs.

The man who came into the hall was a painter. He had a can in his hand. 'Oh, hello,' he said. 'I didn't know anybody was there.'

'Is Mr. Emmerson in please?' She was shaking, not a little with relief at the respite.

'Oh, no. There's just Mrs. Stringer here. Will I get her?'

She hesitated, then said, 'Yes, please.'

She saw him go along a little passage off the hall and heard him speak to someone; then, coming towards her, she saw a woman in her fifties enveloped in a large overall. She had grey hair and a round face and looked motherly.

'Yes?' she asked, looking straight at Cissie.

'I . . . I've called to see Mr. Emmerson.'

It was as if a skin had dropped over the motherly countenance. Cissie saw the mouth tighten and the eyes narrow.

'Mr. Emmerson isn't here. They're abroad on holiday.'

'I mean young Mr. Emmerson.' She knew that the woman was well aware which Mr. Emmerson she was asking for.

'Oh, I'm afraid he's away too.'

'Could . . . could you give me his address?'

'I'm afraid I couldn't. You see . . . you see I don't know where he's gone.'

Cissie looked into the woman's face. She was a working class woman. If you were speaking of levels you could say that she would be considered as far down in the social scale from herself as she was from Ann Emmerson. Yet this woman was an ally of Ann Emmerson. She was not only tied to her in servitude – the latter she would have denied strongly – but all her loyalty was to her mistress; she might be of the lower working class and talk their language, but her ideas, her way of looking at life, her condemnation of all those who didn't conform to a particular pattern, would be the same as Ann Emmerson's.

Cissie knew all this instinctively, yet she felt that she must get behind the hard core of this woman. Her voice low, she said, 'It's . . . it's so important that I should see him. It's for his own good, believe me.'

'That's a matter of opinion, Miss, but as I said I can't tell you 'cos I don't know.'

Cissie took her finger tips and wiped the sweat from her brow, lightly pushing her lank hair back from her face as she did so. She was hot and tired, and she felt at the end of her tether, like a child that had been for a long walk and calls for a house and says, 'Can I have a drink of water, missus?' She wanted to ask just that: could she have a drink of water? But she wouldn't ask this woman for water, nor would she plead any more or cringe before her. She managed to lift her head and straighten her shoulders as she said, 'Thank you. Good afternoon.'

'Good afternoon.'

She knew that the woman was watching her walking away and she kept her steps steady and her back straight until she was out of sight of the house. Then sitting on the grassy verge of the road in the shade of the hedge, she took off her shoe and stocking and straightened the plaster on her heel. And when she had done that she wiped her face with a handkerchief, then said to herself, 'Don't. Don't. You've likely got a long way to go yet and crying is not going to help you.'

* * *

The next morning she phoned the office of Ratcliffe, Arnold and Baker and asked to speak with Mr. Ransome.

'What name is it, please?' asked the secretary.

'Mrs. Thorpe.'

It was a full minute before she heard a man's voice, saying, 'Ransome here. Good-morning, Mrs. Thorpe.'

'Good-morning, Mr. Ransome.'

'What can I do for you?'

'I wonder, Mr. Ransome, if you could give me Mr. Emmerson's address.'

A long significant pause now, then Mr. Ransome's voice saying pleasantly, 'Oh, I'm afraid it's beyond my power, Mrs. Thorpe. You see they're on a cruise. . . .'

'I mean Mr. Laurance Emmerson, Mr. Ransome.'

'Oh! Oh, Mr. Laurance. Well, that's just as difficult. I'm afraid I can't help you, Mrs. Thorpe, because I don't know Mr. Laurance's address.'

Cissie waited a moment, then said, 'Mr. Ransome, please, please if you know Mr. Laurance's address, please tell me. It's very important.'

'Believe me, Mrs. Thorpe, I would if I knew it, but I don't. The only place he might be that I can think of is in Oxford with his uncle.'

'Well, could you give me that address?'

'Dear, dear. Now, I don't really know that either.' Mr. Ransome sounded flustered. 'The name is Emmerson, as it's Mr. Emmerson's elder brother, but that's as far as I know.'

'What do you call Mr. Emmerson, I mean the one at Oxford, I mean his Christian name?'

'Ronald.... Ronald I think.'

'Thank you, Mr. Ransome; you've been very helpful.'

When the phone clicked, Arnold put down the receiver. 'Helpful?' This was all very puzzling. He was under the impression that if anybody knew where Laurie was it would be Mrs. Thorpe. It was all over the town that he was living with her in her flat. John's departure abroad was put down to this fact, more than his need for recuperating after his illness. He hadn't set eyes on Laurie for weeks. But that was understandable; he'd been so knocked about that he didn't want to be seen.... But this was very odd, her not knowing where he was.... If he wasn't with her then where was he?...

It was later in the morning when Cissie got through to Ronald Emmerson's house in Oxford, and when a hearty voice greeted her she asked directly, 'Is Mr. Laurance Emmerson there please?'

'Laurie? No. Who's speaking?' the voice asked.

'I'm... I'm a Mrs. Thorpe.'

'Are you a friend of Laurie's?'

'Yes.... Yes I'm a friend of his.'

'And you expected him to be here?'

'Well... well, I thought he might be.'

'So did we, but he changed his plans. We expected him to come on after he came out of hospital, and then we got a letter from him saying he'd got some kind of job. He wouldn't explain what and was very brief, very brief, but he said he would be getting in touch with us. We're rather worried about him; we feel that after this eye trouble he should have somebody to look after him. John and Ann are away on a cruise, you know, and we promised Ann we'd see to him. It's all very worrying. ... You say you're a friend of his, Mrs. Thorpe. When did you last see him?'

'Oh, just before he went into hospital.'

'Was he all right when he came out? I mean as right as he could be; you can't feel very right losing the sight of an eye.'

She hesitated before saying, 'Candidly, I didn't know he was going into hospital. I saw him just before but he didn't tell me.'

'Stupid boy. Stupid boy. He did the same with his mother. She doesn't know a thing about it. Myself, I think he's going through a very bad patch, mentally disturbed, you know what I mean. Something went wrong when he broke off his engagement. We were coming through for the wedding, everything was settled....'

The voice went on and on. This was John Emmerson's brother but he sounded so different. He was a chatterer. She broke in on the voice, saying, 'Could you give me his address, I mean from where he wrote last?'

'Oh, that was from their new house, Meadow Mere, Bromford Way, but he said he wouldn't be going back there, having got this job, and as I said before he promised to write us later, and he hasn't.'

'Thank you, Mr. Emmerson.'

'I wish I could tell you more. We are very worried this end.'

'Yes, yes, I understand. Thank you. Good-bye.'

'Good-bye.'

Cissie sat staring down at the desk. It was as if he was trying to lose himself, trying to break contact with everyone he knew. The only one she felt who could help her was the woman up at the new house, but it would be easier walking through a stone wall than getting any information out of her. It was some days later when the thought struck her that perhaps he had to attend the out-patients' department at the hospital. After she had phoned she sat with her head in her hands. Yes, they had said, he attended the out-patients' yesterday. No, he wasn't due to come again ... at least not to this hospital. No, they didn't know which one he might attend.

* * *

The weather changed abruptly and autumn came with a rustling stride. There was hard bright sunshine some days with warm patches, but all the evenings were cold, and when the north-east wind blew it seemed to go straight through the body.

Every Saturday and Sunday, whatever the weather, Cissie, Pat with her, would take a trip out to Bromford village where they would look round the church, and have tea at the only café in the main street, then walk back up the road that passed Hill Lane, looking, always looking, for a blue Rover car. Sometimes they even ventured up the lane and came within sight of the house.

Pat knew whom his mother was looking for. She had explained to him enough to make him understand that because of them Mr. Emmerson had lost the sight of an eye, and he was as anxious as she was that they should meet up with young Mr. Emmerson again, even, he thought, if he did make her cry, because for a long time now she had been different, and he didn't like her being different.

There were nights, before it got too dark, when she would leave him in the house to do his homework, with the strict order not to go out, and she would take the bus to Bromford.

Her visits to the village became so frequent that people began to wonder about her, for evidently she didn't come to see anyone, for she just went into the church, then walked up the road. Perhaps, some of the old ones said, she went into the church to pray for someone belonging to her who had died, perhaps along the road there, at the toll bend. Two people had been killed there last year. Yet no one asked her why she came to the village, not even Mrs. Bailey in the teashop. Customers' affairs, she said, were none of her business; serving tea was her business, and the blonde young woman was always good for a tea and left a respectable tip.

Then one Saturday, late in October, as they came out of the teashop, Cissie saw the blue Rover, but driving it was John Emmerson, and sitting beside him was his wife. . . . They were back.

She didn't go to Bromford any more after this, for the thought of meeting up with John embarrassed her greatly now.

It was almost a month after she had seen John in Bromford that he phoned her.

'Mrs. Thorpe.' His voice, quiet as ever, brought a tightness to her throat, and she had to clear it before she could say, 'Yes, Mrs. Thorpe here.'

'This is John Emmerson.'

'Oh, hello, Mr. Emmerson.' There was a slight pause now and she added, 'I hope you are better.'

'Yes, I'm quite well again, thank you.'

'Did you have a good holiday?'

'Oh, yes, a splendid holiday.' Another pause, and now John said, 'I wonder if I could see you?'

Oh, no. No. She hadn't spoken the words aloud. She gathered the skin of her neck into her fist and waited.

'Are you there?'

'Yes ... Mr. Emmerson ... I – I think it would be better if. . . .'

'This is nothing personal, Mrs. Thorpe ... You understand? Nothing personal.' His words were rapid but scarcely audible.

She made no comment on this and again she waited, and he went on, 'I heard only yesterday – it was during the course of a conversation with Mr. Ransome – that ... that you had been inquiring after Laurie. It is that I would like to see you about. I ... I can't discuss it over the phone, you understand?'

'Yes.' Her voice was as low as his.

'Would you care to meet me?'

'Yes.'

'Where?'

'Oh. Oh, I don't know.' Not at home. Not at home. Never again.

'I could be walking through the market about half past five, say on the Education Office side.'

'Yes, yes, that will do. I'll be there exactly half past five.'

'Very well. Good-bye, Mrs. Thorpe.'

'Good-bye, Mr. Emmerson.'

She sat with her hands tightly clasped on the desk before her. During the last few weeks her mind had settled down into a state of acceptance: if a thing had to be, it had to be; if it hadn't, it hadn't. She had done her utmost to make it possible and it wasn't to be, that was all. She had lost her chance. Everybody was given one chance, sometimes two. She had only been given two and she had made a hash of the second but she wasn't really to blame because the chance had been presented to her in such a way that she hadn't recognized it.

It was going to be awkward meeting Mr. Emmerson. The way things were she just didn't know how she was going to face him, and no matter what the result of their meeting would be she knew that she would feel she had let him down, and that he would feel this too, and in a way blame her.

* * *

She saw him coming towards her just past the Education Offices. He was wearing a grey overcoat and trilby and was carrying a dispatch case under his arm. His skin looked healthier, browner, but the expression on his face was one she remembered from when she first met him. He stopped in front of her and raised his hat, and as they stood looking at each other the embarrassment was high between them. And then he said, 'I would rather we could have met at some place more congenial than this but . . . but you understand?'

'It's all right.'

He stood blinking and peering at her; then he said, softly, 'You're looking tired.'

'It's the cold; I don't like the cold weather.' She shrugged her body beneath her coat. 'The nights are drawing in, I think it's always colder in the twilight.' She looked over the roofs of the market stalls housed in the middle of the big square. The fading light was merging them into one. Then looking back at him she waited, and after blinking rapidly again John said, 'Well. . . . About Laurie. Did you know he had lost the sight of an eye?'

'Yes, I did, and . . . and I feel responsible.'

'No. No, you mustn't feel like that. Any blame must be attached to me. I sent him to Bolton.'

'But it was about Pat's business.'

'These things happen. You mustn't blame yourself. Tell me, when you last saw him did you know his eye was bad?'

'No.' She shook her head.

'And when you found out that was why you wanted to see him?' It was a question asked softly.

As she stared at him through the dim light two women with prams pushed past them and they had to move towards the kerb, and the movement seemed to give her time, and courage, to say to this man, who was the last person in the world she would want to hurt, 'Not exactly.' She bowed her head and into the silence that fell between them she whispered, 'I'm sorry.'

'Oh, don't. Please don't be sorry, because if you're sorry it'll make me be sorry for something I value, for a period in my life that I'll cherish to the end of my days.'

She was staring up into his face. 'Don't talk like that.'

'Why not? Why shouldn't I value something good that I experienced? Life for most of us is humdrum routine, so why not welcome the breaks?' He was speaking lightly. 'What we must face up to is that these episodes are merely breaks, they can't go on. . . . It couldn't have gone on.' His voice lost its light tone. 'I realize that now; that period had something of a fairy-tale quality about it. . . . You know, as you grow older you often find yourself reading the books you enjoyed as a child, and groping back into the world of fantasy because you remember nice things, unusual things happening in that world. It was like that with me.'

Again they were staring at each other in silence. And now John, wetting his lips, said, 'But I wanted to see you to tell you about Laurie. It . . . it was a great shock to us when we returned to find he'd had an operation on his eye. We had a further surprise when we found he'd taken up a new way of life. He's taken on a dilapidated farmhouse with four acres of land attached and is working it as a smallholding. It had been a smallholding before, I understand, with pigs and poultry, but he's turning it into a nursery for flowers and such things.'

He stopped speaking and she said haltingly, 'I'm glad; it'll do him good to work outside. Perhaps he's taken after you, you being born on a farm. . . .' Her voice trailed away.

'I don't know about doing him good. Laurie has changed. He doesn't seem to want people about him any more. It . . . it has upset his mother greatly. She . . . she doesn't often see him now.' He paused here and his eyes held hers, and by his look he tried to tell her what he found too difficult to put into words, the rejection of his son by his wife. At one time their close association had been unbearable to him. The irony of it was it didn't matter any more, for the pain and the jealousy had been transferred to his son's association with this girl. But he hadn't realized until he was talking to Arnold that they weren't together. He had never stopped imagining they were. This seemed to be confirmed when after their return they received a letter from Laurie telling them, in so many words, that he didn't expect them to visit him. He said now, 'Would you like his address?'

'Yes. Yes, please.'

He was fiddling with his dispatch case. 'It's quite a way off, between Rothbury and Alnwick. The best way to get to it, if you're going by rail, is to go to Alnwick and get the bus back towards Rothbury. The place is called Slagbottle Farm. Not a very pretty name, and it doesn't do justice to the surrounding country. It's ... it's beautiful in parts, but rather wild and isolated. Look, I'll put it down for you.' Tucking his case further under his arm he put his hand in his pocket and took out a diary, and after writing in it at some length he said, 'There, that should help you to find it. I ... I would advise you to start rather early because after getting to Alnwick there's quite a journey by bus, and they're not very frequent, I understand. ... I haven't been to the farm, but, but I know where it is. I – I took a run out there one week-end.' His face was scarlet as he finished.

She took the flimsy piece of paper from his fingers, and now her hand impulsively gripping his, she said, 'Thanks. Thanks. I've ... I've always thought it, and I'll go on thinking it, there'll never be anyone quite like you.'

His fingers remained slack and still within her hold, and then his hand was free and he was hitching his case up again under his arm, and his voice had a businesslike, brisk sound now. It was a tone she hadn't heard him use before. 'When you see him, tell him I'll take a run over one of these days. Now I must go.' He hunched his shoulders up under his coat. 'Good-bye, and ... and I hope you find the place all right.'

She moved her head in the characteristic way he had come to know so well and enjoyed watching, and not as a father might a quaint mannerism of a favourite daughter, but that is how he must think of her from now on, as a daughter. Yes, a daughter. But how did one take to oneself a daughter when he didn't want a daughter? Well, the years ahead would tell; he'd have plenty of time for practice. . . . All his life he had been practising law, restraint, to live without bodily expression, without love, to smile – that had almost been the hardest, and would certainly be so in the future. To smile for Ann, who, of a sudden, needed his smiles to prove to her that he was happy, that she was making him happy, for now he was not only at long last her husband, but also her son, her lost child. A stronger man would have run from this new burden of affection, but he wasn't a strong man, he was a vacillating man, a weak, kindly man. He wondered at times how he got by in court. Perhaps because in court he was dealing with other people's emotions, emotions which he knew couldn't impinge on himself. In court he stepped out of the weak man and acted a part. He was fortunate, he supposed, in having this form of outlet; other weak men had to be content with dreams. . . . Dreams! Now he, too, would have to resort to dreams; for the rest of his life he could only be with Cissie in dreams. He had been a fool, an utter fool. He could have made her happy; even as he was he could have given her more than Laurie could ever dream of. For the young only took, but he would have given, and she had wanted what he had to give. She wanted more than mere sex; but even there he would have satisfied her, there were ways and means. During all the long twenty-six years with Ann he had never thought along such lines. There had been no incentive. You don't look for ways of loving an ice-coated wall. But with Cissie. . . . Oh, Cissie.

'Are you all right?'

'Oh yes. Yes.'

He had been staring at her so long, sort of holding his breath, she thought he was going to have another attack. 'You sure?'

'Of course. Now I really must go. Good-bye.'

His abruptness now disturbed her. She tried to smile at him but couldn't. 'Good-bye, Mr. Emmerson,' she said. 'And thank you. Thank you so much.'

When he passed her and walked away she should have walked in the opposite direction, but she turned and watched him until he stepped off the pavement and went towards the market stalls and disappeared into the gloom. She had the unnerving desire now to run after him and catch him by the arm and say, 'Come on home, John.' She wanted to lift that look from his face. That lonely look. That lost, empty, hungry look that had first caught at her sympathy. And it had all been there again as he stood staring at her. . . . But in the hospital he had said . . . what had he said? Only, 'I've nothing to offer you, Cissie, and you're young.' But it wouldn't have mattered about what he hadn't got to offer, she'd had all the sex she wanted in her life time. This being the case, then why had she been breaking her neck to find Laurie?

'You can't have them both.' She came to herself with a shuddering shock, not only from the context of her words but the fact that she had spoken them aloud in the street.

CHAPTER THREE

THE FARM

SHE set off early from Fellburn the next morning for Newcastle, from where she took the train to Alnwick, and it was just on twelve o'clock when she reached there. On inquiring, she found there was no bus passing Slagbottle Farm but that she could be set down near a road which led to it.

Out of Alnwick the change in the aspect of the country both surprised and awed her, and this wasn't helped by a low rain sky. There were few houses to be seen, only great stretches of fell land rising to bare-looking hills. Eventually they came to a little hamlet, followed by a long stretch of deep, black-looking woodland, then open country again, and it was while passing through this that the conductor said, 'There's your stop, missus. Go along that road there.' He pointed to a track. 'Fork to the left over the hill an' you can't miss it.'

'What time do you come back?' she asked.

'Oh, around half past three, a minute here or there.'

'Is that the last one?'

'No, there's another around six.'

She thanked him, and he rang the bell, leaving her standing, seemingly alone in a vast wilderness, for wherever she turned she could see nothing but rolling fells.

She set off on the rough cart track, which went uphill for some way. Then over the brow she came to the fork in the road that the conductor had spoken of, and now she found herself going gently down hill and looking across a wide valley. She could see in the far distance the wood she had passed in the bus and, nearer, were small copses. The land here looked less gaunt; altogether it had a gentler aspect.

Then she saw the farmhouse. It lay in a hollow on the hillside. It was as if a giant hand had scooped out the earth to make a place flat enough to build a house. After staring at it a moment or so she went on down the hill and came to a five-barred gate. After passing through and closing it she walked along a footpath that skirted a deep rutted field. And again she was going uphill. At the edge of the field some of the earth had been dug and made ready for planting. She walked now between stacks of seed boxes, then past a greenhouse that was in the process of being erected, and all the time she looked around her. But she saw no one, not even an animal.

Then she was walking up a flagged path, bordered on each side by a tangle of weed and bramble that had once been a garden. And so she came to the back door of the grey stone house. She noticed that the weather boarding on the bottom of the door was rotten and that the door had not been painted for years. She shivered, not only from the cold, which had become intensified in the last few minutes with a thin drizzle of rain, but with a foreboding of fear as to what she would find when the door opened.

She put her hand out and tapped on the door, two small knocks. She imagined she heard a movement inside, but when no one appeared she tapped again, louder this time, and the next minute the door was opened and there he stood, at the top of the three steps, his face at first expressionless until the colour suddenly flooded over it.

Her whole stomach jerked as it hadn't done since Pat first kicked at her from within the womb. 'Hello,' she said softly.

Still with the door in his hand he didn't move. She was shocked at the change in him. He was older, much older, and although his face was flushed to a dark red, his skin indicated pallor. There was an oddness too about his looks. Both his eyelids moved but only one side of his face seemed alive.

Her voice trembling, she said gently, 'Aren't you going to ask me in? I've – I've come a long way.'

As he half glanced over his shoulder she was reminded of the last time she had seen him, when she had half glanced over her shoulder. He had thought then she had someone with her. Now the same fear attacked her making her feel faint and sick, and it sent flying the doubts she had had about the reason for her visit here. When with a jerk he stepped aside and pulled the door wide she walked past him and entered the house.

She had taken no more than three steps into the room before she was brought to a halt with shock. The place was stark and bare, reminiscent of most of the land outside. The floor was made of great uneven slabs of stone. There was a big open fireplace with the remnants of a dead wood fire on the hearth, and in the middle of the room an old wooden table and one chair. On the table was a board on which stood a loaf, some butter, still in the paper, and a piece of cheese, it, too, lying in its wrapper, and towards the edge of the table lay a knife and plate, and beside it a half-empty bottle of beer and a glass.

She turned her eyes from the table and looked at him. He was standing with his back to the door, his hands hanging by his sides. She didn't know what to say. She had thought she would have known, once she saw him, but she didn't. She hadn't expected it to be like this. She hadn't expected him to look like this. He had always looked cocksure, but now he looked ill, yet aggressive. She made herself smile as she said, 'It's . . . its grand country; I've never seen such scenery.'

He seemed surprised at her choice of words and she watched him clutch at them as if with relief as he spoke to her for the first time. 'Yes,' he said, 'it's wonderful.' He cleared his throat then moved stiffly towards the table. 'It makes you wonder why you ever stayed in town.'

'May I sit down?'

'Yes, yes.' He pointed to the chair; then his hand, continuing the movement, covered the table, and he gave a hick of a laugh. 'I'm living rough; I'm not settled in yet, there's so much to do.'

'Yes.' She nodded. 'There's always a lot to do on a new place.'

He scraped his foot, which was encased in a thick, heavy boot, over the stone floor, and then he looked down at it, and she looked at it too. He had changed, all of him. He was wearing dirty corduroy trousers and an old leather jacket on top of a pullover, and his hands were rough, his nails broken. She remembered having admired his hands and the way he dressed. As yet she couldn't understand the reason for the complete change in him. Would losing the sight of his eye do this?

His voice startled her, bringing her eyes up to him. 'Why have you come?'

'I wanted to see you.'

'What for? We have nothing to say to each other; you pointed that out very forcibly the last time we met and you were quite right. I know now you were quite right. Oh yes.'

She leant over the corner of the table towards him. 'Please! Listen. I . . . I hadn't had time to think.'

The seconds piled up before he answered, 'You . . . you wouldn't have needed time if it had been my father, would you?' Now she saw it all, the reason for this self-imposed isolation, the way he was living, the whole disintegrating of him, it was almost tangible. This thing that was eating him was not the loss of his eye, this thing that might take her a lifetime to conquer, this thing that would well up at times and make them blaze at each other, this thing that would be secreted in some corner of his mind for as long as she was alive, was jealousy of his father.

Still leaning towards him she almost convinced herself she was speaking the truth, so emphatic did she sound when she said, 'It had nothing to do with your father. He didn't come into the picture at all, not in that way. I was mad at you, that's why I said what I did . . . and, and I didn't believe you would want to marry me.'

Again some time elapsed before he spoke. 'If my father was free and you had to choose between us you would have him now, wouldn't you?'

'No! No! I wouldn't.' She shook her head wildly. 'He's nearly twenty years older than me, another generation. He . . . he could be my father.' Somewhere inside her she was apologizing to John, begging him to understand.

'You've changed your tune.'

'Look, be reasonable. Just think for a minute. . . . I didn't know you when I met your father. If I'd met you first, well . . .'

'He still wants you.'

'He doesn't. He doesn't.' She was shouting now as if he were at the other end of the house. 'He sent me. . . . Aw, please.' She rose to her feet and pressed her hands over her face and begged, 'Don't let's start again, don't let's row. . . . Please.'

'He sent you?' His lips scarcely moved as he spoke. 'You've been seeing him?'

'No. No.' She closed her eyes. 'He phoned me yesterday and told me where you were.' She knew better at this stage than to say she had met John. 'He had just learned the day before that I had been looking for you, and I have, for months and months, from shortly, shortly after that night. I, I went to the hospital, then to your old home, then to the new place. The woman there wouldn't tell me where you were. I got in touch with your uncle at Oxford. I . . . I went back week-end after week-end, and sometimes of an evening, to Bromford, hoping that I might see you, at least see your car, and when I did see it and your father and mother were in it I stopped going. I phoned Mr. Ransome and begged him to tell me where you were. He said he didn't know, and then he must have told your father about me inquiring and' – she spread out her hands to him – 'and here I am.'

As she finished speaking she felt a faintness coming over her and she turned from him, groping at the back of the chair, and sat down again.

He looked intently at her but did not go towards her.

'Could I have a drink of water?'

Without a word he went out of the room, his boots clattering on the stone floor, and in a minute he came back carrying a cup. He did not put it into her hand, but on the table to the side of her, and she took it up and drank it nearly all. Then, wiping her mouth with a handkerchief, she said, 'It was a long walk.'

'Would . . . would you like a glass of beer, and some bread and cheese?'

'Yes, yes, I would, please. I . . . I've had nothing since breakfast; perhaps that's what's made me feel faint.'

'Help yourself, my hands are not too clean.' Brusquely, he pushed the board, with the loaf and butter and cheese, towards her; then he went out of the room again and returned with a bottle of beer in one hand and a box in the other. He put the bottle to her hand, saying, his manner unchanged, 'I'm afraid you'll have to use the cup, I'm short of glasses at the moment.' Then taking the box to the other end of the table he sat down and poured the remainder of his beer into the glass.

The food was sticking in her throat; she was cold both inside and out, and the beer wasn't helping. There was an unreality, she felt, in their sitting together like this, eating together in this awful room, in this awful silence. 'What kind of farming are you going to do?' Her voice was small.

'It isn't farming, nothing so glorified as that; there's only four acres. I'm going in for flowers, building my own greenhouses.' He moved his head towards the door but he kept his eyes on his plate. 'I'd like to try orchids; there's money in them and this spot is amazingly sheltered.'

'The house looks old,' she said, her voice still undertoned.

'It is. It's over three hundred years. They hauled the stones over the hills from the quarry, and there're timbers in some of the rooms that were once part of the old wooden ships on the Tyne.' His tone was stiff, his flow quick, but he was talking.

'Would you show me round?' she asked gently, and when his eyes flicked towards her before returning to look at his plate, she said. 'My bus doesn't go until half past three.'

'Half past three?' He nodded, then added, 'They don't run very often.' Then finishing his beer, he said, 'It won't take all that long, there's not much to see, only the skeleton of the house. I'm concentrating on the outside first, getting the greenhouses up. They're the most important.'

'Yes,' she said; 'they would be.'

He rose from the box and walked across the room and she left her unfinished bread and cheese and quietly followed him. At the door he flung his arm back and said, 'This is really part of the hall. The stairs used to go from here but they shut them off to make another room, but later on I'm going to have the partition down and it'll make a fine hall.'

They were standing now in the other part of the room, from which led a shallow black oak stairway. There was another door in the far wall, which she took to be the front door, and to the side of it a window which stretched from floor to ceiling, giving a view across the valley.

'It could be very nice.' She looked around her, and he nodded and said, 'Yes, when I get down to it, it'll look all right.'

'This is the kitchen,' he said. 'It's a bit old-fashioned but there's plenty of time to alter things. At present I cook with calor gas but I'll get that old range going one day; there's not a thing wrong with it.'

She looked at the great black open range taking up almost

one wall of the big room, which was also flagged with stone. There was no furniture at all in this room, no table or chairs, nor even a working surface. The cold bareness, that in itself indicated loneliness, made her ache with compassion. His father had been lonely, but that wasn't his fault. But this kind of loneliness, this self-inflicted loneliness, spoke of a sickness of the mind.

'There's another room on this floor,' he said, as she followed him out of the kitchen. 'But I won't use it much, as it'll take too much heating.' He opened a door and she saw a long, low, beautifully shaped room, it had a wooden floor, the boards, worn with use, were over a foot wide.

'It'll be a pity if you don't,' she said; 'it's a lovely room this.'

'Yes, I suppose so.' He turned abruptly away and walked back into the hall and up the stairs. On the landing he said, 'There's five rooms here. Mind your head.'

She had to bend down to go into the first room. It had a dormer window and the walls were plastered. The next three rooms were larger but much the same. The fifth door he didn't open, and as he passed it he said, 'That's just the same,' and she guessed it was where he slept.

As she followed him down the stairs, her eyes on the back of his head, she thought what a dreadful place to be alone in. There flashed into her mind a picture of her flat, and she almost groaned aloud at the comparison.

Downstairs again he walked through the room by which she had first entered the house, saying, 'There's a big cellar underneath. It's full of rubbish, but it'll do for a storage place when I get going.'

He was still walking, in silence now, and she was still following, and when they reached the other side of the house she saw, to her surprise, a large courtyard with two stables going off and a thatched barn that was used as a garage. The thatch was rotten and there were gaps in the roof, and inside the garage stood a van.

'You've got a car?' she said.

'Oh, it's just an old van, but it's a necessity up here. I bring all my stores from Alnwick once a week, and of course I'll need even a bigger one when I get going.'

'Yes, yes, of course.' She nodded.

He walked past the barn now and along a tangled pathway, saying, 'This was a sort of vegetable garden.'

'Has the house been long empty?' she asked.

'No, it has never been empty.' He spoke over his shoulder. 'An old couple lived here. The old man died and she went down into the town. It's too far out for most but it suits me, just what I wanted. Moreover, it was going cheap. Twelve hundred she was asking, that was all. Amazing these days. When I get the house finished it'll be worth six times that, let alone the land.'

It was just talk. He knew it, and she knew it. He would never get the house finished, not without her he wouldn't. Without her he might work out part of his sickness on building the greenhouses, and when they were completed he would move on. This could be a temporary resting place for him, or it could be a home for life. It all depended on her and how she handled him within the next hour. She couldn't just say to him, 'I'll marry you'; it wouldn't be enough, she knew she would have to convince him that he meant more to her than that, that there was nothing he would ask that she wouldn't do for him. Even more than that, that he would have no need to ask.

He was saying now, 'The old man was born in the house and he was eighty-four when he died, amazing.'

She could imagine old people having lived in the house for a long time. It looked like it, and smelt like it. She would alter all that.

Her back was straight and her head was up. Then she stumbled over a bramble. He turned quickly but he did not touch her. Instead he looked at her shoes and she felt he was about to criticize them; but when he saw they were flat-heeled, he said, 'I must get the paths cleared.'

'It's all right,' she said. 'I wasn't looking where I was going.'

When they came to the greenhouse she said, 'It's very clever of you to be able to build it on your own.' And to this he replied, 'Oh, there's nothing in it, it all comes in sections. The difficult part of the job is getting the stuff carted up here, cement and things for the foundations.'

She was surprised he knew how to handle cement. Likely he

hadn't at first, as two burst bags of hardened cement indicated.

'Later on I mean to make up the track to the main road; it'll be easier on the van.'

As he led the way back to the house he looked up at the sky in a casual manner and remarked, 'I think we're in for another shower.'

In the room again she could not control her shivering, for it seemed colder inside the house than it did out. He was aware that she was cold and he walked towards the fireplace, saying as he went, 'I usually don't light up until the evening; I – I'll get it going. Would . . . would you like a cup of tea?'

'No, no thanks.' She paused, then asked, 'Is there a telephone box on the main road?'

'Yes.' He nodded. 'About a hundred yards along from the bottom of the lane.'

'I'll have to make a phone call,' she said. 'Pat is staying with the mother of one of the girls at the office. I would like to get in touch with her. I'd better be getting down,' she said.

He turned from her towards the fireplace again and she saw his left shoulder twitch; then as quickly he turned back and stared at her. His distress was too much to bear without going to him, and the time was not yet. When she moved to the door he muttered thickly, 'If you'll wait a minute I'll take you down in the van.'

'Thank you; it would be a help.'

He went past her, almost knocking her aside, and she watched him hurry along the side of the house. A minute or so later she heard him starting up the van, and then he appeared at the corner, shouting roughly, 'You'll have to come this way.'

She went quickly towards the courtyard where the van was now standing, and he opened the door for her but did not help her up the steep step. And then he was sitting behind the wheel and thrusting in the gears.

Going down the rutted lane she was bumped and jostled, and twice she fell against his arm, until she found that by bracing herself with her feet she could curtail her movements somewhat.

He had not spoken during the journey down but when they

neared the road he said gruffly, 'They don't like you parking on this stretch, it's narrow and on the bend. There's the kiosk along there.' He pointed across the corner of the field.

Out of the van, she would not let herself look at him. She must burn her boats completely before she made the final move. She said under her breath, 'Thanks,' then walked down the road conscious that he was watching her.

It was a funny thing about the burning of boats, you were always frightened; even if you wanted to burn them you were still frightened. She had once before burnt her boats when she ran away from home and married Harry. The result of that burning was her loathing of sex, the abhorrence of even the thought of physical contact. Yet within the next few minutes she was going to set the seal on another episode of physical contact – and not under the sanction of marriage either. She was going to do what she had been suspected of doing for years, and perhaps she would never be really able to convince him that she hadn't. Well, that was as might be, but at the moment she knew instinctively that the only way to help him was to give him her love . . . unreservedly. That's what she had come to do, but she had never imagined he would need it as much as he did.

She lifted the receiver and got through to Jean's mother. Yes, Mrs. Watson said, Pat was fine; eaten a big dinner. And, no, no, of course she wouldn't mind having him for the night. Was she herself fixed up for the night? Oh, that was good. Some of those country people did you well.

As Mrs. Watson continued to talk Cissie was startled by the distant sound of the van starting up. She twisted around, the phone still to her ear, and saw the van turning in the road. . . . She said 'Yes, yes,' to Mrs. Watson, then gabbled, 'I'll have to ring off. There's a bus coming.'

She jammed the receiver down, but moved no further than the door, and from there she watched the van bounding and bumping up the hill. She closed her eyes for a moment, then walked heavily towards the track, and just as she reached it she saw the bus winding its way towards her from the far distance. Another two minutes and it would be here. Perhaps that's what he had thought; the bus would be along in a minute, and it was no use prolonging the agony. When the bus passed the bottom of the road she was a few hundred yards up the track.

Before she reached the fork in the road it was raining heavily. When she reached the house door she was very wet, tired, and sad.

She didn't knock this time but, lifting the latch, she pushed the door open. She watched his head jerk up from his arms on the table. His face looked ghastly, and she did now what she should have done when she first entered the house. She went to him and put her arms about him.

His face buried in her breasts, his body shook convulsively and she muttered over him, 'There now. There now. It's all right.' It was like talking to Pat until, after a while, she brought his head up and, bending to him, placed her lips on his. After a long moment he pulled himself up and held her tightly to him, and, both their faces awash now, they looked at each other. And then she said, 'I – I was just phoning to say I wouldn't be home tonight.'

She saw the greyness seep from his face. And now, her voice high and cracking between laughter and tears, she gabbled, 'We can go in tomorrow and clear the flat, and collect Pat. . . . You won't mind Pat?'

For answer he held her face tightly between his hands, and after searching it with his limited gaze he muttered, 'Oh, Cissie, Cissie.'

Not Cecilia, she noted, but Cissie.

'You'll have to marry me sometime . . . doesn't matter when, just to make it right with Pat.'

'Oh, Cissie, Cissie.' He gathered up handfuls of her hair as he kept repeating, 'Oh, Cissie, Cissie.'

She put up her hands and caught his and pressed them to her head.

It was funny. She was about to throw her hat over the windmill, so to speak. Well it was done every day, but she had always resisted it, not alone, she knew now, merely because she had been sickened of sex, but because in giving way to it she'd really be doing what people expected of her. So she had lived a way of life that belied her looks, just to keep her self-respect. But now that didn't matter any more; nothing mattered, except his peace of mind and happiness, and she could give him both.

. . . Yes, she could do that so long as they didn't talk about his father. . . . And as long as she herself stayed shut away in this wild separate world and didn't see him. . . . Oh John, John I'm sorry.

Further examples of Catherine Cookson's renowned ability to capture the flavour of the Northern scene and its people, past and present:

THE DWELLING PLACE BY CATHERINE COOKSON

When Cissie Brodie's parents were taken by the fever in 1832, Cissie suddenly found herself the head of a family of nine brothers and sisters. She was just fifteen and the youngest was but a babe in arms, yet she decided that rather than have the family split up in the workhouse, she would try to find work to keep them all, for they would be happier together. But how? And where would they live?

In *The Dwelling Place*, Catherine Cookson tells with compassion and warmth of Cissie Brodie's heroic fight to rear the family under appalling conditions of cold, near starvation and persecution in the class-conscious society of nineteenth-century England.

0 552 09217 7 85p

FEATHERS IN THE FIRE BY CATHERINE COOKSON

Every once in a while circumstance traps a group of people in a pattern of tragedy and violence from which they struggle vainly to fight free. Thus it was with the Master of Cock Shield Farm, Angus McBain, who was too easily tempted to sin, too sinful to escape a hideous retribution ... and Jane his gentle daughter who devoted her life to caring for her deformed young brother ... Amos, the legless child whose tortured spirit transformed him into a demon capable of every cruelty – even murder ... and Molly Geary, the 'fallen' servant girl, whose love for the child she had borne in shame gave her strength to become a truly courageous woman ...

0 552 09318 1 £1.00

OUR KATE BY CATHERINE COOKSON
An Autobiography

The *Our Kate* of the title is not Catherine Cookson, but her mother, around whom the autobiography revolves. She is presented with all her faults, yet despite these, Kate comes out as a warm and lovable human figure. And against this central character, we see the child Catherine going to 'the pawn', fetching the beer, and collecting driftwood from the river – for the family struggle through an era when work was scarce and social security non-existent.

So *OurKate* is a story of a person and a period. It is an honest statement about living with hardship and poverty, seen through the eyes of a highly sensitive child and woman whose zest for life and unquenchable sense of humour won through to make Catherine Cookson the warm, engaging and *human* writer she is today.

0 552 09373 4 85p

THE INVITATION BY CATHERINE COOKSON

When the Gallachers received an invitation from the Duke of Moorshire to attend his musical evening, Maggie was overwhelmed. Naturally, she did not see the invitation as the rock on which she was to perish; nor was she prepared for the reactions of her family. Her son Paul, daughter Elizabeth and daughter-in-law Arlette were as delighted as she was but the effect on Sam, Arlette's husband, was to bring his smouldering hate of his mother to flashpoint. Maggie herself, however, was to be prime mover of the downfall of the family she loved too dearly . . .

0 552 09035 2 85p